MURDER
MOST FOUL

GUY JENKIN

Legend Press Ltd, 51 Gower Street, London, WC1E 6HJ
info@legendtimesgroup.co.uk | www.legendpress.co.uk

Contents © Guy Jenkin 2025

The right of the above author to be identified as the author of this work has been asserted in accordance with the Copyright, Designs and Patents Act 1988. British Library Cataloguing in Publication Data available.

Print ISBN 9781917163682
Ebook ISBN 9781917163699
Set in Times.
Cover design by Rose Cooper | www.rosecooper.com

All characters, other than those clearly in the public domain, and place names, other than those well-established such as towns and cities, are fictitious and any resemblance is purely coincidental.

All rights reserved. No part of this publication may be reproduced, stored in or introduced into a retrieval system, or transmitted, in any form, or by any means electronic, mechanical, photocopying, recording or otherwise, without the prior permission of the publisher. Any person who commits any unauthorised act in relation to this publication may be liable to criminal prosecution and civil claims for damages.

Printed in India

Guy Jenkin is a multi BAFTA, RTS and Emmy award-winning writer, director and producer. His television series include *Outnumbered*, *Kate & Koji* and *Drop The Dead Donkey*, all co-written with Andy Hamilton. He also wrote and directed a number of TV films including *A Very Open Prison* and *Crossing The Floor*, and two feature films, *The Sleeping Dictionary* and, with Andy Hamilton, *What We Did On Our Holidays*. This is his first novel.

To Bernadette

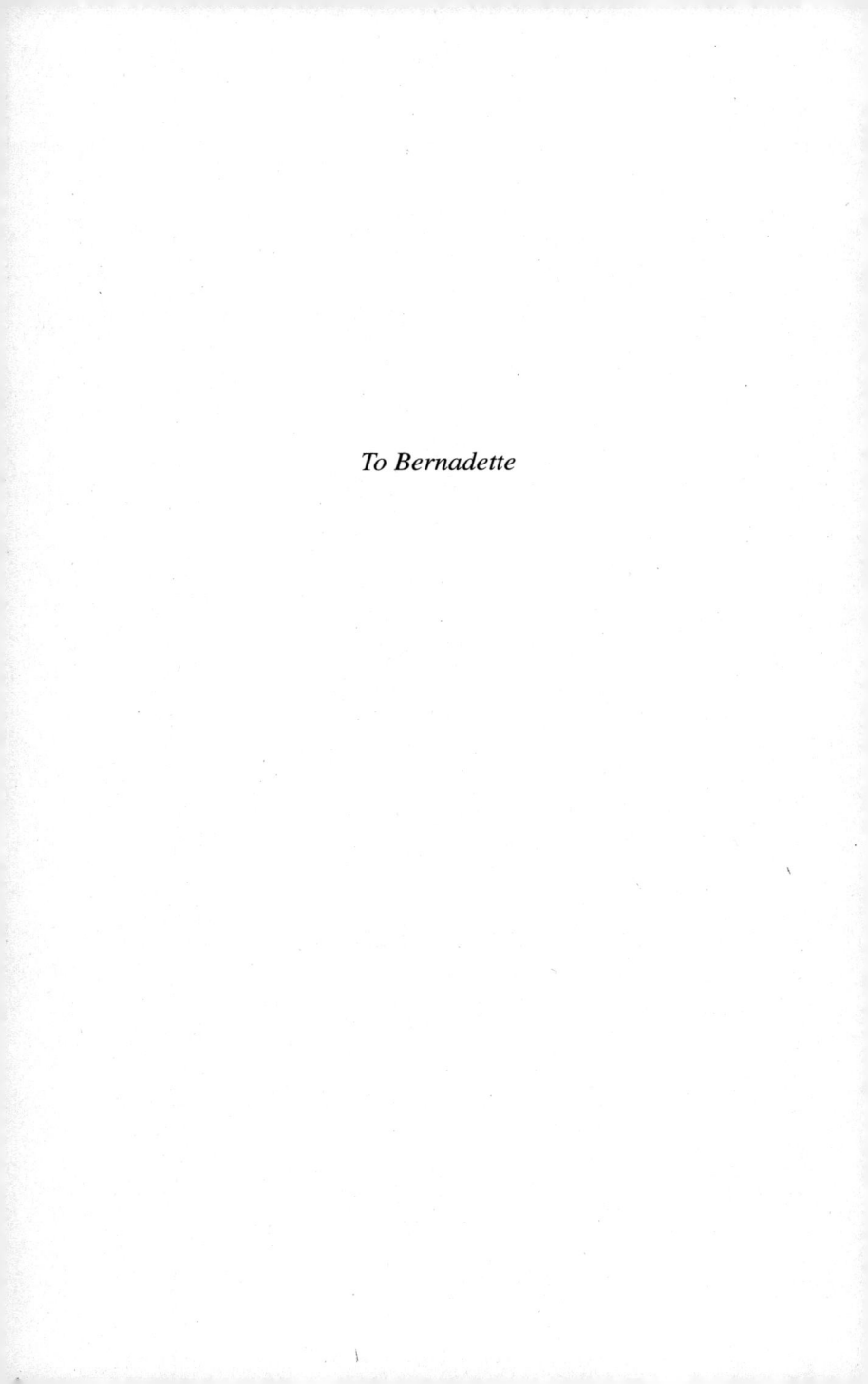

ACT ONE

LIZZIE

Lizzie was afraid of spiders and witches and Spaniards but not of dead men. She'd seen a lot of them back in Holland. She poked this one cautiously with the toe of her bare foot but he didn't move. He was slumped against an upturned boat on the Thames shore in a sitting position, his lips mauve and curled back into a grimace. She reached out and touched his hand. It was cold but soft. He had the teeth of a gentleman and smelt of perfume. She reached forward on her tiptoes and took his silky black cap. It reminded her of the hats her father had worn before they fled. She rubbed it against her cheek for a moment, then stowed it under her dress and ran off down the alley.

WILL

A man walked a lion down the street. It was an old, skinny lion but it was a lion, and the iron choke chain the man held in his hand would never hold it if it didn't want to be held, but for now it padded head down with the blank expression of a predator. That was one man who wouldn't get mugged, not even in Deptford.

Why the hell had he, Chris and the others come all the way here for a night out, to this town of bars and brothels perched on a swamp? Not that he could blame Deptford for what had happened. To say Will would never drink again would be a lie, but he was going to drink less. He wasn't going to drink so much that he ended up swearing at his best friend and sleeping on the floor of a dockers' bar. He couldn't be sure, but he thought he might have been urinated on while he was sleeping, perhaps by a dog, possibly by a docker.

As he plodded glumly along Deptford Strand he could hear the thump of axes and smell the boiling wood-tar from the dockyard. He turned a corner and the low sun was glinting in the puddles, splintering the street into shadow and glare. Ahead of him, walking with that lopsided gait he had now, was Tom Kyd. The last of Will's money had been stolen while he slept, but surely Kyd would lend him the boat fare back to London and save him a boggy hour-and-a-half walk. Will called his name and Kyd stopped.

'Chris has been hurt,' he said.

Will's hangover was driven out by a sense of cold dread. 'How?'

'In a fight.'

'Is it bad?

'They won't say.'

Kyd started walking again. Not long ago he had drawn crowds wherever he went as the writer of *The Spanish Tragedy*, London theatre's biggest ever hit, but since his arrest and interrogation people crossed the road to avoid him, as if blasphemy was something you could catch.

'Is he still in Deptford?' asked Will.

'He's at Eleanor Bull's house.'

'Where's that?' Will shouted after him. 'Are you going there?'

Kyd shook his head and kept walking towards the ferry. After what Topcliffe the torturer had done to him in his dungeon following his arrest, it wasn't surprising that he was walking away from trouble.

'Where's the house?' yelled Will.

Kyd looked around him to see if anyone could hear, as if even this was dangerous. 'Oxestalls Road. Between the Cock Tavern and the Russian wharf.'

Kyd hurried on and Will was left alone again. Oxestalls Road was close. If Chris was in trouble he needed to run there, but after last night his body didn't even like walking that much, and he knew it was going to kick up a fuss. It did. Everything hurt, he gasped for breath and he had to fight back a wave of nausea. His feet slithered on the slippery cobbles, and he could feel the cut in his chest start to bleed through his undershirt. A group of women were cleaning fish on a doorstep and one of them shouted something after him that he couldn't hear, but which made the rest of them laugh. A small boy ran effortlessly alongside him then raced ahead and ran backwards ahead of him yelling encouragement from a mouth smeared with red fruit.

He thought the place would be hard to find, but a small

crowd was gathered in a semicircle around the door of a dilapidated three-storey house. Blocking it was a short, greasy-haired man. The white of one of his eyes was yellow and his face looked like a sunset over a plague pit. Will recognised him as Skerries, but couldn't remember his first name. Skerries called himself a Catholic and had been involved in the Babington Plot to kill Queen Elizabeth but he must have been a double agent because he'd walked free and stood in the front row to heckle as the others were hanged, drawn and quartered.

Will stepped into his eyeline. 'Where's Chris?'

Skerries looked at him and considered whether he could be bothered to reply. 'We're waiting for the constables,' he said. 'We're doing this right.'

Another shiver went through Will and settled in his guts. If they were waiting for the constables, it was bad.

'How bad is he?' Will asked, still panting from the run. 'I'm his friend.'

This time Skerries didn't answer.

'You know who he is, don't you?' said Will. 'He wrote *Tamburlaine* and *Doctor Faustus*. He has connections. He works for Lord Strange and you don't want to cross His Lordship.' Will sounded like the people he hated, but he had to try.

Skerries ignored him and picked at a scab on his chin.

A high-pitched male voice from inside the house shouted, 'Any sign?'

'Not yet,' said Skerries.

Will, still panting from the run, yelled as loud as he could. 'Chris, can you hear me?'

There was no reply.

Skerries sighed. 'Step back and wait for the constables like everyone else.'

Chris filled his head. Chris in the thunderstorm, daring God, if He existed, to strike him down. Chris playing Zenocrate in a rehearsal of *Tamburlaine*, kissing Alleyn on the lips.

Chris's face last night as Will called him a talentless fraud. He knew he couldn't just stand there.

'He's my friend,' he said. 'I need to see him.'

He tried to push sideways between Skerries and the door frame, expecting to be shoved backwards, but not expecting the quick elbow to the throat. He gasped for air, tottered, fell and cracked his head against something. Darkness reached for him with liquid black fingers.

ANN

It was mad to be in a shop buying shoes when her father was a shoemaker. When she'd threatened to come home with a pair, he'd told her that he'd throw them on the fire. 'Why don't you make me some new shoes yourself then?' she'd said to him, but you couldn't make shoes in the pub.

Leave it to him and she'd end up like her sister Jane on her wedding day: wearing old shoes that had been left at the shop for repair and never collected. Jane, aged thirteen, walking down the aisle in shoes too big for her, and a belly too big for her, dead in childbirth six months later. Her father had always been careless with his daughters. Now he'd sent Ann to sell the Dutch linen and Flanders wax up in London, during the worst plague in half a century. Still, she was a good haggler, and with the shortages she had done well. She kept a few coppers in her purse in case she was mugged, but she had three gold angels in her hose, and she was going to spend part of one on some shoes that didn't leak, her father be damned.

She'd ducked into a shop at random to avoid a bunch of blue-robed apprentices lurching down the narrow street chanting something filthy about Dutch women. The shoemaker's wife sat, with a baby on her breast, on a stool by the door. She was watching Ann to make sure she didn't steal anything while the shoemaker was out back. Ann wasn't going to let herself become that woman, trapped by babies and business, her world as narrow as that shop door. The bent-backed shoemaker came back in and handed her a pair of cream pumps with a flourish.

'The finest shoe leather you can buy,' he said. 'Full-grain Welsh kidskin.'

She ran her fingers across the surface. 'They're split-grain cowhide,' she said, 'Split-grain cowhide soaked in milk.'

He opened his mouth, but nothing came out. The wife on the stools laughed.

A drunk apprentice fell over outside so his head and shoulders were inside the shop. The wife shifted the baby to the other arm and reached for a wooden cudgel, but one of his mates reached a beefy arm inside the shop and yanked him out.

'You heard? Marlowe's been stabbed in a brawl in Deptford,' she heard one of them shout.

Ann dropped the shoes and ran out into the narrow street. The apprentices were only a few yards away, arms around each other, a walking, drunken heap. She ran after them and tapped one on the shoulder.

'Do you mean Christopher Marlowe?'

The one she tapped turned around and the mate he was holding on to fell over. He had a meaty face that looked her over from head to crotch. He licked a bead of sweat off his upper lip. 'Ooh, hello.'

'Did someone say that Christopher Marlowe's been stabbed?' she asked.

'You his girlfriend?'

'I'm his sister.'

'With him it's the same thing, isn't it?' said the meat-faced one and they all laughed.

'Come with us, Marlowe's sister,' shouted the one on the ground. 'You won't regret it.'

He sprung to his feet in one leap, without using his hands. They were all walking towards her. One of them dropped his breeches and hopped forward with them around his ankles.

Ann's heart was beating fast, but her mind was making

calculations. What to do, what not to do, how to get out of this. In Canterbury, the family name would have helped her. They'd know there'd be consequences. But not here. She backed away and reached behind for the safety of the door into the shoemaker's and felt it being shut. She heard the bolt being pushed across.

'Hey, Marlowe's sister,' shouted meat-head. 'Ever been boned by a butcher boy?'

So that's why they smelt of blood: they were butchers' apprentices. She wanted to run but sensed that would make her even more like prey, so she kept walking backwards. The one who had jumped to his feet came running towards her, but then he flew past her doing cartwheels. Another reached to grab her arm. He got hold of a piece of her sleeve which ripped as she yanked her arm back. He tipped back his head and howled.

She was retreating across a junction now, and another gang dressed in blue were coming down the alley chanting, 'Clap your hands if you hate the goldsmiths.'

She pointed at the butcher boys and shouted, 'They're goldsmiths!'

'We're butchers,' yelled one of them, sounding hurt, but it was too late. She squeezed herself against the wall as the goldsmith-haters pounded, screaming, past her and flew into the other gang in a blur of kicks and punches.

A voice shouted, 'No blades, boys.'

So, they had rules.

Ann felt relief for a second before she remembered Christopher had been stabbed. Although had he? London was full of rumours. Queen Elizabeth, aged sixty, was pregnant with a miracle baby. Another Spanish Armada had set sail. A Catholic rebellion had started. A Protestant rebellion had started. Lord Cecil had killed Elizabeth and made himself king. When she didn't even know if the rumour about Chris was true it would be stupid to try and get to Deptford now. She was only one street away from her cousin's house, where she was going to stay the night, and God knows the streets weren't safe after dark.

She heard footsteps behind her and looked over her shoulder. It was one of the butcher boys – she could smell the blood. He was tall but skinny, a stickman in the shadows. She thought she might be able to fight him off.

'Go for the balls,' her father had said, probably the only good bit of advice he'd ever given her. She stopped and turned, and he stopped a yard away from her.

'Are you really Christopher Marlowe's sister?'

'Yes,' she said.

She could just about see his face. He was shaven-headed and gaunt and his Adam's apple bobbed as he talked.

'I know where Marlowe's secret lover lives,' he said.

That was it. He turned and walked back towards the sound of the fight. Ann was a minute's walk from her cousin's house, where there'd be yeoman bread and Lincolnshire cheese waiting on the table.

WILL

Will came round. His chest hurt, but his throat hurt more, and his head hurt more than that, and when he moved he thought he'd be sick. Consciousness was overrated. He rolled slowly onto his side. There was a crowd of people watching him and, when he looked up, a man with one yellow eye looked down at him. He considered getting onto all fours but, no, it was too soon. That would lift his head much further from the ground than he wanted it to go right now.

A woman in the crowd shouted at Skerries, 'Let him in you fat, yellow-eyed twat.'

Was that blank verse? Almost. 'Skerries', that was it. The man with the yellow eye was Skerries. Other things from longer ago came back to him.

A thrown bottle. Someone pulling him away. Him standing in front of Chris with a knife saying, 'Right, I will do it.'

Then there were two large feet in expensive felt boots caked in red mud next to his head, and a large voice said, 'Where is he?'

'Out back,' said Skerries.

The new man wasn't a constable. Constables always told you they were constables. And constables couldn't afford boots like those. That was it – constables. Skerries was waiting for the constables. The pain in his head seemed to increase the more it had to remember.

Skerries opened the door and the big feet walked in and down the corridor. Skerries turned to follow and slammed the door behind him. Will's foot had been left next to the door frame and he stuck it out so it just stopped the door from closing. He waited for Skerries to come back and do something nasty to it, but he didn't. Now he needed to get on all fours. As he did, the woman in the crowd called to him.

'Your head's bleeding.'

That must be why he couldn't see out of one eye. He wiped it and his hand came away sticky and black in the dim light. He held on to the door frame and pulled himself onto his feet and his legs grudgingly held him up. He pushed cautiously at the door and it opened up some more.

'I wouldn't go in there if I was you,' said the woman.

He stepped into the dark corridor. He could hear lowered voices but not Chris's. A floorboard creaked and he stopped. The voices continued so he stepped forward again. Now in the light of a room at the end of the corridor, he could see the back of the man with the big boots. He wasn't that tall but square with huge, muscular shoulders. He looked like he could hold up the world if Atlas ever wanted a break. Another floorboard made the smallest creak and the man spun around, hand on his sword. He looked at Will with that same blank, predatory face as the lion.

'You should have stayed lying down,' said Skerries.

A new man appeared in the doorway, and spoke in the high-pitched voice Will had heard coming from inside the house earlier.

'Who are you?'

'Don't talk to him, Ingram,' said Skerries.

So the one with the squeaky voice was called Ingram. He was no oil painting either, unless you counted Hieronymus Bosch. He was tall and scrawny, his pale flesh stretched over a bony skull, and he really liked colour – a gaudy purple cap, a sweat-stained yellow and orange shirt, and two bright fistfuls of rings. His face was white – like the underbelly of a dead fish.

'Come into the light,' said the big man.

Will stepped forward, and said, 'I'm a friend of Chris's.'

Chris was lying on his back on the floor of the room, with the handle of a knife sticking out of one eye. There was clotted blood in his hair. He was dead.

Chris's hands, which would never hold a quill again, were clenched tight. His face, which would never laugh again, was a mottled purple and his unstabbed eye looked like it had never been alive.

'We didn't have any choice,' said Ingram. 'He came after us like a madman.'

Will swore and ran at them. The big man moved out of the way as if beating up Will was beneath him, and this time Skerries just tripped him up. Will landed on the bare wooden floor, his head only a couple of feet from Chris's face.

'What is it with you?' said Skerries.

Will felt like there was no floor beneath him, as if he was falling into some deep vault of darkness. He clenched his fists and clamped his teeth together. There was a knock on the door, he heard footsteps in the corridor, and two men stepped into the room.

'We're constables,' one said.

They walked up the corridor. The big man grabbed Will with one leg-sized arm and hoisted him to his feet.

The first of the red-coated constables said, 'I'm Quinn and he's Troutbeck.'

The constables looked like ex-soldiers from the body parts that were absent. One had a bit of chin missing, a jagged scar down one side of his head and only a stub of ear. The other limped and had only two fingers remaining on one hand. They took in the situation.

'Mine's a pint of porter and he'll have a drop of the Dutch,' said Quinn, the one with no ear.

Skerries shouted towards the stairs. 'Eleanor!'

Will's pulse raced in his chest and thumped inside his

head. Too much blood everywhere. He was seeing them speak and hearing the words but it was as if he wasn't there.

'So,' asked the constable. 'Who's dead?'

'Christopher Marlowe.' Skerries said.

'The-face-that-launched-a-thousand-ships' Christopher Marlowe?'

Skerries nodded. 'We've done this right. Nothing touched since it happened.'

'So who killed him?' asked Quinn, who seemed to do all the talking.

Ingram put his hand in the air. The rings glinted.

'Got a name?'

'Ingram Frizer.'

The constable repeated it.

A woman appeared on the stairs wearing only one slipper. Her lank hair hung down over her eyes like a curtain between her and the world. She had sprigs of lavender, sage and bay tied to one wrist to ward off the plague.

'Eleanor, they want porter and Dutch,' said Skerries, 'and Dutch for us.'

She spoke with a surprisingly genteel accent. 'What is this? A pub?'

'Well, yeah,' said Skerries. 'Just about.'

Eleanor stood grasping the stair post with both hands like it was her only friend. 'You know where it is. You get it.'

Skerries stared at her for a moment like something would happen to her when everyone had gone, but then he went and got a bottle and cups from a cupboard.

Will didn't want to look at the body, but his eyes were drawn to it. He didn't know what he thought about souls, but, looking at Chris, more than just life seemed to be missing. A plump black and white cat appeared and rubbed its flank against Chris's face and purred. A long tongue licked at a lump of blood by his ear. The big man scooped it up gently and put it on the window ledge. So he was nice to cats. It jumped through the open window into an alley and out of sight.

Quinn took names. The big man was Bob Pooley. The woman who was now sitting down on the stairs was Eleanor Bull. Quinn repeated each name after it was given and Will realised that he couldn't write and that this was his way of remembering.

He turned to Will, and said, 'Who are you?'

Will tried to stop his voice from quaking as he said, 'William Shakespeare.'

'William Shakespeare,' Quinn repeated. 'You one of those play writers as well?'

'Yes.'

'Pay well?'

'Not really.'

The constable made a face like he didn't believe him. 'How did you get that?' said the constable.

Will took a moment to remember his bloody face. Skerries got in first.

'He wasn't here when it happened.'

Will pointed at Pooley. 'Nor was he.'

Pooley sounded hurt. 'I was. Not like I'm going to lie about being at a killing and get myself in trouble. I went out looking for you lads, and when I couldn't find you I came back here.'

Skerries poured out the drinks for the constables and the killers. Will stared longingly at the viscous swirl of the liquor, but Quinn turned to dismiss him.

'We only require those persons who were here when the death occurred.'

'I know Chris,' said Will. 'He's my friend. I can help.'

The constable exhaled wearily. 'You write the plays, we'll do our job.'

They were waiting for him to leave, five fighting men with liquor in their hands. Chris wouldn't have walked meekly out of the house. He'd have danced backwards down the corridor insulting them, or got them laughing and won them over, or just stayed put and taken the beating. Will didn't know what to do so he just did nothing. Ingram Frizer stepped forward.

'Will, I'm sorry about your mate, I am, but we didn't have a choice. If he's your friend you know what he was like. We had a stupid argument about the bill and he was suddenly like a madman. He picked up my knife and I tried to get it off him but we struggled and this happened. I didn't mean it. I don't want to be known as the man who killed Christopher Marlowe for the rest of my life. But it was him or me.' Frizer's face was close to his, and he saw a louse wriggling in his hair. 'You know what he was like,' he repeated. 'He was never slow to reach for his knife.' He put an arm around Will's shoulder and somehow Will found that he was allowing himself to be walked to the door. 'It won't help him to get yourself hurt. He wouldn't want that.'

Will shrugged the arm off his shoulder but Frizer was still talking.

'I'll tell you what, when I come out of prison, if you still want revenge, you challenge me and I'll fight you fair and square.'

Will could tell Frizer thought there was no chance of that happening. They were at the front door now.

'Go toast his memory, that's what he'd want. Loved *Two Gentlemen of Verona*, by the way.' Frizer slipped a couple of coins into Will's pocket. Will felt like he should take them out and throw them at Frizer, felt like he should punch him in the face, but he was overwhelmed with a terrible tiredness, and he could barely move his limbs as he walked away.

'Is it really Christopher Marlowe in there?' asked the woman who'd told him not to go in there.

Was it? Was it really still him or was he now just a piece of meat? It didn't seem real. A knife in the eye. A trick from a play with a wooden dagger and pig's blood. Yet Will had always known this would happen to Chris one day.

'You know what he was like,' Frizer had said, and Will did. There had been that fight in Hog Lane where Watson the poet and Marlowe killed Bradley, when they were the ones who claimed self-defence and stood over the ditch where the body lay until the constables came. There had been the other knife fights in London and Canterbury where he had ended up in front of the magistrates. Chris was addicted to trouble and like many addictions it had ended up killing him.

A man lurched in front of him. It was Tom Kyd. He looked like one of the many corpses from his plays. His eyes were sunk deep in their sockets as if shrinking away from what they'd seen. He'd lost his hat and Will noticed for the first time that one half of his hair had gone completely white, which made him look even more lopsided.

'I thought you left,' said Will.

Kyd shrugged. 'I came back.' He was holding on to the wheel of a broken cart to keep his bent body upright. 'They were saying at the ferry that he's dead.'

'He is,' said Will, and for the first time it seemed completely real and inescapable. Kyd closed his eyes for a moment and dipped his head, whether in prayer or sorrow Will couldn't tell.

'You're bleeding,' said Kyd.

Will wiped his head. 'Skerries knocked me over.'

'Not there.' Tom pointed down. The cut on Will's chest had started oozing blood through his doublet again.

'I must have done that when I fell.'

Tom shook his head. 'No, you had that when I saw you before.'

Will shrugged. He wasn't going to tell him how that happened. 'Shall we get a drink?' he asked Kyd.

'No, I'm going to wait until they bring him out. I want to see him one last time.'

Will had seen enough. He said goodbye and turned away into a gust of rain.

BELLA

It was back in Lisbon, when she'd been Margarita, or was it Beatrice? She had met a Basque captain who had sailed to the edge of the northern ice, who said that the native people there had forty different words for snow. The English should have forty different words for grey. Grey clouds in grey skies over grey roofs above the grey mud of the River Thames. It was summer. Of course, the captain had almost certainly lied. In her experience, divide any figures a sailor told you by at least three. Four if they were Italian, she should know. All those enormous waves and whales and mermaids and monsters. One day she would see for herself and sail to the lands where ice mountains covered in white bears floated in the sea. Charles would come with her and she would show him how to stick out your tongue and let the snowflakes melt on it. They would have a little creaky cabin and keep themselves warm with wolfskins and vodka.

She wondered if the small pipe of hashish she had smoked had been enough to take her away from everything that had happened, but if she was drifting in a cabin with Charles it must be working. Perro made a contented, growly dog noise and opened an eye. She lay with her jowls resting on big, muddy paws, a small pool of drool spreading on the wooden floor. Bella had always liked the smell of wet dog. It was more honest than men's perfume which never quite covered their stink. She looked out the window. Grey England was dark now. She could lie back in the black pillows of night and forget the English, their food, their clothes, their teeth, their breath. In Seville you would not sit next to a lord at dinner and watch a neat line of lice crossing the cushion from his clothes to yours. How did this grubby nation produce such poets? Maybe they flourished in the filth like cabbages in manure. But no, now she was moving back to the thoughts she was trying to exile.

She tried to return to her warm nook in the frozen north. It was time to move on. If only she could leave England, this bog surrounded by sea – if only she could. Perro grumbled and rolled over onto her side and knocked over the bowl of oranges that a man who wanted to marry her had sent. She could not remember his name. There was a knock at her door. Whom had he sent with his message this time? Throckmorton was in love with her, Hesketh hated her and Walls was indifferent.

'Come in,' she said.

It was Hesketh. He had a bony head that came to a point and a neck so thin it was an executioner's dream. He looked at her impatiently as if her existence wasted his time; she suspected he hated anything foreign or beautiful. There was a time she would have seen him as a challenge and day by day worked him like clay until she could do anything with him. But now, she was weary of moulding mediocre men. His bow was a bob like a wagtail and he got straight down to business.

'Marlowe's been stabbed in a fight in Deptford,' he said. 'He's dead.'

'Chris stabbed? No, it can't be true,' she said.

'Well it is, because it's happened,' he said. 'You need to get back down there.'

'With the object of achieving what?' she asked.

Perro stood up, stretched and yawned. Hesketh looked at the dog nervously and handed her a note sealed with wax. The rain spattered on the window and the long trip to Deptford played out in her head. The streets full of shit, the propositions from drunks, the haggling with the ferrymen, the shouts of

'Filthy Moor'. The tide would be against her, the boat ride long and the foul spray would be in in her face. And Deptford would be Deptford. Hesketh gestured at the door.

'There's two men downstairs who'll go with you.'

She shook her head. She wasn't going to walk around London with two thugs trailing behind her. How would she explain that? Besides, Perro was worth two men in a fight.

She smiled. 'How as a little girl I dreamt of going to Deptford. And now twice in twenty-four hours.'

He looked baffled and she realised she was only amusing herself. She called Perro over to her. She spoke to dogs in Dutch, men in English and dreamt in Arabic. If only she could be dreaming now, a goose-down pillow for her head and the dog at her feet, but no, she had to go back to Deptford and reality. She put on her cloak still wet from the rain and picked up the small bag with the dagger and the vial of poison. Grey, grey England, and now one of its few blazes of colour had been extinguished.

Was that her fault?

ANN

Ann was standing in a queue outside Deptford courthouse, waiting in line to see the corpse of her dead brother. Chris's body had been taken there for the inquest and an enterprising nightwatchman was charging people to come in and see it. She should have gone straight to her cousin's house, but she'd known she wouldn't. She'd gone to the front of the queue where a constable with most of an ear missing, who must have been in on the scheme, was taking money at the door.

'I'm Christopher Marlowe's sister,' she'd said.

He had barely looked at her. 'And...?'

'Can I see his body, please?'

'Yes, if you join the queue.' He'd taken money from a fat woman who had squeezed, wheezing, past her.

'Are you really going to make me queue up and pay money to see my dead brother?'

'Looks like it, doesn't it?' he'd said.

He had seemed like the sort of man who would go soft and let her in if she cried, and she'd felt tears coming, but she wasn't going to give him the satisfaction and had walked to the back of the line.

No one had paid Christopher much attention in Canterbury but here it was different. There was a big queue shuffling forward in the darkness. She counted the front ten and then took the distance they made up and estimated how many of similar lengths there were in the queue. She reckoned there were about fifty-five people there at quarter to eleven at night. Were there any other calculations she could do to keep her brain from thinking about things she didn't want to think about, how her brother was no longer in the world, how she would get through all those minutes and hours and days without him? The fog from the creek swirled and coiled in the drizzle, carrying with it the sulphurous stench of the brick kilns. A small girl was selling fried chicken feet and a tiny woman appeared carrying two buckets hanging from a pole across her shoulders.

'Beer, anyone? Ha'penny a cup,' she shouted, like it was an execution.

A man was coming towards her out of the darkness, and before she could see his face she knew it was Will.

'Ann?' He started a fumbled sentence.

She put him out of his misery. 'I know Chris is dead.'

There was dried blood on his face and in his hair and on his shirt. His clothes looked like they had been stolen from the dead on a battlefield.

'I'm sorry,' he said.

A man with an enormous head, who smelt of fish, stepped up close to them. 'This is a queue.'

Will turned to him. 'This is Marlowe's sister.'

'You're not though, and you're pushing in.'

They tried to ignore him.

'It is definitely him, is it?' she said.

He nodded. She couldn't help it. She put her arms around him. There was that old familiarity, her face against his neck, his breath on her hair. The man with the enormous head was tapping her on the shoulder.

'He's pushed in.'

Ann turned to him. 'What are you going to do about it?'

She heard her father's voice as she said it. She was a Marlowe alright.

'It shouldn't be allowed,' he said, but she could see he was only talk and wouldn't be doing anything about it. She turned back to Will.

'You've not changed then,' he said.

'Nobody does.'

His face had always struck her as too ordinary to be an actor. He was clever and quick and funny but he still looked like a glovemaker's son from the provinces. It was the actors, Alleyn and Tarleton and Burbage, who you couldn't take your eyes off, who you believed as an emperor or a potentate, who made everyone want to be with them and be their friends. Yet really Will was the extraordinary one, who could make words come together in ways you could never imagine, and tell stories that made you forget where you were. She looked at him, those brown eyes which showed his emotions whether he wanted them to or not, his face bruised and flecked with blood.

'How did it happen?' she asked.

'A row over a bill, they say. There were three of them, all criminals of some kind.'

'He always liked criminals,' she said. 'We always knew that one day he'd start a fight with the wrong men.'

She could see him thinking.

'What?' she said.

'There's something that Frizer, the one who stabbed him said – "You know what he was like, he was never slow to draw his blade." Yet they said he picked up Frizer's knife. Why didn't he draw his own?'

'Maybe he didn't have it,' said Ann.

They had reached the door. The one-eared constable who had ignored her earlier ignored her again and looked at Will.

'You?' he said.

'Yes, me,' said Will. Ann reached for her purse to pay but Will said, 'I have some money. I might as well spend it on this.' He handed it over to the constable. 'Tuppence admission,' he said. 'That's twice what you pay to get into a two-hour play.'

'That's real life for you,' she said.

Then he must have remembered what they were doing and reached out and gave her hand a squeeze as they walked into the hall.

Christopher's body was laid out on a table at the front ready for the inquest, lit by the nightwatchman's lanterns. His lips were curled back, his whole face a purple bruise, the knife sticking out of his eye. She imagined it plunging in – the brutal thrust, the noise it made, his face as he put together what was happening, as he knew he was dying. She wanted to pull the knife out of Chris's eye, and go find the men who had done it, and cut their throats one by one, and stand over them and stare into their dying faces.

The queue moved forward. You got thirty seconds for your tuppence. A young man ahead of them, with a beautiful face made interesting by a broken nose and straggly blonde hair wet from the rain, stood staring at Christopher, then lunged forward and put his arms around Chris's head, sobbing. Was this what she was supposed to be doing? Another constable who was guarding the body limped over to him, sighing.

'No touching,' he said. 'Come on. Off.'

He grabbed the blonde man's shoulders, but he only had two fingers on one hand and the man was strong and shook him off. Will stepped forward and went behind the table and grabbed the man's arms and tried to prise them away from Christopher. For a moment it looked like Chris's body would be pulled off the table but then the blonde man went slack and let himself get pulled away.

'Alright, alright,' he said. 'I'm going.'

He shook himself free and walked off, stopping at the door to blow Christopher a kiss.

The constable – she'd heard him called Troutbeck – shook his head. 'We've had a fair few of those. First one who's been a bloke though.'

He had a tough, weather-battered face, that looked like it

had been carved out of wood, carved out of wood by someone very drunk.

He turned to her. 'You really his sister?'

She nodded.

'I'm sorry, love. You can touch him if you want.'

Her hand moved forward. She wasn't sure what to touch – should it be his hand or his face? It hovered over his cheek, but she couldn't bring herself to make the final contact and her hand shrank back to her side. She watched as Will reached out towards Chris's right hand with its thumb and first two fingers stained with black ink, the mark of the writer that gentlemen with their pure white hands disdained. Will's hand was the same, and he touched the tip of his black-stained first finger to that of Chris's – a writer's salute. She turned and fled.

Will followed her out, wiping away a tear with his hand. Was she the only one who couldn't cry? Crying in the Marlowe family had been a sign of weakness and at once made you the target for teasing and abuse. As a child she kept one fingernail jagged so, when she felt tears coming, she could clench her fist and push it into her palm so the real pain shocked her into silence.

Outside, the queue had shrunk to a dozen or so. Will took a step towards her then half a step backwards as if he wanted to comfort her but was worried touching her would be misconstrued. The light from a lantern flickered inside a window and she saw he had an inch-long splinter of wood in his cheek.

'Shall I get that out?' she asked.

He looked blank.

'There's a splinter of wood in your cheek,' she said. 'Bend forward and hold still.'

He did. The rain was washing the blood off his face and pink drips fell from his chin. There was plenty of the splinter sticking out to grab hold of, but it didn't come easily. He winced.

'What's three times fourteen?' she said.

'Eh?'

She yanked hard and he yelped as it came out.

'My mother used to ask us sums to distract us from the pain.'

'It doesn't work,' he said.

'I know.'

There was a sharp stench as an old ox plodded around the corner pulling a cart full of barrels of urine for the tannery. The carter plodded after it, even older and scrawnier than the animal. Church bells were chiming the hour in the distance. She lost count but thought it was eleven o'clock.

'His knife, the one with the inscription,' Will said. 'It's still in his sheath.'

'What?'

'He has the sheath sewn inside his doublet. I reached in and it's still there.'

'When?'

'When I helped pull the man off his body. That's why I did it.'

'Was that the knife given him by the woman who claimed she was a pirate?'

'Yes,' said Will. 'He prized it, and if he'd had it, he'd have used it, not grabbed Frizer's.'

There was only one explanation. It was murder. The three men had lured him to that house to kill him. She felt a rush of rage that, for a moment, pushed away the pain of loss.

Someone called to Will, a dark-skinned woman with a huge dog. Ann remembered Bella, who always seemed to be there with the theatre crowd. She was speaking to Ann but Ann wasn't listening. She must avenge her brother. Who would want Christopher dead? The list was endless.

WILL

Bella knew someone with a house in Deptford where they could stay and be close to the inquest in the morning. She always knew things like that. It was a fine place backing on to Deptford Creek with some steps leading up to an iron-studded oak door. Will worried about going into such a house looking as he did, his face a mess, his clothes muddied and blood-spattered. He made it worse by tripping and stumbling as he climbed the steps.

'One's much higher than the others,' he said pointlessly as Bella knocked on the door.

The gentleman who lived there stayed upstairs and a grumpy Dutch maid came down in her nightgown and showed them into a room of dark wood and red rugs with leaded windows that looked on to the creek. She lit a fire and bought them cold duck and beer, dropping the plates the last couple of inches onto the table in protest at having been woken. A window was open and moths fluttered around the lamp. Will tried a bit of duck but he could only taste the grease.

He thought of Chris and what had happened the night before. Was it really only yesterday? It was one of those rare times Chris had money in his pocket and he had treated them all to a trip to Deptford where he said drink was cheap and anything goes. In the boat with Chris were Tom Kyd, Will, Bella, Chris's new friend the Widow and a man called Barking Bobby whom Chris had met in a bar that morning.

There was always someone like that with him, a Mad Teddy, a Frenchie, a John the Dice, drunk men with nicknames and tall stories who were Chris's best friend for a day. The trip had been to cheer up Tom Kyd after his ordeal, but Chris had started it by making him miserable.

'So you gave them my name to get yourself out of Topcliffe's dungeon, did you?' he'd asked Kyd.

They were running the tidal race between the pillars of London Bridge so Kyd had to shout his denials over the noise of the river. Chris kept on at it.

'Maybe you should have bitten out your own tongue so you couldn't blab, like Hieronimo did in your play.'

'I said nothing. Nothing.'

'Just funny how you're released, and I'm summoned. One in, one out, eh?'

'I swear to God I didn't say anything about you,' said Kyd.

'Excellent,' said Chris. 'A man arrested for atheism swears to God he didn't do it.'

Barking Bobby chuckled, though possibly just at something in his head.

Chris said, 'Bet we'd get the truth out of you if you were back in the Scavenger's Daughter.'

It was something you didn't name – a torture machine those who had suffered said was worse than the rack. Tom looked like he was about to vomit. Bella told Chris to shut up and Will backed her up. It was from then on Chris started picking on him. Did Chris have some notion of what was coming? Was he trying to drive his friends away to protect them or was he just being a bastard? He was capable of both.

Ann kicked Will's foot. He hadn't been listening. She was asking Bella a question.

'We think it was murder, do you?'

Bella considered. Her face was in shadow but now and then a reflection of the single candle flickered in those black eyes. 'I think it's very possible. He was an atheist and he slept with men.'

'Wouldn't they have to kill half of London if they were crimes?'

'He was too honest to deny it,' said Bella.

Ann considered this with a frown. She was smaller than the other Marlowes – and darker. Will wondered whether that blotched red lump of a man really was her father. Ann with her black hair and her face of shadows within shadows – small, dark and fierce. Will had once called her an angry wren – which had made her angrier.

'Was Christopher really that different from all the others?' she asked.

Will remembered Chris, standing on a table in a pub, shouting, 'Write this down, informer. The Holy Ghost raped the Virgin Mary. Oh, I forget, you can't write it down, you're illiterate.'

'Yes, he was,' he said. 'He loved to cause trouble, to provoke everyone, he couldn't stop himself.'

Ann wasn't convinced. Her face was scrunched up and those small vertical lines that he knew so well, that warned of trouble, appeared in her forehead.

'We told him to be more careful,' said Will. 'Lords can be atheists but the sons of shoemakers can't.'

Bella nodded, the amethysts on her necklace glinting in the candlelight.

A dog howled somewhere and others joined in. Perro raised her ears, opened one eye, then went back to sleep.

'So you two are telling me, what?' said Ann. 'That he was killed by the government? By Lord Cecil?'

'It's possible,' said Bella. Your queen is losing her grip. There's no named successor, there's plots everywhere, so they're frightened and when they're frightened they're most dangerous.'

'And they're most frightened of a playwright?'

'The theatre's grown bigger since last you were here,' Will said, 'and yes they are frightened of its power. They were looking to close it and the plague just gave them an excuse.'

'No, I understand,' said Ann. 'You're very important.'

Will saw the anger rising higher. You couldn't disagree with her without it becoming personal. He should have just kept quiet.

'What I don't understand is this,' she said. 'Lord Cecil and the Royal Council had summoned him to be questioned about atheism in twelve days' time. They would have interrogated him and got names out of him like they got names out of Kyd, and they can't do that now he's dead. So why did they kill him?'

'That's true,' said Bella, 'but the government is not of one mind. It's not just Cecil. There are ever-changing factions with ever-changing plots. They kill someone at lunchtime for a reason they have forgotten by dinner.'

'Well,' said Ann. 'We're still going to find out who killed him.'

'We,' noted Will. Yes, he wanted justice, but like Bella he wasn't sure they'd be able to disentwine the twisted snarl of rumours and lies, the tangled knots within knots, that could turn suddenly into a noose around your own neck.

'To find out will be full of hardness,' said Bella, sounding more foreign as she always did when she was tired. 'Even his friends only knew half his life. He only slept a couple hours a night. While the rest of us were asleep, he was off to meet someone new.'

'And last night,' Ann said. 'Is that what he did? Go off to meet someone?'

Bella hesitated. 'I left early.'

Will took a breath.

'Did something happen?' Ann asked.

Will hadn't touched the rest of the duck on his plate and Bella reached for it and held it out to Perro. The dog rose, sniffed it to check what it was, then turned her huge head sideways and took it gently between her jaws. Ann was waiting for an answer.

'We quarrelled.'

'About what?' Ann asked.

The dog was licking Bella's fingers to get the last of the duck fat.

'Oh, small stupid things,' he said. 'I don't even remember the details.'

He did. It had started with Chris teasing him about the other Anne.

'Lock up your grandmothers. Shakespeare's in town.'

Will's wife was only eight years older than him. Just eight years, but he knew that to say that would just encourage Chris, better to let him get bored. Only this time Chris just kept going. In his campaign to quarrel with all his friends he'd left his best friend until last.

'You must remember what you quarrelled about,' said Ann. 'It was less than a day ago.'

'About writing,' he said.

They'd quarrelled about that too. 'What have you written?' Chris had said. 'Two comedies, three histories, where I added the best bits, and a tragedy where you write about murder, rape and revenge like they're a joke.'

Chris just wouldn't stop. Chris in the pub, knocking back a glass of that expensive French liquor someone had bought, standing on a step, illuminated by a lantern like an actor on a stage, Will below in the shadows like a groundling. How did Chris always manage that?

'Nothing's ever happened to you so *Titus Andronicus* sounds like a play about slaughter and revenge written by a glovemaker's son from Stratford-upon-Avon.'

That's when Will had thrown a glass at him, which just made Chris laugh. Will shouted anything he thought would hurt Chris – that he thought his audience were stupid, that he used big words, cheap tricks and shiny costumes, noise and colour to disguise that he had no talent, though all the time he knew Chris was a genius.

'Did you part friends?' Ann asked.

Will just shook his head. He couldn't bear to tell Ann how

it had ended. The fire was dying. The rain was heavier. The dog was asleep.

'Shall we go to bed?' said Bella. 'There's two bedrooms we can use.'

'You two have a bed each,' he said, 'and I'll sleep on the floor down here.' He'd fall asleep easily enough on a floor. That's what he'd done last night.

'No,' said Bella, 'Ann and I will share.'

'I'd rather not,' said Ann, adding, 'I'd rather not share with the dog.'

Chris was lying dead with a knife sticking out of his head and these social dances were still going on.

'I'm fine down here,' he insisted.

Ann huffed in frustration and said, 'Will and I will share. We all know we've done it enough times before.' And that was it. They walked up the cramped circular staircase and she said, 'You know this doesn't mean...' and left the sentence unfinished.

'I do know,' he said.

She was ahead of him, her dress hiked up in her hands to climb the narrow steps, her worn 'shoemaker's daughter's shoes', as she used to call them, creaking on each step. Her brisk, businesslike pace was leaving him behind. They undressed with their backs to each other and slept in their underclothes beneath a scratchy horsehair blanket that still smelt of horse. Will felt her presence in the dark in her small movements and her breathing. Snoring came from the room next door.

She whispered, 'Is that Bella or the dog, I can't tell.'

Will smiled and, though it was too dark to see, knew she was smiling too.

The stray dogs were howling again. Kyd said they did it when the tide turned, but he was full of stuff like that.

'Didn't Chris used to sleep with Bella when he first came to London?' asked Ann.

He shrugged. 'They whispered, they fought, they shared

plates of food, they did all the things lovers do, but you know how it was with Chris. You'd find out he was sleeping with the one he never spoke to.'

She murmured in agreement, and he knew what she was thinking of. How they had first tried to keep it quiet so it would not get back to the other Anne. Secret kisses in dark corridors and fingertips touching under the table. Their secret route through the market gardens to the small back door of the Rose Theatre where the key to the padlock was hidden behind a loose plank in the wall. The nights curled up in the costume store wrapped in the brilliant purple and gold capes worn in *Tamburlaine*. In truth, it was probably more for the furtive excitement than the secrecy. He missed it when the secrecy had to stop because it was obvious that everyone knew.

They were alike, him and her, raised with small-town pretensions and the smell of leather. Would he have married her if he hadn't got the other Anne pregnant when he was eighteen? Would she have had him? Probably not. He could tell she was now asleep by her regular breathing. His eyes attuned to the darkness, and he could just make out her shape, the blanket rising and falling, a thin arm and hand. He had forgotten how she slept with fists clenched – as Chris had died. Maybe it was a Marlowe thing. What a day. Chris dead. And Ann alive.

He imagined he could smell that particular smell of Chris's tobacco and the pungent scent only he wore. Then he realised he was really smelling it. He turned the pillow over quietly so as to not wake Ann, and the smell was stronger. Had Chris been here? Was this where he had slept the previous night? His head was racing again.

LIZZIE

'I found it on the head of a dead man,' she had said, when Mama had found the silky cap tucked under her as she slept. Mama had not believed her. Lizzie liked to make things up as they were much more exciting than their drab life in London, but this she hadn't.

'You must have stolen it from a drunk,' her mother had said, and tried to grab her so she could slap her. 'What if someone saw? They think Dutch refugees are all thieves already.'

'If they already think it, what does it matter?'

'Don't talk back,' Mama had said. 'What would Papa think if he could hear you? He'd think I was a terrible mother.'

Papa's letters from Holland had stopped eight months ago. Mama had said he was fine, but how could she know? It had all gone wrong after the Spanish reached Bruges, and Lizzie, Mama and her brother had fled to London. From then on, she was not allowed to be called Yolente any more, and had to be called Lizzie after the English queen so they fitted in, and she had to speak English and sleep on straw. That was why she was now running away from home.

She found a crowd of people waiting outside the big building in the middle of the town and made her way through the gaps between their legs to the front to see what was going on.

'You're too nosy,' Mama was always saying to her. 'Curiosity killed the cat.'

Well, she wasn't a cat so that was alright. The people were trying to get through a door. Two big men stopped most of them, but she was little and ducked under their arms and into a crowded corridor. A man who smelt of fish shouted that she was pushing in as she squeezed past him into a big room. At the front of it a body lay on the table. It was him. She'd been right all along, she knew what dead bodies looked like. She had seen enough of them back in Holland when the Spanish came for them.

ANN

They'd let too many people into the inquest and a fug of sweat and wet wool rose from the crowd, who swayed forward to get a better look every time a famous face joined the privileged few sitting on their chairs at the front. Ann recognised Lord Ferdinando Strange, who ran her brother's acting company, 'Rich' Spencer, the unimaginatively nicknamed richest man in London, Admiral Lord Howard, impresario and retired pirate, and of course, Alleyn and Kemp, who being actors had arrived late. The only commoner among the expensive seats was the cobbler's son lying on the table at the front, dead. Ann wasn't stupid enough to expect fairness. She knew how this world worked. But did it count for nothing that she was his sister? She wouldn't have got in at all if it weren't for Bella talking to someone she knew. Bella knew everyone.

Ann understood herself well enough to know she took refuge in anger, but today she needed something more. She mustn't just let things happen one after another, or that raw onrush of grief would take her over. She must plan and achieve and organise. She must hope Will's idea for the inquest worked out and build on it and use it as a rampart between herself and the black beyond.

Quinn, the constable who had been on the door the night before, shouted for silence and announced, 'Rise for Thomas Danby, the queen's coroner.'

Danby walked in with little, exact steps, a small man,

preceded by his large stomach. There was still a murmur of conversation, and he banged the staff he carried violently on the floor. On the table, Christopher's head moved a little. The lips were still curled back, the face now entirely a purple-black from the bruising. Someone had placed a coin over his unstabbed eye. The queen's head was uppermost on both sides. Had she ordered his death? Ann found that hard to believe, that she would stoop to kill one lowly subject. The sixteen jurors walked out, local tradesmen in their Sunday best who looked like her father's friends, back when he still had friends.

Danby was in a hurry and told the constable to measure the knife wounds. Quinn pulled the dagger from Christopher's eye and there was an 'aah' from the crowd. The constable grinned at the audience's approval and, caught up in the excitement of being onstage, measured where the blood went up to on the blade of the knife, and announced in a hammy voice, 'There is only one wound on the deceased. The knife penetrated his skull by two and one-eighth inches.'

He walked over to Frizer and measured the nick on his brow, which the three killers claimed had come from a thrust by Christopher.

'The injury sustained by Mr Frizer is one and a half inches in length and one quarter of an inch in depth.'

It would have been easy enough for Skerries to have done that after Christopher was dead, thought Ann.

A gangly young man in a black gown stood up. 'I am Jacob Faunt, lawyer for the accused, my lord.' He bowed in a hunched grovel to Danby and stayed bent over as he asked permission to represent the 'three unfortunate gentlemen who find themselves here'.

Where had he come from? Who paid for him? Danby's face was a tight scowl at rest, but now its hostility deepened. His plump head jutted forward.

'I can't hear you properly when you're bent over like that,' he said. 'Which is a good thing. The last thing we want is a lot of speeches.'

They were going to bury Christopher in Deptford churchyard after the inquest. She had started off arguing – she usually did – but what else could be done? She couldn't afford to have the body taken to Canterbury, and anyhow her father wouldn't thank her if the rotting corpse of his son turned up on a cart outside the shop. So the gravedigger was digging a hole for his coffin now. Alleyn, who had played all of Chris's heroes onstage, would deliver the elegy. He'd asked her this morning if she wanted anything said.

'No,' she'd said, 'I want something done.'

She struggled to see through the crowd, tried to stand on tiptoe, but Bella's dog was asleep on her feet. Ahead of her a man grumbled at a woman whose tall hat blocked his view.

Frizer stood up to tell his story. There had been a row over the bill and 'Marlowe was suddenly like a madman'. The same phrases kept coming up, and she thought they must have rehearsed them. Frizer claimed Marlowe had grabbed Frizer's knife from his belt and attacked them. Frizer had leapt out of the way to avoid being stabbed and got the nick to his head. Frizer had grabbed Marlowe's arm and in the struggle the dagger had gone into Marlowe's eye and he had died instantly.

Danby turned his scowl on Frizer, 'How were three men with military experience unable to subdue a single man?'

Faunt, the lawyer, rose to his feet like a telescope being opened but Danby waved him to sit down.

Skerries answered, 'We thought we could, sir. Mr Pooley and myself tackled him when Mr Frizer grabbed his knife hand, but unfortunately the act of wrestling him to the floor led to the knife going into his eye.'

They're going to get away with it, she thought. The jurors sitting there, itching in their Sunday suits, would have heard of Christopher Marlowe and the fights and the atheism and the men he slept with. To them a knife in the eye was divine punishment for a filthy sodomite and the men who had done it were God's holy instruments.

Ann finally shifted the dog off her feet and craned her head to see Will standing waiting with the other witnesses. Would he get out what he wanted to say before Danby shut him up? Her easy familiarity with Will in bed the night before had made her fearful. She had pretended to fall asleep, frightened of where talking might lead, but then again, she was frightened where it would lead without him – to a small-town life where women gossiped while men got drunk. Only sons were sent to university to write plays and be spies, and have hundreds of people fight to get into their inquest. Christopher was dead at twenty-nine. Would she exchange his life for hers if it was offered to her now? She was twenty-two, so that would be seven years of excitement and adventure, able to think, feel, speak, love, and then sudden death with a knife in the head? Yes! She'd say 'yes' in a blink of an eyelid.

It sounded like the pact with the devil in Christopher's *Doctor Faustus*. She'd seen it sitting in the half-a-guinea seats up onstage with the lords and the ladies, Alleyn striding the stage, the mounting terror of the end, the blank verse breaking down into a torrent of beautiful, terrible poetry as he moved towards death and eternal damnation. Alleyn had been looking straight at her as he spoke the words.

'See, see where Christ's blood streams in the firmament. One drop would save my soul, half a drop. Ah, my Christ!'

Was the most thrilling moment of her life watching make-believe? Will said it was the greatest five minutes of poetry ever written for the English stage. But not to tell Chris that. She had not. Chris had said Will was a much better writer than him, he just needed to find something to write about. But not to tell Will.

Will was the only man she could make laugh, and for a long time she thought it was because she had a strange sense of humour, but then she realised. He was the only man who truly listened to her. Christopher said it was because he was an actor.

'The good ones,' he said, 'they learn that half of it is listening.'

She smiled to herself. Much as she loved Will, he wasn't a very good actor. Though, of course, she didn't love him. She couldn't.

She was surprised to hear Will interrupt Pooley as he gave evidence. 'May I speak?' he said.

'No,' said Danby.

'It's just that this man wasn't there when it happened,' said Will.

'I was, sir,' said Pooley.

Danby seemed intrigued enough to let it go on.

'I was at the door when he came in,' Will said.

'I was coming back from looking for the constables, sir,' said Pooley.

'He said to Skerries, "Where is he?"' said Will. 'It only struck me this morning. If he had been there before he would have known where the body was. There was a crowd outside. There'll be others who heard him say it.'

Will went to go on but Danby held up a hand.

'Enough of this. Pooley, did you say, "Where is he?" I can ask for witnesses.'

The lawyer shot upright quickly this time. 'He did say it, but he was asking where Frizer was.'

'I didn't ask you,' said Danby, but Pooley took the cue.

'That's right,' he said. 'I did know where the body was, sir, but I didn't know where Mr Frizer had got to.'

'That's clearly a lie,' said Will.

'Shut up,' said Danby. 'You're not onstage now.'

Alleyn in the front row chuckled unkindly.

'I can send anyone in this courthouse to prison, and right now, I'd lay a bet on you being the first. Sit down.'

Will sat down. Pooley was still standing.

'Sir,' he said, 'I've known the other two lads for years. We all did jobs for Lord Cecil together.'

Next to her, Bella let out a breath. Had Pooley just threatened the queen's coroner? With Walsingham dead, Cecil had no competition for the most frightening man in England. But Danby just scowled at Pooley.

'You sit down too. Everyone sit down.'

Faunt spoke from his seat. He indicated Will. 'As this man

has insisted on giving evidence, Your Lordship, would you generously allow me to put a couple of questions to him?'

Danby sighed. 'Very well, a couple of questions, but that means a couple. I'm counting.'

Faunt asked hesitantly. 'May I stand, Your Lordship?'

'Yes, yes,' said Danby.

Faunt unwound his long body unctuously and turned to Will. He gave a dramatic pause.

'Get on with it,' said Danby, who knew bad acting when he saw it.

'Mr Shakespeare,' said Faunt, 'I believe you last saw Marlowe the night before he was killed. What were your final words to him?'

Will hesitated.

Faunt went on. 'Were they, "I'm going to kill you"?'

The audience buzzed. Will looked shaken and Ann, at once, knew it was true. It hadn't just been an argument, it had been a bitter falling-out.

'We quarrelled, yes,' said Will to Faunt. 'We said some things we didn't mean.'

'Or perhaps you did mean,' Faunt hurried on. 'And then you turned up at the house of Mrs Eleanor Bull the next day with blood on your shirt. Where did that come from?'

'I fell,' said Will.

'Did you indeed?' said Faunt.

'That'll do,' said Danby.

Why was the lawyer doing this? The three men had admitted they killed Christopher. Was he just sowing doubt and confusion or was he suggesting to the jury that his clients were shielding the real killer? Faunt tried to speak again and Danby told him to sit down.

'I told your father he shouldn't let you go into the law,' said Danby. 'It's not a fit occupation for a gentleman. Now let's get on with this.' He waved towards the jury. 'These men have shops to open.'

His short arm stabbed towards Pooley.

'Do you have anything to say that's different to the other two?' He answered his own question. 'No, I didn't think so.'

'Thank you, sir,' said Pooley, who could be threatening and obsequious at the same time.

'So let's get on to Mrs Bull,' said Danby.

A man from the audience was pushing his way forward through the seated celebrities at the front. It was the blonde man who had hugged Chris's corpse the night before. He had a knife in his hand.

'You killed Chris,' he shouted.

He was heading for Frizer. A part of Ann urged him on. A large part.

'Constables!' shouted Danby rather wearily.

The constables did not seem in a hurry to get between the blonde man and Frizer. He strode by Danby who waited until he had passed and then picked up the staff with which he had called for silence and hit him hard on the back of the head. The man went down heavily and the constables jumped on him.

Danby turned to Frizer. 'This seems to happen to you a lot.' He sighed heavily. 'We will clear the court and continue in five minutes.'

There were groans of disappointment but everyone filed out. There was deep mud just outside the door that had to be stepped through or jumped over. Ann slipped as she landed and reached out to stop herself falling over and found herself holding on to the coat of a young girl.

'Sorry,' said Ann.

The girl gave her a quick smile. 'Sorry about Chris,' she said. 'I'm the Widow.' She looked very young.

'The Widow?'

'It's what Chris called me. He was my friend.'

'Are you a widow?'

She nodded. 'I married at thirteen but the plague got my husband within two weeks.' She tugged Ann's sleeve.

'What?' said Ann.

'You need to listen to what this man is saying.'

She pulled Ann towards a group of three walking away from the courthouse. A red-faced man in a claret coat was sounding off. He was like her father but with a northern accent.

'Last time, Skerries said he killed him, and Frizer was the witness. Skerries even had the same little cut on his head. Look close at him. You can see the scar.'

The man he was telling whistled. 'Bloody hell.'

'Claimed self-defence and walked free in five weeks. Not a soul heard about it down here.'

Ann sped slightly ahead of them so they had to stop. 'Where was this and when?'

The man's face was close to hers, broken veins and eyes hidden under swollen lids. Now there was more fear than bluster. 'I wasn't talking to you.'

'I'm Christopher Marlowe's sister,' she said.

'Well, he's dead now, isn't he?' he said as if that ended the conversation, and started to walk off. She stepped in front of him again but this time looked at the woman with him.

'Who was the man they killed?'

The woman looked down at the ground. The man put an arm around her shoulder and started to walk again.

'Do you want them to get away with it?' said Ann. 'Again.'

The man pushed his wife along and walked faster. 'Get away with what? I never said a thing.'

Ann stamped her foot in frustration. There he was, his red face all puffed up and boastful about what he knew, and then suddenly he was a little scared thing. The Widow was looking at her anxiously.

'How did you know Chris?' Ann asked.

'He was kind to me. He gave me a little money.'

'What for?' said Ann.

'Nothing like that.'

Ann felt relief.

'I didn't have anything after my husband died,' said the Widow. 'People say he did bad things, but he did good things too, he just didn't make a song and dance about them.'

'Lend me your shawl for a moment,' said Ann.

She passed it to Ann obediently and Ann wrapped it around her head and shoulders. The red-faced man's wife had split away from him and headed for the privies that backed on to Deptford brook. Ann tried to walk behind other people but she had to pass the man waiting for his wife. She walked past him, head down beneath the shawl, and he didn't glance at her as she headed into the toilets.

She saw the woman at once, already hitching up her skirts. When she saw Ann, she cursed under her breath.

'Please,' said Ann, 'I promise I won't say where I heard it.'

She got nothing from the square, thick-necked face.

'He's my brother,' said Ann. 'Think how you'd feel if your husband had been murdered.'

'Relieved,' she said.

Ann couldn't stop herself from laughing and the woman did too. 'Where did they murder this other man?' asked Ann.

'They don't do the murdering,' she said in a northern accent Ann couldn't place. 'If you've killed someone, you pay them to come in afterwards and they take responsibility and do their self-defence act.'

Ann formed another question but the woman cut her off.

'That's all you're getting, love.'

'Is it Lancashire you're from?' asked Ann as the woman pushed past her.

'Do I look like an arsehole?' said the woman. So Yorkshire, thought Ann.

She could have done with using the toilet herself but she had to get to Will. He could tell Danby this too when the time came.

She spattered mud around her as she ran back to the courthouse. She couldn't see the Widow to hand back her shawl. The side entrance she'd come out of was surrounded by a throng of people. Just like last night, Quinn's red coat was blocking the door.

'The coroner says no crowd for the rest of it, so go home,' said Quinn.

He stepped aside to let Sir John 'Rich' Spencer through with a woman who could have been his daughter but wasn't. Spencer had supposedly been handsome as a young man but many fine meals had inflated him and the flesh of his face had engulfed his features.

'Why are you letting him in?' shouted an old man. 'Is it because he's rich?'

'That's it,' shouted Spencer, grinning as he propelled the woman through the door with a hand on her arse.

Spencer was the man who had seen the plague heading to England from Venice, Vienna and Marseilles and bought up all the plague cures and preventatives. His warehouses were said to be packed with mercury and vinegar and bergamot. Rumour had it that when the Armada looked like it would be a success, he had tried to make a deal with the Spanish for the monopoly to import sherry.

The crowd tried to follow Spencer through the door and someone was pushed into Quinn by the crush. He waved his cudgel. 'Anyone else shoves me, we're all going to be back here tomorrow for another inquest.'

Ann squeezed along the wall until she was close enough to the door to shout at the constable. 'I need to get a message inside.'

Quinn ignored her.

'It's important.'

She knew as she said it that it wasn't going to work. She looked for Bella. She could get in anywhere but there was no sign of her.

She thought about offering Quinn the money she had kept for the shoes, but she'd have to get the people in between her and him to pass the coins along, and even in London that was too public a bribe. She took a chance.

'I have vital evidence. Frizer and Skerries have done this before and claimed self-defence. Up in Yorkshire.'

The crowd around her went quiet to listen.

'You need to tell the coroner.'

Quinn glared at her.

'He'll be angry if you don't.'

'Not half as angry as if I do,' he said. 'I'm not interrupting him.'

More people were gathering around her.

'They didn't even kill him,' she shouted. 'You pay them if you've killed someone, and they come along and say it's self-defence. You need to tell the coroner.'

The constable turned the side of his head with the ear missing towards her. 'Can't hear a thing, love,' he said.

He backed further into the doorway so she couldn't see him. People around her were asking questions but it was just a clamour of noise. She pushed through the faces shouting at her to walk around the courthouse to find another door, a window, anything, but there was nothing but blank stone and the thick wood of the locked front entrance. She banged on it with her fists but the big door just absorbed the sound. She gulped back big sobs. Her defences had failed, her plan wasn't working and the raw loss of her brother tore through her. The one bright, exciting, dangerous member of her family gone.

Someone took her hand. It was the Widow, and the girl led her away. The crowd followed her, still shouting questions like she was a prophet. Inside the court they might not know the truth but everyone outside did. That was London for you. The crowd, one by one, gave up and fell away until it was just her and the girl. She took a look at her. She had a small, even face covered in big, uneven-sized freckles like someone had thrown a handful of mud at her. Ann remembered she still had the shawl and gave it back to her.

'What now?' said the girl.

'I find out who had Christopher killed and kill them,' said Ann.

The girl nodded.

'Bit of breakfast first?'

WILL

Eleanor Ball was nervous. She clutched the sprigs of lavender she held in her hand so tightly, that its crushed scent reached Will.

'Were you there when he was killed?' Danby asked.

'No, but—'

'Next witness.'

Skerries gave her a nod to continue. They must have agreed a story, Will thought, but when she tried to speak again, Danby just said, 'Sit down.'

Faunt stirred.

'Don't,' said Danby, like he was talking to a dog. 'Next witness.'

Will was the next witness and he knew from what had happened to Eleanor Bull what Danby's only question would be. He had to try what he'd promised Ann, so he rose quickly and spoke fast. 'I wasn't there when it happened, but I do have one brief fact that I think the court would want to know.'

'It doesn't,' said Danby.

'If you judge it worthless, you can imprison me for wasting the court's time.'

Had he just said that out loud? It appeared he had because there was an appreciative murmur from the privileged few that had been let back in. Here was the drama they'd turned up for. Danby put his hands behind his head, leant back and considered. Everyone was waiting on him, and he liked that.

'Very well,' he said. '*Ludi incipiant.*'

A few of the crowd laughed just to show they understood the Latin.

'I don't suppose you know what that means, Mr Shakespeare?' said Danby. The college men always used that against you. Even Chris would start speaking in Latin when they argued, just to irk him. 'Go on then,' said Danby. 'The stage is yours, but the court is mine.'

Will spoke directly to Danby. 'They keep saying that Marlowe grabbed Frizer's knife from his belt, but why would he do that when he had his own knife in a sheath inside his jacket?'

Danby looked interested.

'It's still there now,' said Will.

'How do you know that?'

Will thought of the limping constable's kindness to Ann and, besides, it was best not to make enemies of them. He lied. 'I saw it when they brought his body to the courthouse.'

'Let's see then,' said Danby.

Quinn stepped forward but Danby wasn't going to let anyone steal this moment. He waved the constable away, got up and stepped forward to the body.

Danby opened Chris's jacket, and with a conjurer's flourish, he held it open so everyone could see inside. There was a gasp.

The sheath was empty. Will kept looking for the knife, even when clearly it was not there. The horrors of Marshalsea Prison flickered inside his skull.

'But it was there,' he said.

Skerries was grinning. Faunt was on his feet.

'Oh dear, my lord, it looks as if the witness is going to prison.'

That probably saved Will.

Danby snapped, 'I make the decisions here, Faunt. His evidence has been worthwhile. We now know Marlowe had no knife of his own.'

'Someone must have taken it,' said Will.

Danby passed close by Will as he returned to his chair. 'Say nothing else.'

Will didn't. But who had taken the knife? The constables? It could just have been plain theft. Or had someone got them to search the body after they closed the courthouse? But how did they know? Had someone overheard his conversation with Ann?

Danby turned to the jury. 'Let me sum up.' He pointed at Frizer, Skerries and Pooley. 'If you believe them, it's self-defence; if you don't, it isn't.'

Faunt made as if to stand.

'No,' said Danby, and continued to the jury. 'You could retire to talk this over, but bearing in mind that even as I speak, your apprentices are robbing you blind, and possibly impregnating your wives, shall we just have a show of hands?'

The jury nodded.

'So,' said Danby, 'those for self-defence?'

LIZZIE

Lizzie had gone to sleep in someone's garden and she woke up with a snail crawling across her neck. She put it in her pocket along with the soft black hat.

She wanted to go home but didn't know where she was, so she did what her mama had always told her to do, and asked a well- dressed woman the way back to Skinner Street.

'I'll tell you the way,' said the woman. 'Go to the sea, swim back to Holland, and then stay there.'

They could still tell she was Dutch from the way she spoke.

'I'm called Lizzie, after the English queen,' she yelled out as she ran away.

Why did they hate her just because she came from Holland? Strangers shouted that they took English jobs, but the English weavers wouldn't let her mama work even though she could do tapestry stitch much better than them. They shouted that they brought disease, but her family had been healthy until they had to live in the rotting hut with the white and orange mould on the walls that looked like scary faces in the light of their only candle. Once a man had put his face close to hers, and speckled her face with spittle as he shouted that the Dutch worshipped the devil. She had never worshipped him. Never. She ran and ran on angry legs past all the people who hated her, but then gasping in air she smelt the stinky smell of the tannery and knew where she was.

Lizzie's mother hugged her when she came home. She

hugged her too tight, and Lizzie could feel her heart going fast. Grown-ups never stopped surprising her. She had expected a beating.

Mama scrubbed her when she saw the silvery snail trail across her neck, and Lizzie told her about the man on the table in the big building and how he was the dead man she had found. Her mama's forehead wrinkled as she thought about it. She went back to speaking Dutch and made Lizzie swear on her Bible that she was telling the truth, and then she went back to English and said they must do their duty as citizens and for Lizzie to put on her best dress.

'Better dress,' Lizzie corrected her. 'I only have two.'

WILL

Ann was angry, walking fast, her head down like she was heading into a stiff breeze. Chris's friend the Widow was with them and had to break into little running steps to keep up. They were walking away from the fine merchants' houses on Broadway towards the competing stenches of the slaughterhouse and tannery. The leather from Deptford was too poor quality for the gloves his father had made. They cut across Deptford Strand past the tumbledown shacks, most built illegally on waste ground. Many were made from the curved timbers culled from abandoned ships, their sides buckled and bowed so they looked as drunk as the rest of Deptford.

'So did none of the jurors think they were guilty?' Ann asked.

'One,' said Will.

When Danby had asked who was for self-defence, nine or ten had put up their hands right away, then most of the rest, seeing which way it was going, had too, except for a little, wiry man on the end who sat there glaring with his arms folded.

A passing man, who had the bow-legged walk and ape-like arms of a sailor, spat a black stream of something at Will's feet. Will started to turn, but Anne grabbed his sleeve.

'So are you sure you really felt Chris's knife last night?' Ann asked.

He nodded. He was. He'd felt the cool of the ivory handle and the grooves of the Latin inscription.

'Could it have been the blonde man you were struggling with who took it?'

'No, he was already being dragged away when I reached inside Chris's doublet.'

'But, maybe, he'd been sent to get it, and when he didn't, he ran into the inquest the next day threatening to kill Frizer to create a diversion so they could send everyone out and get rid of it?' Will could see why she was asking questions but his bruised head ached and he wanted to stop thinking for a moment. 'But to know about it they'd have to have overheard us talking about it,' he said, hoping this would end it.

'We told Bella. Or that Dutch servant could have been listening, or just someone in the street.'

Big spots of rain started falling and women bustled out from the shacks to bring in washing.

'Perhaps, Danby the coroner was in on it,' she added.

To Will, Danby didn't seem like a man who'd like being told what to do. 'I don't know,' he said, shaking his head, which made it hurt more.

'So they've killed Christopher and they're going to get away with it,' said Ann, as if it was his fault.

'They've been sent to the Marshalsea,' said Will.

'But they won't be down in limbo,' Ann said. 'They'll have good rooms and good food. And whores, they'll have whores. Someone with money's paying them. How else did they get Faunt? And he'll get them the queen's pardon in no time. How long was Christopher in Newgate?'

'About six weeks,' said Will.

After Chris and Watson, the poet, had killed Bradley in a sword fight about no one knew quite what, they too had ended up being judged at an inquest. The magistrate had been most concerned that Chris had been carrying a sword when he wasn't a gentleman. The witnesses had said Bradley started it, though Will suspected Chris had bribed them. The verdict had been self-defence just like today. There had nearly been another fight with Bradley's brother outside the doors of the courthouse.

'Could Chris have been killed in revenge for Bradley?' Will asked.

'It was the thrust from Watson, not Christopher, that killed him,' said Ann.

Will hesitated, then decided not to say anything. He didn't know for sure which of them stabbed Bradley with the sword, only that one morning Chris had told him that he'd killed a man. Was that Bradley, someone else, or a lie?

'I feel guilty,' Chris had said, 'at how little guilt I feel.'

It must have been in early spring, because they had been watching one of the gangs hired to kill dogs as the plague got worse. Chris kicked open a gate so a slinking grey lurcher could escape.

'And now I've saved a life,' he said as a dog catcher swore and called him a sodomite.

'You'll have to save more than a dog to square things up,' said Will.

'How many?' asked Chris. 'Five? That would weigh about the same as a man.'

'Would it weigh as much as a man's soul?' Will realised he was once again playing Chris's straight man.

'Do souls exist?' Chris had asked. 'I've repeatedly tried to sell mine but there haven't been any takers.'

He'd laughed, watching the dog catcher fall over trying to throw his net over a nimble black mongrel.

'You should kill someone, Will, it's good research for a writer.'

Chris had always told Will that he hadn't lived. Very well, he hadn't killed anyone, but it was not as if murderers made the best writers. Could Frizer write a tragedy? He doubted it. And anyway Will had seen danger. What of his six months on the road with the players when he'd left Stratford? Winter nights sleeping, stacked together in the cart for warmth, waking with their faces white with hoar frost. The horse had died and they'd eaten it. He'd gashed his arm in a sword fight in the first act when the Sultan was too drunk to remember the moves. He bled for three acts and fainted when he was supposed to bring the King of Persia news that his daughters were dead.

'Think less and live more,' Chris had told him. Well, Chris had thought very little and now he was dead.

'You really think Bradley could have had something to do with it?' Ann was asking.

The rain was getting heavier and the Widow held her shawl above her head, but Ann just strode on, curls of black hair plastered to her cheeks.

'I don't know,' said Will. 'But after the inquest Bradley's brother swore he'd kill both Watson and Chris.'

'You think he hired Frizer's gang to kill him?'

'Or he killed him and brought in Frizer and Skerries to do their self-defence racket.'

'We need to find out if that story is true,' said Ann. 'And who they killed up there. And we need to talk to Watson in case someone has tried to kill him. And Bradley's brother, we need to speak to someone who knows him and see if he has enough money to hire Skerries' gang.'

She was frowning with her head bent forward in that way of hers and counting on her fingers as she marshalled the thoughts in her head.

'And we need to find out where Chris went after he left the pub, and whether he stayed at the Deptford house where you thought you smelt him. And who that blonde man with the knife is.'

Will's bruised head pounded and the wound in his chest throbbed. He felt like he was being beaten up from inside. Ann was running out of fingers. She stopped talking and stared at him.

'What did I just say?' she asked him.

'I'm sorry,' he said. He was giddy with tiredness.

'Don't you want to find out who killed Chris?'
'I do.'

He did, he really did, but what he most wanted was to be with Ann. He hadn't realised how much he had missed her until he saw her again. He shouldn't think thoughts like these with Chris rotting in his coffin but, in truth, mixed in with the exhaustion and pain and grief, he felt a kind of joy at being with her.

'Well, we need to get on with it,' she said. 'Because we've only got nine days.'

'Why nine days?'

'Because that's when I'm getting married.'

LIZZIE

Lizzie saw an apple core on the ground at her feet. Did snails eat apple cores? They probably would if they were hungry. Lizzie picked it up out of the mud and wiped it off a bit before she put it in her pocket. Her mama was trying to explain in her bad English about how Lizzie had found the body, to a man in a red jacket at the door of the courthouse. Lizzie had known it was a mistake to come. She tried to get as far away from the man as possible, but her mother held tightly on to her hand and pulled her back.

'Blah, blah, blah, blah,' said the man. 'Today's all blah, blah, blah.'

'Tell him, Lizzie,' said her mama.

Lizzie could see that he didn't want to be told. He didn't want them to be 'good citizens', he wanted them to leave him alone and go back to Holland.

Three men came out of the door with another man in a red jacket with one ear missing who said, 'We'll all get to Marshalsea quicker if I don't chain you up, so swear you're not going to run away, right?'

'How about we run away into the Cock Tavern on the way?' said one of the three men who had a horrible yellow eye. 'We'll buy you a drink?'

Lizzie's mama jabbed her with one finger and gestured at the first red-jacketed man. 'Tell the constable.'

'I saw Christopher Marlowe dead yesterday at lunchtime down by the river,' said Lizzie.

'*Rot op*,' he said. 'Weren't expecting that, were you? I've been to the Low Countries. I fought with Dudley at Zutphen.'

'You'll tell someone, won't you?' said Lizzie's mama, but he wasn't looking at them any more.

WILL

Ann was marrying a shoemaker who had been one of her father's apprentices. He was taking over her father's failing business. What could Will say? He was already married. It hadn't been a love match between him and the other Anne. After the families had met to organise his wedding, his mother had said, 'Put it off for another month. She may still miscarry.'

The titled poets who wrote of the sweet romances between swains and maidens hadn't spent much time in the English countryside.

His father just said, 'Couldn't you have just waited?'

He couldn't. Eighteen and impatient, he couldn't wait for sex and love and a life that stretched beyond the narrow world of his parents' business.

It had happened at a Michaelmas fair where he'd got in a drunken fight and lost. Anne, the other Anne with an 'e', had got drunk too and quarrelled with her sisters. She'd taken pity on him and mopped up his bloody face with her handkerchief.

'Won't that stain?' he'd asked.

'Not if I soak it in a pail of cold water,' she'd said. That had been their courtship.

His lip had started to bleed again when they'd kissed, and he had the metal taste of blood in his mouth as they walked sideways, still kissing, into the barn. He'd not known there were horses there until he heard their heavy movements and panting breath in the darkness. By the time they'd finished his eyes had grown accustomed to the dark and he could just make out a tiny foal on the ground next to its mother, still too weak to stand. Had it been born while they drunkenly copulated? It kicked its legs around and struggled to its feet and tottered towards the mare to suckle and they laughed at the surprise of it. That was the closest he ever felt to her.

His family had blamed her for trapping him into marriage, twenty-six and needing a husband, but Anne didn't think like that. She barely thought. She wanted things then and there. He had left her, with his daughter Susannah barely baptised.

He'd told himself that it wasn't them he was leaving but the cramped confines of Stratford-upon-Avon. He told himself that Anne didn't love him or even seem to like him, and that he sent them money and went back to see them when he could, and that most of the theatre people had left a wife in the countryside, sometimes two or three. All the things he told himself might have worked if it hadn't been for Ann Marlowe, Ann with no 'e' as he called her, and as time went on just 'no e'. She didn't let him get away with anything, and told him he was a bad husband and a bad father. How she squared her disapproval of his adultery with the nights she spent under his sloping roof in Shoreditch he wasn't sure.

It was Susannah and then the twins, Judith and Hamnet, whom he missed. He had set out in March to get home for Susannah's tenth birthday but the plague was just getting a grip on London and travellers from the capital weren't welcome. The cart was stoned before they even reached Hertford and he turned back.

He, Ann and the Widow were approaching the Queen's Head where they had arranged to meet Alleyn and the others before going on to Deptford graveyard for Chris's burial. The pub looked as if it had been designed by drunks and built by fools – every wall bowed out, leaning in or cracked, windows racked into strange shapes by subsiding walls, not a right angle in sight. As they came around the corner a press gang moved in to block both entrances, but then the two thugs at the front door stepped back, separated and bowed low. Lord Strange came out. They stayed bowed low, hoping to be thrown a penny. Lord Strange took a silver sixpence from his pocket with a silk-gloved hand.

'Heads or tails?'

They hesitated.

'There's only two to choose from,' he said.

'Heads,' said one of them.

He spun the coin high and caught it.

'Tails.' He showed them and put the coin back in his pocket.

Lord Ferdinando Strange financed the most successful theatre company in London. He dressed himself as a shopkeeper dressed his shop window. Today he wore a purple cloak with a red silk lining and a red hat plumed with purple feathers, one of his more modest outfits.

'William, William,' he said as he saw him. 'So now Chris has gone, you're the top scribbler in London, eh?'

Will felt Ann tauten beside him.

'Ann Marlowe,' Will said. 'This is Lord Strange.'

'Lord Strange,' said the Widow. 'Is that a stage name?'

'No, he's a lord,' said Will.

'But not a real one?' said the Widow.

'I'm descended from Henry VII on my mother's side and Henry VIII on my father's side,' said Lord Strange, enunciating carefully as he always did when talking to common people.

'Oh,' said the Widow. She curtsied.

'I expect you're sorry about my brother's death?' said Ann.

Strange considered this as if it was a serious question. 'Yes,' he said. 'This morning I was rumoured to be responsible for it.'

'Why was that?'

'They said he was intending to desert Lord Strange's Men for the Admiral's Men, so I had him killed.'

'And did you?' asked Ann.

'I didn't,' said Lord Strange. 'And he wasn't. Anyhow, thankfully there are now new rumours. Have you heard that Frizer and the other ones did the same thing in Yorkshire?'

'Yes,' said Ann. 'I may have started that.'

Lord Strange stared at her. His top lip remained slightly open at rest which gave him a constant look of disdain, and his eyes had a strange, cloudy deadness. It was good that his obsession with theatre didn't run to acting.

'How's the new one coming along?' he asked Will.

'Nearly there,' said Will.

'Hmm,' said Lord Strange. 'Chris kept saying that about his new one. You don't know if he finished it before his... you know?'

Will had no idea Chris had a 'new one'.

A man with a bad limp ran out of the pub door with the press gang after him. They soon tackled him to the ground, and when he kept struggling one of them hit him in the head with the hilt of his dagger.

Strange's lip curled a little more than usual. He shook his head and murmured, 'People,' before turning back to Will.

'I'm having a word at court about reopening the theatres,' said Lord Strange, 'with less audience so they don't worry about spreading the plague, but with higher prices. We'll put on one of Chris's plays and clean up after all this publicity.'

He walked away to where his three beautifully liveried servants were waiting. His servants probably had servants. Ann was seething.

'Apparently he's very good with horses,' said Will.

'But he is fantastically rich,' said Alleyn, joining them, 'so we fawn over him incessantly.' He turned to Ann. 'I am so sorry for your loss, and for the world's loss. The only alchemy that ever worked was what Chris did with words.'

How were actors so eloquent when they spoke, while writers just sounded like everyone else? There were these great, dark underground rivers flowing through people, but when they tried to speak of them it came out as trite nothings. It was only when Will put words in the mouths of made-up people that he could touch some of it.

Ann spoke to Alleyn. 'I'm sorry I didn't say earlier when you sent a message about your elegy, but yes, there is something I would like you to include.'

'Ah,' said Alleyn, looking down from his great height past his Roman nose and finely honed jawline. 'I'm frightfully sorry, but I cannot speak at the funeral any more. As Lord Strange mentioned, we are attending a meeting about reopening the theatres. I shall make very little contribution, I'm sure.' He bowed his head in mock modesty. 'But I'm a necessary appendage, much as I hate to get involved in politics.'

That wasn't true, he loved politics, and couldn't keep out of it.

'Oh,' said Ann. 'Can Burbage—'

Alleyn interrupted – gracefully, of course. 'He will be at the meeting too, I fear. And Tarleton. It requires the presence of all London's leading thespians, if only as ornamentation.'

Kemp came over. He was the greatest comedian in all of Europe, he often told Will. He played all the fools for Strange's Men. His face was built for comedy but refurbished by alcohol and today he was far too drunk to be funny. He stared at them slack-faced, his head too big for his body and his mouth too big for his head. Spotting a drunk, the press gang came walking over.

'Fuck off, I'm Kemp,' he said, then pointed at Will. 'And you can't take him, he's my writer.'

They weren't going to take Will. When he had first turned up in London, with one patched set of clothes and nowhere to sleep, he had to keep his eyes open for the press gangs, but now they left him alone. Chris had teased him that he'd become respectable.

'He's writing a play about Richard III,' said Kemp to the press gang. 'Tell him he better write a part with some laughs.'

He unbuttoned his flies and Will thought he was going to piss on his feet, but he walked a couple of steps and leant with one hand against the pub wall.

'If only he was this good when he acts drunk,' whispered Alleyn.

'So who'll do the elegy?' said Ann.

'You could,' said Will.

'I couldn't. I wouldn't get the words out.'

'It should be Will,' said Alleyn. 'It probably should have been him in the first place. We all know he's a fine speaker.'

That was untrue for Alleyn didn't rate him. He'd overheard his reply when someone asked who Will should play in *Titus Andronicus*. 'Probably the pie'. Just because Will didn't overact like the rest of them.

'Just do, you know, wonderful, lovely, gorgeous, wonderful,' he said to Will, 'stay off anything political.'

Alleyn turned to go, but Ann was quickly on to it. 'Why does no one want to speak at Chris's burial? Have you been warned off?'

'Good God,' said Alleyn, his jaw tilted up as when he played Tamburlaine. 'I am not the sort of man to be "warned off" by anyone.'

Ann continued to stare angrily at him. He may have been England's greatest actor but he wasn't fooling her. Kemp was no longer urinating, but still leaning against the wall. The wall leant one way and Kemp the other. Alleyn grabbed him by his collar and led him away, swearing at a Dutch beggar who stretched out his bowl towards him.

'Did anyone warn you off doing the elegy?' Ann asked him.

Nearly all the theatre people had left by the time the cart with Chris's coffin turned up, but Bella joined Will and Ann as they followed it to the graveyard. She had found somewhere to change and had replaced the pearl-trimmed mauve gown that she had worn at the inquest with a simple black dress and cape. A glazier's wagon ahead of them had turned on its side and the glazier was sobbing and shouting as he tried to pick the few unbroken panes from the street before they were trampled.

'Whose house did we stay at last night?' Ann asked Bella.

'It's owned by "Rich" Spencer,' she said. 'He told me that if I mentioned his name I could always stay there.'

So she even knew "Rich" Spencer.

The cart with Chris's coffin crunched across the broken glass.

'And who is it who does live there?'

'No one permanently. There's a couple of gentlemen who stay there. I've never met them, they always send their servants down.' Bella barely concealed her irritation at being questioned.

'Could Christopher have stayed there the night before he was killed?' asked Ann.

'I very much doubt it. Spencer disliked him.'

Bella pulled on the chain attached to Perro's collar and led her across to the side of the street where there were only a few shards of glass.

'Will smelt him,' said Ann, 'that particular scent he used, it was on a pillow.'

'Surely,' said Bella, 'there are others who smell the same.'

'It was Chris,' said Will.

'What a keen sense of smell you have,' said Bella. 'If you fail as a playwright you can work as a truffle hound.'

Did Will trust Bella? Was her calculated air of mystery meant to captivate or simply conceal? Where was she from? Arabia, Sicily, North Africa? She had money, but what did she do? Even her age was uncertain. Was she late twenties, thirty, forty even? She told stories of travel to the Levant and Arabia Felix and the New World – a whale that carried her to shore after a shipwreck, how she survived a sandstorm stitched into the belly of a dead camel, how she made her way past the Yellow Eunuchs into the great harem of Constantinople, and there joined in a conference of the sultan's one-thousand wives who voted on which policies they would persuade him to undertake. Will suspected these were tall tales told her by others and that her own untold tales were darker and sadder. Once, when the boy actors all had the Thames fever, she had read the part of Margaret of Anjou in rehearsal and played her with a ferocity that the male actors struggled to match. Was that her? He couldn't tell for sure, she changed constantly. It was like trying to grasp the sea.

The cart was stuck again. A man was shivering uncontrollably in the street, his teeth chattering, his hands clamped around his head. 'It's not the plague,' he kept saying, so everyone around him thought it was, and stepped away from him. 'It's just the fen ague,' he yelled, 'I've had it for years.'

A woman shouted at him to get out of the way so she could pass.

'But it's not the plague,' he said again and stayed put.

The plague drove people mad, but it drove them mad in different ways. Some hid away as if the plague wouldn't find them in the dark. They bought food from the plague vendors, who soaked their clothes in vinegar and took the coins slipped out under the door and left the bread or cheese on the doorstep. These people had nothing to do and too much time. Their minds ran out of sane things to think about, and they obsessed on wild rumours whispered through walls and windows by others like them. A priest in Cheapside told his congregation that the Dutch carried the plague but never caught it themselves. A tailor in Limehouse killed his family with an axe because the plague told him to.

Then there were those who presumed they would die and tried to pack a life into each day. Couples copulated in the back rooms of pubs. Drunk men fought wildly not fearing death for it was coming for them anyway. Some gambled away all they had and woke up still alive, owning nothing but their clothes. Some were kind because that was their nature, but others turned to goodness because they felt the flames of hell licking about their feet, and they sought salvation with a loud charity that did little good.

Catholics said the plague was God's punishment for abandoning the True Faith, though on its way north it had stopped off to kill a third of Catholic Venice. Puritans declared it was God's will and your fate was inescapable, yet still hid lavender, bay, rabbit's feet and holy trinkets behind the furniture.

Doctors multiplied. They swore that their salves and potions, their chopped-up newts and mercury and arsenic and owl droppings could save you, but, walking among the sick, they died fastest. They were at once replaced by the reckless and desperate, for to be a doctor in a plague year was the quickest route to a fortune.

Will knew many who had died. Three actors, the boy who had played Helen of Troy in *Faustus*, the two women who made the costumes, were all dead, and his landlord and the family that had sold cheese from a barrow beneath his window. If puritans were right and death was preordained, God seemed to be murdering the men and women he had created at random.

To Will the plague seemed a living thing, creeping through London in the evening mists, slinking under doors and reaching its long fingers up the stairs as you slept. He felt that anything he touched could kill him, that every breath he took was a lottery. There were days when he wondered how he could be both sick of life and scared of death. Ann jabbed him.

'It's him,' she said.

'Who?' asked Will.

'There. Look.'

Will didn't know who she was pointing at.

'The blonde man,' she said, 'the man who tried to stab Frizer at the inquest, the man who hugged Chris's body.'

She was walking forward past the cart, pointing, but Will couldn't see the blonde man.

'It's him,' she said stubbornly, and started to run.

Will followed. The bruise on his face was throbbing. She ran close to the shivering man and into the crowd on the other side. There was a narrow, crowded lane off to the right – a fish market, the ground glinting with fish scales, dogs waiting for discarded tails and heads.

'He must have gone down there,' she said.

'He'll be in prison,' Will said.

'It was him.'

'Maybe he's got a brother.'

'Oh, identical twins who keep getting mistaken for each other,' she said. 'Wherever would you get an idea like that?'

'They won't have let him go,' said Will.

Another voice beside him called out. 'I saw him.' It was the Widow.

Ann looked triumphant. 'See!'

The Marlowes were bad losers and bad winners. Will knew from betting against Chris. The cart driver was using his whip to try and shift the man in the road.

'Maybe he's one of them,' said Ann. 'Maybe they released him because he helped them get rid of the knife.'

She must have seen the doubt in Will's face.

'You heard Pooley,' she said. 'He claimed they work for Cecil. If Cecil sent word they'd release Satan.'

Robert Cecil, Secretary of State, son of Lord William Cecil was the queen's hunchbacked advisor who had ordered Kyd's torture and summoned Marlowe to the Queen's Court, the man who was rumoured to control the queen through witchcraft, who had probably started the rumour himself, who ran hundreds of informants who in their turn paid thousands more. 'Cecil's in the corner,' someone would say, putting a finger to their lips when conversations slipped into politics. Chris, of course, prefaced his diatribes with, 'Cecil, are you listening?'

'If you're up against Cecil,' said Will. 'There's no point trying.'

'Me? I thought it was us,' said Ann angrily.

Something in Will loved her when she was angry, but then, of course, she was angry most of the time. She and Will could argue about anything from an odd look to which of mankind's inventions had most changed the world. He said the printing press. She said gunpowder, of course she did. When it had ended up with them shouting, she claimed that it proved her right, for words had been superseded by belligerence.

Barking Bobby walked past them. 'Mate,' he said to the man in the road, 'I've had the plague twice so you don't frighten me.'

'I'm not talking to some African.' said the man, taking in his colour.

Bobby ignored this. 'There's a bloke here who needs to get buried, so you don't move, I'm going to deck you.'

Barking Bobby was short and plump, with more chins than teeth, but he had a way with a threat that made you believe it, and the man moved.

'Are you sure you saw him?' Will asked the Widow.

'Yeah, I saw his wrist.'

'You saw his wrist?'

'Yeah, that tattoo of a cross with four crosses in the gaps.'

It came back to Will. The arm he'd grabbed wrestling the blonde man away from Chris's body had that tattoo – the Jerusalem tattoo of those who had made the pilgrimage to the Holy Land. Ann really had seen him.

He had walked into the courtroom with a knife so why was he walking free? Was he one of Cecil's men, as Ann had said, used to clear the court so they could remove the knife from the sheaf? Or perhaps Danby was being more independent than they wanted and they needed to have a word with him. Or perhaps he was just employed to remind the crowd that Chris slept with men, that he was one of those 'lewd theatre types' who were always getting in drunken brawls in the afternoon while honest men worked. That could explain him embracing Chris's corpse the night before.

The questions multiplied and there were no answers. One thought wouldn't go away though. He was sure that he'd seen the blonde man with the Jerusalem tattoo before.

ANN

She shouldn't have told Will that she was getting married. When her father had told her that John wanted to marry her she'd hesitated.

'You're thinking of that married playwright, aren't you?' he'd said.

For once he'd been right. Did John know about Will? He had to. In Canterbury everyone knew everything about everyone else. What else did they have to talk about apart from the price of leather and wood and silver and beef and brass? Did John mind about Will? She didn't know him well enough to tell. Still, he was marrying her. Why was she marrying him? This was the question she tried never to ask. Why did it keep coming back into her head? Why was she surrendering to a life she never wanted? Because it was going to happen sooner or later, so why not now? Because she liked other people's children so surely she'd love her own. John was sober, clean and educated. One of them would probably die before he became fat, opinionated and drunk – most likely her in the lottery of childbirth. It just took one bad one, and four men were lifting you into your coffin. With Jane, she was so small, her father had lifted her alone. Young men bled to death, killed by young men's knives. Young women bled to death, killed by young men's babies. And now, here she was trying to answer the question she promised herself she'd avoid, when she should be concentrating on finding out who killed Chris.

There was a big crowd at the burial, a rough crowd. The titled and famous had gone home. Strangely, Faunt the lawyer was there, and crooked Tom Kyd, Bella and Barking Bobby. Was he from Barking, was he barking mad, or did he just bark? Who knew?

The gravedigger, weathered as a dead tree, leant on his shovel gnawing meat off a bone of some kind. The vicar sped through the rites in a fast mumble. He'd had a reluctant, wet, fleshy handshake and wouldn't look her in the eye. Everyone was in such a hurry to get Chris under the ground where he could do no more harm.

Another twelve hours and word of his death would reach Canterbury. Her father would be heartbroken. He might be in debt and quarrelling with his neighbours, but did they have a 'playwright son in London'? He thought he'd created Christopher by sending him to university.

'I could have been you, if I'd had a father like me,' he'd shouted in one of their frequent rows.

And her mother – she would grieve silently. As her father got louder she got quieter. She faded into the dark corners of the house, as if she hoped everyone would forget she was there. And soon Ann would be back there too. She'd sent a message, with a cartman she knew, to say that she'd stay in London a few more days to sort things out, but be back in time for the wedding.

The vicar's mumbling ceased. It was time to lower the coffin.

'It has to be men on the ropes,' the vicar had said, looking slightly to the right of her face.

She wasn't having that. It was her, Will, Tom Kyd and an elderly actor who'd been asleep when the rest of them fled. Tom's right hand was next to Will's on the rope. There was only the slightest tinge of black ink. His claim that he'd been busy writing a new play was a lie. Tom gritted his teeth and groaned as he took the weight, and Barking Bobby stepped forward to help him, his chins quivering with effort. The coffin slurped into the wet clay. To Ann, it looked like the gravedigger had sold them short and dug a grave more like four feet deep than six. There were some who'd like him buried a hundred feet underground, thought Ann. The gravedigger stepped forward, shovel in hand as soon as the coffin touched the dirt, but Will stepped to the edge of the grave, ready to speak. The gravedigger sighed and stopped, but did not move back, so he stood beside Will, his long shovel in his hand, as Will began.

'Many things have been said about Christopher Marlowe. That he was Satan's ambassador on earth, that his eyes glowed in the dark, that dogs fled from him, and women were drawn to him and woke in his bed not knowing how they got there. A lot of these rumours were started by Chris.'

Will had asked Ann what to say.

'Make them laugh,' she'd said. 'He'd like that.'

She saw Will had expected a laugh there, but there was a hostile silence and a few of the crowd hissed and booed. Will was rattled, but went on.

'The truth is that he was a genius, his eyes were dark brown, and dogs loved him as much as women and men. He was publicly outrageous and privately kind.'

There was more hissing and some shouts from the back she could not make out.

Will raised his voice. 'He was accused of atheism, murder, counterfeiting, homosexuality, espionage, incest, alchemy and black magic, at least a couple of which were untrue.'

Again no laugh, but louder booing.

She heard a shout clearly. 'You should know about murder!'

Some men started a slow handclap. Will's eyes were panicky. He could not understand what was going on. She began to.

'Few knew his real secret,' he said.

'What about your secret?' a woman shouted.

'That he wrote plays, not in a whirlwind of alcohol-fuelled genius, but in long, sober hours.'

Without realising, Will was speaking in time to the rising crash of the slow handclap. It was getting hard to hear him.

'Bolted in his room by his landlady at his request,' he said as if the clap was part of his performance.

They were throwing things now. A stone that fell short thumped on the lid of the coffin. The gravedigger moved sideways so as not to be in the target area.

Will was yelling in a sort of fury, and not stopping, not ducking. A bit of rotten fruit hit him on the head.

'He created blank verse!'

'Murderer,' they chanted.

'He was our guiding light, our leader, the man who made it all possible, the man who created modern theatre.'

He stood stiff and still, frozen in a storm of missiles and abuse. A stone smacked into his face.

The crowd were moving forward, inching in small, slow steps, a monster stalking its prey. Ann grabbed his hand and pulled him away.

'What's happening?' he said.

'Walk fast,' she yelled, and he did what she told him.

The Widow, bless her, was walking with them and she saw Bella leaving too, and in amongst the baying mob she was sure she glimpsed the blonde man.

Would the crowd be satisfied now they'd made him run or did they have the scent of blood? A bald man with no teeth broke into a trot. He had a metal spike in one hand. More followed.

The bald man jumped the grave and started moving fast, his mouth a panting red hole.

There was a black blur of movement and he was screaming. Perro was clamped to his arm. The men running behind him stopped and watched Perro drag him to the ground.

Bella spoke a command in a harsh foreign language and Perro let go and sat down on her haunches, licking the blood off her nose with a long pink tongue. The man showed no signs of wanting to get up and Bella called again and the dog loped over to her.

Will wiped blood off his cheek. 'I don't understand,' he said.

'Later,' said Ann. 'Keep walking.'

'Wait please,' called a child's voice.

Ann turned and out of the low sun came a sickly woman and a small girl.

'Are you Christopher Marlowe's sister?' asked the woman in a heavy Dutch accent.

'I am,' said Ann, still walking fast.

'I try to speak to the man at the courthouse but he did not listen,' said the woman.

She pushed the girl forward. The little girl trotted to keep up. She was only slightly taller than Perro.

'Tell them, Lizzie,' said the woman.

'The men who say they killed Mr Marlowe are lying,' she said.

'We know,' said Ann.

'She saw him dead down by the river at about two o'clock,' said her mama.

'That couldn't have been him,' said Will.

'He had a black jacket, and he was sitting down,' gabbled the girl. 'And he only had one shoe, and staring brown eyes and purple lips and he smelt nice and had gentleman's hands but with swollen fingers.'

And then she reached inside her dress and pulled out something black and glossy.

'That's Chris's hat,' said Will.

They came out into a small street of shops mostly selling cloth. There was a short gust and the rain started again and the shopkeepers rushed to get the bright-coloured racks of fabric back undercover. One saw Will and stopped what he was doing. He called a young boy over and whispered into his ear. The boy shot off, running between the flapping cloth.

'We need to get away from here,' said Bella.

'How did you get his hat?' Will asked the girl.

'Not now,' said Ann. 'Run once we get around the corner.'

Will still hesitated and Ann shoved him. He called over his shoulder. 'Where can we find you?'

'We live in the blue and red house on Skinner Street,' the mother shouted.

They turned into an alley but Lizzie's small, serious face peeped around the corner after them. 'It's not really a house,' she said, then disappeared.

The four of them splashed down the alley that was more puddle than not.

'What's happening?' said Will. 'I don't understand.'

Ann took a breath. 'They think you killed Chris.'

He looked at her as he ran and stumbled.

'I heard someone saying it in the pub,' she said. 'I thought it was just another rumour that would go away. But...' She was out of breath. 'It hasn't.'

'But why?'

'He was the top playwright in London,' said the Widow. 'And now he's dead, you are.'

Ann tried to give her a look to shut her up, but on she went.

'And you said you were going to kill him the night before he was killed. And there was that blood on your shirt.'

Bella interrupted. 'Let's try and get a boat at the Upper Watergate. If we go straight to the Stone Wharf they might try and cut us off.'

They slowed to a fast walk.

'But who started it?' said Will.

'Faunt, that lawyer, with his speech in court,' said Ann.

They were in the street by the crooked pub. Ann looked behind them. A couple of the crowd were following. Will led them off into another alleyway.

'And me,' she said. 'I started it too.'

'You?'

'I didn't mean to, but I put it about that Frizer and Skerries get called in, when someone else has done a murder, so then the mob were looking for someone else to blame.'

A wall had fallen in and blocked the alley, but they clambered over the heap of the stones instead of going back.

'We need to find out who killed him,' said Will. 'By now

everyone in London will think I murdered Chris. Everyone in half a day's ride of London – more and more people every minute. We have to find out who was behind it.'

'Yes,' said Ann, 'I thought we'd already agreed on that.'

BELLA

Throckmorton searched her at the second gate. As his hands touched her, his face went red beneath his floppy yellow hair. He took away the small dagger from her bag, but she had hidden the vial of poison in her underwear, just out of curiosity to see if he would find it, and he had been too embarrassed to reach there. He was jealous, and she knew he enjoyed hurting men, and she wondered if he had heard the old rumours about her and Chris. One thrust from that muscular arm would ram a knife deep into an eye socket. She smiled at him.

The yellow rose climbing the brick walls smelt of nothing and the chaffinch that pecked at the ivy was silent. She had taken a little something in her tea – enough to relax her, but not dull her sense of danger. Throckmorton showed her into the dining room where he sat working at the end of a long fruitwood table with an intricate inlay of shells and bone. He looked up briefly when he heard the rattle of Perro's chain. If they were intent on taking away anything dangerous, Perro was the first thing they should have confiscated.

He went back to working on his papers and the only sound was the scratching of his pen. He paused to sprinkle powdered cuttlefish bone on the page to dry the ink. When he finally looked up he stared silently at her for a long time as if studying an unusual insect through a magnifying glass.

'Bring me up to date on who you're spying for,' he said.

'Only you.'

He smiled indulgently.

'If I betray their confidence to you,' she said, 'you'd think I'd betray your confidence to them?'

'Do any of them have the hold over you that I do?'

'No, they just pay me money.'

'I like you, Bella,' he said, 'but I don't confuse that with trusting you.'

Others like him told you nothing of what they thought, but he gave you glimpses, like a man revealing the hilt of the dagger in his belt as a warning.

'I told you about the hidden knife on Chris's corpse, didn't I?' she said.

He nodded. 'The door,' he said.

She turned silently and opened the door behind her to check the corridor outside was empty. It was and she closed it.

She felt a listless torpor enfold her and badly wanted to sit down. Her mind drifted off to the voyage she had taken to the far north.

The ice stretched to the horizon. At first, she had thought the orange glow where the frozen sea met the sky was the sun rising, but then she saw it was a distant fire.

A sharp crack made her jump. He had banged a candlestick on the table.

'Bella,' he said, 'if you work for me you must numb yourself less.'

'I'm sorry,' she said. 'You're right.'

'I need you to do something for me,' he said, still holding the candlestick.

'And what is that?'

She saw his anger rise. 'Does the captain ask the galley slave if he would like to row today? Let us try again. Bella, I need you to do something for me. Now you say "yes".'

'Yes,' she said.

ACT TWO

ANN

Waking up on the two mornings since Chris had been murdered, Ann had taken a moment to place where she was. When she did, it came with the stab of knowledge that her brother was dead. She had suffered grief before, and she knew a morning would come when her first thought would no longer be 'Chris is dead', but she feared it would take a long time. It certainly would be the first thought on her wedding day.

She got up from where she had slept on the floor, and shook Will awake. He opened his eyes groggily and she saw him go through the same moment that she had. She wished she had fully dressed herself before she woke him rather than standing there in just a thin smock. And yet she wished she could have spent the night in his arms, just for some comfort.

The bruise had spread all down one side of his face and the wound in his chest had bled through his nightshirt.

'How did you get that cut?' she asked.

He hesitated. 'Can I tell you another time?'

She didn't suppose it really mattered, and dressed hastily. Will's room was messier than the last time she'd been there. When she looked for some clean clothes to replace his torn and bloody ones, there weren't any. She picked out some that looked only moderately dirty, chucked them to him and looked out of the window as he dressed. An old man in the house opposite winked at her, so she just turned and faced the wall.

'Pike or peacock?' asked Will.

It was a bad joke from the days when they couldn't even afford bread, and faced the day on empty stomachs. She felt herself smiling and was glad to be facing the wall. She and Will had barely been apart since they had met at Deptford courthouse and being together had started to seem normal. She wondered if her husband would be able to make her smile on such a grim day.

'Let's get something to eat on the way,' she said.

'The way where?'

'The way to Chris's room. We might find out something there.'

Will opened his mouth to say something, but then didn't. Was it that he thought there was no hope of finding Christopher's killer? Well, there wasn't if they did nothing. She felt irritated, then saw him grit his teeth as he stood up and headed for the door. He was coming, wasn't he? No one else would do that.

Christopher's room was ten minutes' walk away in Houndsditch, in a house built backing on to the old Roman wall. As they reached the end of Cripplegate, they heard the rhythmic banging of pans, and as they turned the corner, they met a woman who had been sat backwards on a donkey being led through the streets by a gang of drunks – an adulteress. She sat in silent misery, not bothering to wipe away the smears on her face, where the crowd had thrown muck at her. Will glanced at Ann. She was sure he knew what she was thinking – that this could be her. He went to take her hand but she yanked it away.

The woman had been sat on the donkey, wearing only a thin smock, which was soaked from the rain so her breasts showed through. A teenage boy gawped at her, mouth half open, too bewitched to throw the chicken carcass he held in his hand at her. Ann kicked him hard and, as he turned, slapped the carcass from his hand. He stepped angrily towards her, but Will pushed him backwards.

A bare-chested man opened a casement window, and tried to empty a pisspot on the woman, but only hit the donkey, whose long tongue licked it appreciatively.

'This is what they do for entertainment when the theatres are closed,' muttered Will.

When they reached Chris's room, the lock was smashed and a dead cat was nailed to the door. She pushed it open cautiously. The room was wrecked, furniture smashed, clothes slashed and papers spread across the floor. The breeze of the door closing behind them sent a mass of feathers from the ripped mattress floating up into the air. Written on the wall, possibly in shit, or more likely cat blood, was the word, *Madge*. She turned to Will who was staring at it too. He shrugged apologetically as if he was responsible for all of London.

'It's slang for homosexual.'

She hadn't thought they cared so much in the big city. She'd thought it was a Canterbury thing, where they hated anything different, where men who liked men were classed with witches and lepers, where a fourteen-year-old boy who couldn't whistle, that certain sign of degeneracy, was beaten so badly he could no longer talk or walk and certainly not whistle. She felt the savagery recently visited on Chris's room like the savagery inflicted on his body. Her legs felt weak, and she went to sit on the half-broken bed, then realised someone had pissed on it.

'Why the cat?' she asked.

'I think it's because he's a catamite,' said Will, again apologetic for their stupidity.

He was staring at the floor.

'They've lifted up the floorboards'

She stepped over to look. Every few feet a board had been lifted.

'Bigots don't bother to search under floorboards,' he said.

'And thieves don't bother to pretend they're bigots.'

'They were looking for something.' Will looked around carefully.

Real thieves or not, they had stolen Chris's rings, his quills, his tobacco, everything that could easily be sold. Will said he couldn't spot anything else missing. There was virtually nothing for Ann to take as a keepsake as everything left was ruined or too heavy to carry. In the end she found a couple of silver buttons that had been torn from a doublet and put them in her purse. Under the bed she saw some clothes that hadn't been savaged. She gathered them up.

'These are clean,' she said. 'Put these on. Your clothes stink and you're not far off Chris's size.'

She held up a leather jerkin. He looked hard at it. 'That isn't Chris's. It's far too big, look at the shoulders.'

It was true, he always wore his doublets fashionably tight. She looked closer. 'Kidskin. Probably Italian?'

He nodded. She and Will had no idea who had killed Chris but they knew their leather.

'It's expensive,' he said. 'Odd for someone to just leave it behind here.'

She went through the other clothes. They were Chris's, and she persuaded Will to put on a pair of burgundy pantaloons, a fresh linen shirt and a yellow doublet. In Chris's bright finery, he looked like an actor onstage.

'We should go,' she said.

'Yes.'

But he took a couple of steps over to Chris's bed and smelt the pillow. His face told her the answer but she asked anyway.

'Yes,' he said, 'the same.'

WILL

They'd been walking away from Chris's rooms past the women carrying dough to bake in the communal oven when Ann had announced, 'We need to go back to Deptford.'

'Deptford?' Will had said. 'The Deptford where a mob tried to murder me twelve hours ago?'

'They won't recognise you,' she said. 'You're not that famous.'

He pointed to the large bruise on his face. They would recognise him from that.

'Rumours come and go. They'll have forgotten,' she said.

'I don't think they will have.'

'Oh well, the men in that mob didn't strike me as early risers.'

So they had walked down to the river and Ann had paid the fare for the fast boat back to Deptford and here they were outside Eleanor Bull's house with Ann banging on the door.

'Eleanor!' Ann shouted. 'We just want to talk to you for five minutes!'

A woman stuck a head wrapped in a towel out of a nearby window. 'Not at this time of day you won't!' It was the woman from yesterday who had called Skerries a fat, yellow eyed twat.

Will remembered the cat that had jumped out of the window.

'We might be able to get in round the back alley.'

The alley ran between the houses and the mudflats beside the Thames. The gate fell off its hinges when he tried to swing it open. The passage was high with flowering nettles and when he stepped forward snail shells crunched under his feet. The window into Eleanor Bull's house was shut. Ann tried to prise it open.

'Don't help me then, will you?'

He wasn't sure whether Ann was angry with him, Chris's murderers or the world. Last night in his room she had refused his offer to have the bed to herself. In the end she slept on the floor wrapped in a bear fur, her face poking out so she looked like a small mythical beast.

He tried to get a grip on the window frame, and his hands sank into the rotten wood. Ann did the same and something gave way and they wrested it open. As he stepped over the ledge and into the room he could hear a scraping noise and a woman muttering. Ann, with her short legs, struggled to get in, but would not be helped. The muttering kept going and they stepped around the corner into the room where Chris's body had lain. Eleanor was on her hands and knees scrubbing furiously at a large rug.

'What?' she said without looking up. She did not seem surprised that they had broken into her house. She dipped a brush in a pail of soapy water and there were soap suds in her hair.

'A good rug ruined,' she muttered.

'How?' asked Ann.

'His blood. It won't come out. I think he had the devil's blood running in his veins.'

'That's his sister you're talking to,' said Will.

'So will she buy me a new rug?' She scrubbed furiously, grunting with the effort.

'She just needs to know what really happened so she can go back home and tell her mother and father.'

She ignored him. 'Come out, you bastard,' she said to the stain, still scrubbing. 'Who'd have thought he had so much blood in him?'

'Leaving it to soak is best,' said Ann.

'I'll tell you what's best. Not bleeding to death on my rug.'

She finally stopped scrubbing. The hand holding the brush was shaking. Her eyes shone emptily.

'Tell us what happened, and we won't tell anyone we got it from you,' said Will.

'My cousin's a lady-in-waiting,' she said. 'I have direct access to Her Majesty the Queen so you had better stop asking questions.' She went back to scrubbing.

'We're not going to get anything out of her,' said Ann, who reached in her bag and got out a small flask Will hadn't known was there. She took out the stopper and he smelt raw alcohol. She put it to her lips, but only pretended to drink. Eleanor stopped scrubbing.

'What's that?'

'Nothing.' Ann put away the flask. 'Let's go.' She looked at him to play along.

'Yes, let's,' said Will.

Ann rolled her eyes. It was probably not his finest bit of acting but Eleanor was only looking at the flask.

'What you got?' She stood up.

Ann got the flask out again, pulled out the stopper and held the flask at arm's length so Eleanor could smell it. Eleanor breathed in the fumes and her face softened, and for a moment looked upward as if seeing a vision. Ann pulled the flask back and turned to go. Will was surprised at her casual ruthlessness and then surprised that he was surprised.

'Wait,' said Eleanor. 'Give us a little-bitty swig.'

'What happened to my brother?'

'It was just like they said. Honest, it was.'

'You're going to have to do better than that,' said Ann.

Eleanor stared at the flask. 'Do you want to know his last words?' she said.

He saw a longing in Ann.

'No,' he said, 'we want to know what really happened.

Someone else killed him and Skerries and his lot came to sort it out, didn't they?'

Eleanor stubbornly shook her head. 'Do you want to hear his last words or not?'

She had seen the longing in Ann too.

'What we want to know,' he said, 'is who killed Chris?'

'Frizer, I told you.'

'Did Chris mention his family?' asked Ann.

'Give me that itsy-bitsy swig and I'll tell you.'

'We'll ask her the other questions in a moment,' said Ann. She held out the bottle so Eleanor could just drink a little. 'So what did he say?'

'You could see the light going out in his eyes,' Eleanor said. 'Then he muttered, "My God look not so fierce on me", and he was gone.'

Eleanor snatched at the bottle with both hands and tipped it back. Ann wrestled to stop her, and the alcohol slopped down Eleanor's face. Will reached to help but before he could get there, the little flask flew across the room, hit a beam and smashed. There was a small puddle of liquid on the floor among the shards.

They stared at Eleanor. Eleanor stared at the puddle.

'My God look not so fierce on me?' said Will. 'So you've seen *Doctor Faustus*.'

'No,' said Eleanor.

'That's what Faustus says just before he dies,' Will said.

'Maybe that's why it came into his head,' said Eleanor.

She was looking at the puddle slowly disappearing down a crack between the floorboards. Will realised she was waiting for them to go so she could try and lick it up. Will would never do that, not unless he was really desperate and it was a much bigger puddle.

They left by the front door. The woman with the towel around her head shouted to Will. 'So was it you who murdered him, love?'

They walked off.

'You said you were going to kill him the night before though, didn't you?'

'It's just one of those things you say,' Will said to Ann.

'You don't have to prove you didn't kill him to me,' said Ann. 'Just everyone else in London.'

The woman shouted up the road after them, 'I don't blame you, he was a pervert.'

Will swore and closed his eyes for a moment as he walked, but when he opened them London was just the same.

Two very small, barefoot girls ran after them, and one of them threw a very small stone at Will. It hit him, and they ran off giggling.

Around the corner came a tall figure in long black robes, with a painted mask with a long black beak. Will jumped sideways and grabbed the knife he'd put in his jacket pocket but it was just a plague doctor with his tall black boots and arm-length black gloves and the ampules of dark liquid clinking at his waist. Ann looked at Will's hand clasping the weapon. It was the best he could find at home, a kitchen knife with a long blade but no point.

'What's that for?' Ann asked.

'What do you think?'

'You'll be fine as long as you're attacked by a cabbage.'

He could still smell the vinegar the doctor had doused himself in and the bergamot oil from the long beak of his mask and a sickly stench that must have been from the vials. Ann must have smelt it too.

'They use bird blood and chopped-up toads in Canterbury. An apprentice my father quarrelled with took up as a plague doctor, but they caught him stealing from the dead, so they buried him alive in a plague pit with the bodies.'

'Well,' said Will, 'he won't be doing that again.'

Ann stopped to buy some pickled eels from a stall and, when she offered them to him, the vinegar got into the cut by his mouth.

'I know, I know,' said Ann.

'What?'

'I shouldn't have given her a drink just for his last words.'

'What she told you might be true.'

'But it wasn't, was it?'

Will said nothing. It wasn't true. Chris was not very poetic in fights. There hadn't been a lot of poetry when they screamed at each other the night before Chris died on that floor.

Ann was still muttering, 'I'm such a fool. She played me.'

'It was just bad luck the bottle smashed,' he said.

At least when Ann was angry at herself she wasn't angry with him. A small boy looked up at Will and hid his head in his mother's skirts. Will had forgotten his bruised face.

'Do I look that bad?' he asked Ann.

'Yes.' She peered at his face. 'Bend down.'

He did. He could see two of himself in her grey-green eyes.

'I missed a bit of that splinter. I'll need a small knife.'

Something bothered Will. 'The splinter,' he said, 'it was from a wooden floor.'

'Yes. And?'

'I got the splinter when they tripped me up right next to Chris. And his body was right next to me. There was no rug there.'

'So where's the blood on the rug come from?'

'They killed him upstairs?'

She did that thing where she tilted her head to one side as if weighing a thought in some scales. 'That rug's too big to fit in a room upstairs.'

'So why's it covered in blood?' he said.

'We just seem to end up knowing less and less,' said Ann. 'Why did I offer her a drink for his last words?'

Will tried to speak but now she turned the anger on herself.

'I could have got it out of her, I could. I'm so stupid.'

'We do know more,' said Will. 'We just have to put it all together.'

'I just want him back, I'd sell my soul to have him for another twenty years.'

Ann made a small keening sound, so full of pain that even

95

among everything that was going on, it shocked Will. He didn't know how to comfort her. To put his arms around her seemed to be against the rules they'd wordlessly created for each other, yet he wanted to help somehow, and he craved her touch.

A loud boom stopped everyone. It rumbled on and on and the windows rattled and the black shapes of crows and ravens rose from the roofs.

'It came from Greenwich,' said a well-dressed man with a loud voice. Will couldn't see how he knew, but everyone looked east towards the royal palace.

A man mending a roof shouted, 'There's smoke rising near Blackheath.'

'There's always smoke rising near Blackheath,' said Will. 'It's the brick ovens.'

A little boy ran out of an alley yelling, 'The Catholics are attacking Greenwich Palace. They've blown up the North Gate.'

Ann looked at Will questioningly.

'I doubt it,' he said. 'Last Sunday, James of Scotland blew up the Tower and it still seems to be there.'

They were probably just blowing up the houses put up illegally in Southwark. They could have just knocked them down but 'Rich' Spencer and the rest of the London aldermen loved a bit of gunpowder.

Ann poked him suddenly with her finger. 'What if they used the rug to carry his body there? What if he was killed somewhere else? What if that little Dutch girl was right and she really did see him dead by the river?'

Yes, thought Will, here was something that did make sense.

Someone kills Marlowe on the mudflats down by the creek, but whoever ordered the killing doesn't want it to look like murder so they call in the clean-up men, Skerries, Frizer and Pooley. Skerries and Frizer get there first and they go to Eleanor Bull's house because it's near to the body and they know she'll say anything for a drink. Even in Deptford, you can't carry bodies far in daylight, so they take her rug, bundle up the body in it and carry what looks like a rug to her house. They know the routine and this time it's Frizer's turn to be the killer. They stab the dead man in the eye and send word out that he's been killed in a fight. That's when Will turns up and Skerries elbows him in the throat because they don't want anyone else in the house before Pooley gets there to be another witness.

Some tanners, standing on a corner with their greasy leather aprons and blackened faces, were staring at Will and muttering. Will and Ann walked swiftly away, and when the men didn't follow them, they went back to talking.

'They carried him in the rug,' said Ann. 'I bet that's what happened,' and she rolled up her sleeves as they talked.

Will remembered the gesture, how she did it without really thinking about it when she was getting down to do business. For a moment she was exultant, then her forehead crinkled.

'They said at the inquest that the only wound was the knife in the eye, so how was he murdered?' Will considered. 'If the constable at the inquest was telling the truth that must be how he was killed originally.'

'But it was Frizer's knife.'

'Then Frizer must have stabbed him in the same wound.'

It struck him that they were calmly discussing blades being plunged into Chris, into Chris alive and Chris dead.

'But the little girl,' said Ann, 'didn't she mention that his eyes were open?'

Will could see the Dutch girl's face, earnest and concentrating as she told them what she had seen. 'He only had one shoe, and staring brown eyes,' she had said.

'You're right,' he said. 'She was very exact. You'd think that's the first thing she would notice if he'd been stabbed in the eye.'

'We must talk to her. It's good we came to Deptford. Do you think you can find her house?'

Will remembered her description of the blue and red house that wasn't a house on Skinner Street. He thought he could.

BELLA

Bella was weary of Deptford; it made London seem civilised. Here they left the hanged men dangling on the gibbets so long that even the crows could find nothing more to pick away. Here, her dark skin seemed to be an insult to everyone. Men spat, women cursed and children threw stones. She was sure it would be worse if Perro was not walking beside her. There were times she wanted to whisper a word to the dog, unslip her chain and watch their faces change.

A crowd had gathered outside the blue and red shack. Behind them, the ships creaked at anchor in the river and cormorants on the mooring posts spread their wings to dry in ragged black shapes. They were close enough that she could make out their brilliant green eyes.

Why had the Dutch family been killed? Where was the need? It was just a child and a mother who no one would believe. Had they just done it to tidy things up? The English loved tidiness. In Seville, where they stuck a stiletto between your ribs just to say 'hello', they wouldn't have bothered. In Venice, where they had dug the canals so you never had to walk more than ten yards to dispose of a body, it would have been beneath them.

Painted on the door of the blue and red shack was *Holland Barstads*. Was the misspelling to make it look like the killers were stupid, or were they just stupid? Stupid men sent to kill children.

The crowd were listening to an old man holding himself up on two sticks.

'Couldn't sleep with my gout. I was looking out at the storm, and I saw two blokes go into that hovel of theirs. Thought they were just robbers not murderers or I'd have shouted.'

'Did you see their faces?' asked a woman holding a baby in each arm.

He shook his head stiffly.

'But there was a third man in the shadows over by the gates to the farriers'. Big bloke, in shiny high boots, saw his face in the lightning, wish I hadn't. Like looking into Satan's eyes.'

Bella wondered how he knew.

The crowd was growing. A free tragedy performed on a Deptford street corner.

They jostled to get closer as constables carried out the bodies with their bloody nightclothes pulled up over their heads to hide their faces. If the aim was dignity it did not work.

If it had been her, she would have made them vanish with money or threats but it would not have come to this. That stupid mother stomping around London, sure that England was different, sure that if she made enough noise wrong things would be put right. She had not worked out that the English, beneath their ham-fisted handshakes and red-faced proclamations of justice, were as corrupt as the rest. And that poor little girl, that poor clever girl. Two ravens cawed as they flapped heavily down onto the roof of the shack and peered over the edge.

She yanked Perro's lead and walked away. The dog looked up to her anxiously, sensing her agitation. She was walking fast and she realised she was angry. She did not know that she could still be angry. She thought she had moved beyond the more exhausting emotions. She must be calm and remember the details of what had happened.

She had learned the Roman method of *Loci*, to hold things in her head. Her memory palace was the white stone house on the hill above the cypress forest. She walked through the iron-studded gates into the courtyard where she kept the faces she needed hanging from the fig and orange and lemon trees or ranged around the lion's-head fountain that gushed rusty water after thunderstorms. The dead faces she dropped down the well and she put new ones in their places.

The dark kitchen held, amongst its copper pans and pots of cloves and cinnamon and saffron, rumours and stories and secrets each smelling of a different spice. In the library, where the little yellow moths fluttered around the books they were turning to dust, were numbers and codes each linked to a volume – to *Meditations* or *Metamorphoses* – to *Triumphs* or *The Inferno*. Now she walked up the creaky stairs into the day room that looked out into the treetops where she kept the memories of Charles among bowls of oranges and sun-faded yellow cushions. Her breathing had slowed, but now, to leave her house of memories she had to pass the stone steps that led to the cellar. That was the fee she had to pay for a visit. She could not always get away without being drawn into the basement, where they kept the wine and the oil and the broken fragments of old statues, and where she kept memories she had never wanted, but could not banish. They reached out from the alcoves and dead ends and clutched at her as she ran blindly through the darkness.

Will and Ann saved her from these nightmares. Will called as they walked towards her. Perro nuzzled him with her bristly muzzle and Will scratched her behind the ears. She preferred women, but she liked Will. She moved on to sniffing Ann, and would not be pulled away, and Bella saw that there was a smell the dog recognised.

'We're looking for that Dutch girl?' said Will.

'She's dead.' Bella was brutal. She needed someone else to be upset. 'Anti-Dutch vigilantes killed the family in the night.'

Will was angrier and Ann sorrier. She thought it would have been the other way round.

'We think that little girl may have been right,' said Will.

He would have gone on but Ann poked his arm to stop him. Her dark face was clenched in a frown. So Ann did not trust her; it was a good thing that she had that instinct for survival but she was less sure Will did. Sometimes he did not seem that different from that blonde block of a Dutch woman, clumsily blundering around London in order to get herself killed. They had their heads together whispering, as a water cart passed by, drips splashing from the barrel.

'It's worth trying,' she heard Will saying.

Ann turned to her. 'Do you really think they were killed by vigilantes?'

Bella hesitated. Things were going to happen. Men and women would do what they did because they were who they were. She had learnt by now she could not change anything, but she could make it all happen quicker. And then it would be over. Her head was full of smoke, and she wanted to curl up on the ground with her arms around Perro. She wanted to crawl into the coffin with Chris and sleep – lie in the dark until everything was over while London raved and thundered above the wet clay.

'No,' she said, 'I think they were killed to keep them quiet.'

Will and Ann were whispering again, heads close together.

'Can you get a message to Danby?' Will asked her.

ANN

The gates of Greenwich Palace were still standing despite the rumours. The guards at the front gate sent them to the side gate. The guards at the side gate sent them to the back gate.

'You do the talking,' she said to Will. 'They're more likely to listen to a man.' Then she couldn't help herself and went and asked, 'Is the queen in residence?' like some country yokel on a trip to London. What an idiot she was.

The sergeant of the guard, a great, ugly lump of a man who could have been a bouncer at the gates of hell, just laughed at her. Anyway everyone knew the queen was there in Greenwich Palace shuttered away from the plague with the rest of the court, or rendered mad from having caught it, or held prisoner by Cecil, depending on which rumour you believed.

Danby kept them waiting for two hours, outside on a knobbly elm bench in the drizzle. Will had been thinking it through.

'Is this the right thing to do?'

'You were the one who wanted to go back to Danby,' she said.

'Yes,' he said. 'We have no power, and those with no power have to rely on justice. That's why the law is so important.' Sometimes he still sounded such an innocent. He must have sensed her scorn because he raised his voice.

'What else can we do?' In Canterbury, Ann had seen what else could be done. The Marlowes dealt out justice themselves, mostly by night, in alleyways and on dark country roads. It wasn't that just or that pretty but it was that or nothing. Maybe, though, Will was right and in London it was different. They had no large, rambunctious family to call on, and even if they had, it would have been no good. Three thousand people lived in Canterbury; in London it was two hundred thousand. 'So do you trust Danby?' she asked. 'He's full of himself but I think he's his own man. It's just I worry we're going back to him before we have enough evidence.'

He was off again, thinking about everything so much that he did nothing.

'We know Christopher was killed down by the creek,' she said. 'The little girl saw him.'

'She's dead.'

'Exactly. She was killed because she saw him. That's evidence, she was right.'

Will scratched at the last bit of splinter in his cheek. 'But it's all supposition, and we still haven't worked out why she never mentioned the wound in his eye.'

'She could have missed it,' said Ann, knowing she hadn't. The girl had given them all those details, the purple lips, the swollen fingers, the staring brown eyes.

An idea was starting to form in Ann's head.

'There was this brutal goldsmith in Canterbury whose wife put poison in his food and killed him. She was sentenced to be boiled alive.'

'They don't like just hanging people in Canterbury, do they?' said Will.

'Well, in the end she was hanged because they couldn't find a pot big enough, but the thing is, when they found him he had purple lips.' She remembered something else. 'And swollen fingers. The girl said he had swollen fingers.'

'You think he was poisoned?'

'Yes.'

She watched Will nodding almost imperceptibly to himself as he considered. 'So Chris was poisoned and died out on the mudflats so Frizer and Skerries went and fetched the body and carried it to Eleanor Bull's house so they could make out it was a drunken brawl.'

'Yes, I'm sure that's it.' Yet something bothered her. She knew there was still something that wasn't right.

Danby's valet finally came to collect them. The sergeant of the guard in his embroidered coat, high black boots and fine plumped hat watched them pass through the gate with a sneer of contempt. They followed the valet along a path across a sodden lawn, dotted by bent-backed gardeners in white smocks.

Will whispered to her. 'That still doesn't explain the blood on the rug.'

That was it. There was always something that didn't quite make sense. A young man in a wolfskin cape with a deerhound on a lead walked towards them, and the valet stepped off the path onto the grass, nudged them to do the same, and whispered that they mustn't look him in the face. The dog sniffed her but the young man walked by as if they weren't there.

They climbed a flight of polished wooden stairs to a corridor that smelt of oranges, with a painted ceiling of green and gold, and panelled walls delicately carved with brightly painted flowers and leaves, so you seemed to be walking through a fantasy forest. Rush matting silenced their footsteps, but cages with singing birds hung from the walls, their sweet song echoing down the long hallway. They were led into a smaller corridor and to a south-facing room, heated with several clay pit fires and full of real plants. Danby sat behind a huge desk that dwarfed him.

'I've got four minutes,' he said.

He saw her glance land on a plant pot in front of him. Reaching out of it was a red and white speckled trumpet-shaped arm that looked more like flesh than vegetation.

'A Portuguese captain brought that chap back from the

Gold Coast. It eats insects. He says there's bigger ones inland that eat monkeys.'

He was ready to spend the remaining three and a half minutes on botany, but she nudged Will who told him what they had discovered. He explained that Frizer, Skerries and Pooley had done the same thing in Yorkshire and how a witness had seen him dead earlier. He hesitated before mentioning the poison, but in the end he did, and that seemed to get Danby's attention. He thought for a while.

'So you want me to reopen the case?' he said finally.

'We hoped you would do that,' said Will.

'Really?' Danby said. 'You do realise what you're doing, don't you? Right now, the law holds Frizer responsible for Marlowe's death, but if what you say is correct then we still have to catch his murderer, and half of London thinks that you killed him. If I reopen the case I may end up hanging you. So are you sure you want me to?'

'Yes,' said Will.

Will could still surprise her. There were times he seemed to like trouble.

'So,' said Danby, 'are you an atheist like your friend?'

'No,' said Will, 'and I don't think Marlowe was an atheist. He just liked to shock people.'

'His corpse suggests he succeeded,' said Danby.

He seemed to be enjoying himself. He picked at a plate of confectionery, poking at some spun sugar and marchpane, before popping a morsel of pink marzipan into his mouth.

'What play are you writing now?' he asked Will.

'A tragedy about star-crossed lovers,' said Will.

'I heard you were writing a play about Richard III who overthrew the rightful king and whose very name is an insult to Her Majesty.'

'That as well,' said Will.

'Oh, that as well.'

'Richard's a villain.'

'But will he be one of your lovable villains?'

Ann was sweating in the overheated room.

'No,' said Will. 'You'll hear booing from the groundlings.'

'I heard booing during Titus-whatever-it-was,' said Danby. 'But that's just because it was shit.'

Ann didn't think that was true, Chris had said the crowd had loved all that killing.

'I'll tell you what,' Danby went on. 'I don't like being made a fool of. If you can bring me firm evidence that Marlowe was poisoned and that gang were just clean-up men, I'll hang the three of them and you can kick away their stools yourselves.'

'Sir,' Ann said. 'What constitutes firm evidence?'

'Constitutes,' said Danby as if the word in her mouth was a presumption. 'Someone who knows what they're talking about would "constitute" evidence. Now off you go.'

'And, sir, may I ask,' said Ann, knowing that she might not, 'the blonde man with the knife who you knocked out yesterday, is he in prison?'

His large head swivelled on his little body and looked at her. 'I won't be cross-examined by a cobbler's daughter,' said Danby. 'Get out.'

As they were led back down the corridor, a smocked servant removed a dead bird from one of the cages and replaced it with a living one.

WILL

The Thames was swollen by the ebb tide, whipped into the waves by the wind, a brown torrent sweeping to the sea. The Greenwich ferry yawed sideways towards the jetty; in the front a drunken wedding party and in the back two men sitting on a struggling donkey.

Will had been thinking. 'What if they went with the rug to get him and he wasn't dead, and that's when they stabbed him. Or he was and they stabbed him to make sure. That would explain the blood.'

Ann was staring at the river.

'I'm sorry,' he said. 'I know we're talking about Chris being stabbed but that would explain it.'

The boat touched the jetty, but the donkey broke free and leapt over the side into the river. One of the men wearily jumped in after it. The wedding party laughed and cheered.

'What do you think?' he asked her.

'I don't know,' she said. 'I don't know. I don't know. I don't know.' Her eyes had a wet sheen. 'Why am I doing it? Why? Why am I marrying him?'

She put her arms around him and dug her hands into his back and buried her head in his doublet like an animal hiding in its lair. Will's heart filled his whole chest.

'Do you love him at all?' he asked, hoping the answer was 'no'.

'No,' she said.

'And me?' he asked, hoping the answer was 'yes'. 'Do you love me at all?'

'No,' she said. 'Do you love your wife at all?'

Will knew there was no good answer to this question so he told the truth. 'No,' he said. 'Nor does she me, but we both love our children.'

It sounded cold out loud yet as he said the words he could feel the pang of fear that something would happen to them, the ache of longing to see them. The man in the water struggled to stay on his feet in the fierce current. He lunged for the donkey's halter but slipped, fell and surfaced, spitting out foul water. The donkey swam for the shore but was carried downstream with the tide.

'Don't marry him,' said Will.

'Without him my father's business will collapse. I don't care about my father but my mother and sisters will be destitute. And me, what do I live on? No one will employ a single woman.'

'You could stay in London.'

'What, with you? Married Will Shakespeare. What does that make me?' She seemed to be vibrating in his arms. 'I've three choices. Whore, beggar or wife. Which would you choose?'

He didn't know. He didn't know anything. The donkey brayed, lifting its big head above the water, as it drifted downstream towards the North Sea. The man in the water looked imploringly towards the ferryman, who shook his head. The man in the river beat the water with his hands in frustration. Ann abruptly let go of Will, stepped back and brushed a loose hair out of her eyes.

'Ignore me, ignore this,' she said. 'I don't know why I said it out loud. All brides have moments like this, don't they?'

'I'm not sure they do.'

'Well, never mind the others, I'm having one, but the thing is it doesn't mean anything. What matters is that I'm going to get married in seven days so we have to be quick and get proof Chris was poisoned.'

Her face was tight and clenched and her eyes still damp as she turned away from him.

The donkey was a distant dot.

LIZZIE

Lizzie tried to forget what had happened the night before, but that made her think about it, and that made her remember again and again. She had woken from a dream where she was eating a whole saffron cake and found someone was in their shack, standing over Mama. Mama had made a noise Lizzie had never heard her make before, and when the man moved away, Mama was just a motionless shape on the mattress.

Her little brother, Henry, had run towards the shape of the man, but another man grabbed him from behind and made a couple of quick motions with his hand and Henry went quiet. Tom, whom her mama was minding for Auntie Rosa, had been standing by the door breathing hard. One of the men had said quietly, 'It's alright, lad, don't you worry, you just stay there,' and stepped towards him, like someone trying not to scare a bird.

Lizzie had burrowed down where the straw was deep.

The man who talked had said, 'One and two halves, yes? All done.'

Then they had left, and she had heard them fumbling outside the door for a while, then it went quiet. Lizzie had stayed under the straw for a long time, scared by how fast her heart was beating, then when it started working like it should, she had crawled out of the back of the hut under one of the broken planks.

She had nowhere to go. Her aunt worked as a servant but she did not know where. She had spent the day out on the Thames shore with the mudlarks looking for debris they could sell. The children told stories, like of the day a small boy had found a huge pearl buried in the mud, or when they had found a man's severed hand still clutching a knife. She felt safer out there among the children, but now the tide was coming in and she was hungry, and she followed the others into the alleys behind the dockyard. She reached inside her apron pocket and found the snail and the apple core. She ate the apple core and dropped the snail and stepped on it, then wished she had not. The shell was cracked but not crushed. It was only its home broken and the soft living thing inside was still alive. She placed it among the nettles at the side of the path. It would be fine.

THE WIDOW

Plans were funny things. Everyone talked about them as if they were real, but once a plan met life it might as well not exist. Three months ago the Widow, aged thirteen, had fallen in love and got married – just not to the same person. Her parents had caught her kissing Margarite, the Dutch girl who bought the eggs. Her mother had told her that if she ever found her kissing a woman again she would kill herself. Her father had said that he'd kill her. So she had been forced to stop seeing Margarite with her bad jokes, and her crinkly smile, and those chapped lips she couldn't resist, and they had married her to a thirty-eight-year-old candle maker whose fat, creamy body looked like a melted candle.

Five days later, the first wave of plague that breezed through Garland Street killed him, along with her mother, father and Margarite, four of them in five days. Her uncles, moving at the same speed as the plague, turned up, sold everything her family owned, and spent it on beer and women. She told them that she was the candle maker's widow so his possessions belonged to her. They asked if she wanted a slap. When they went back to Essex, they tried to take her with them, but fearing a second husband before her fourteenth birthday, she ran away and for three days just kept walking the streets of London.

She met Christopher Marlowe in a doorway in the clothing quarter. Late at night, exhausted, she had taken shelter from a thunderstorm in a shop door and fallen asleep. She had woken to a heady waft of scent and found a beautifully dressed gentleman sleeping next to her with his head on her shoulder. She had stayed still, breathing in that perfume that seemed to come from her dreams of princes and pashas and palaces. Finally, he had spoken without opening his eyes.

'And who are you?'

She had told him. When she knew him better she asked him why he thought God had spared only her from the plague.

'Because God knows that London needs more prostitutes,' he replied, but when he saw her lip wobble he gave her a gold coin that saved her from the stew houses. She wondered if he wanted her for 'down below', as her mother would have put it.

'Don't worry,' he said, 'when it comes to teenagers I prefer boys.'

Like nearly everything he said, she didn't know if it was true. It was funny how he, with his drinking and swearing and brawling, was the kindest of all of them.

Now he was dead and her rent was due on Friday, and she had to find a way of surviving all over again. She wondered if the package he had given her to keep was valuable and she could sell it. She'd promised him not to peek at it, so she didn't, but she had a feeling that if she told the wrong person about it she might end up the same way as Chris. She'd only told Kyd about it the night before Chris had died and now she wished she hadn't even done that. So there it was under her mattress. She could feel it beneath her when she went to bed, and both the lump and thinking about it gave her sleepless nights. Chris would have found that funny. Poor Chris. Poor Margarite. Poor Mama. She tried to do her crying for all of them at the same time because otherwise she'd be crying all day long.

WILL

Finding murderers seemed to involve a lot of walking. They'd only been able to get a boat to the south bank at Southwark and had got stuck on London Bridge. A cavalcade of wagons, a flock of geese and a file of schoolboys were all backed up behind a stubborn carter who refused to pay the soldiers at the north end the bribe needed to enter the City of London. Angry muleteers cracked whips in each other's faces, shopkeepers kicked geese and the schoolboys cheered as their schoolmaster traded punches with a farmer; only the oxen chewed patiently, steaming in the drizzle, their huge heads bowed by their yokes.

Will and Ann were heading towards the Bell Savage, a pub on Ludgate Hill where Thomas Kyd liked to drink. They needed an expert on poison and Kyd knew everything there was to know about mandrake and monkshood, about autumn crocus and yew extract, hellebore, hemlock, henbane and deadly nightshade. He'd enthusiastically researched these tinctures, toxins and venoms before he had written *The Spanish Tragedy*, London theatre's most successful play ever. There was yet more poisoning in his 1587 play, *Hamlet*. It was a poor play, Will thought, but the story had possibilities.

They finally squeezed themselves across the bridge, and Will led them on a shortcut through the transept of St Paul's Cathedral, weaving through the throng of vendors and businessmen gossiping and making deals, past the diamond merchants gathered beneath the altar holding up their stones so they glinted in the light, past the turbaned Turks, their gaudy silks draped over the pews by the shrine to Saint Erkenwald, past the gold-toothed pawnbrokers under the Rose Window, their ledgers bound in scarlet goatskin, through a hubbub of haggling in half a dozen different languages. They ducked under the string of extracted teeth a dentist had hung as an advertisement over the north door and out into Cathedral Close.

A crowd had gathered around a door where a pamphlet had been tacked up. Will could hear those who could read explaining to the others: it was 'Tamburlaine', the rogue pamphleteer, who had taken his alias from Chris's play, *Tamburlaine*, the story of a goatherd, Timur the Lame, who had risen up to enslave emperors and conquer dynasties, a play written by a cobbler's son who had risen up to conquer the London theatre.

'Tamburlaine' nailed up his notices in the night, verses condemning Dutch refugees fleeing the Spanish in the Low Countries for carrying the plague and diluting pure English blood. Many had thought it was Chris himself who wrote the pamphlets, but much as he loved the mischief, he didn't hate the Dutch and he'd sworn to Will that it wasn't him; besides, Chris couldn't have written verse that bad if he'd tried. Whoever it was either had unusually loyal friends or high influence, for there was a reward of one hundred crowns for their capture and no one had turned them in.

Ann cursed when she saw why the crowd had gathered, for 'Tamburlaine' and his pamphlets was surely one reason why the Queen's Court had wanted to question Chris, and that summons surely had something to do with his murder. When Will tried to get a closer look though, she tugged at his sleeve. When he turned around a couple of merchants were staring at him, their heads together, talking in low voices. One of them called out to his friends and one by one heads started turning away from the pamphlet and towards him. Did they really believe he'd killed Chris? He opened his mouth to reason with them, but Ann yanked him away.

'Just walk.'

He did.

'Don't look round.'

It was hard not to, and as they turned into Paternoster Lane he glimpsed behind them. The crowd weren't following.

Kyd wasn't at the Bell Savage but Kemp, the comedian, was.

'Oh, look out. It's Will Shakespeare, London's favourite murderer,' he said.

'Can you keep it down a bit?' said Will. 'The mob's out to get me.'

'Going to kill any more playwrights today?' said Kemp loudly. 'If you are, start with Beaumont and do Fletcher while you're at it. Fucking pastoral bollocks, where's the laughs in that?' Kemp was in a good mood. 'My arsehole's funnier than those two,' he said, knocking back his drink. That was true enough. He'd entertained them once by farting 'Greensleeves'.

Will and Ann had found him with Barking Bobby and a couple of actors in an upstairs room. In the cobbled yard below Will had once played the Earl of Shrewsbury, the Bishop of Rochester and Third Messenger in the dreadful play *Sir Thomas More*. Back then, pub yards had been the theatres of London.

'We're looking for Kyd,' said Will.

'Oh, so he's your next victim, is he?'

Kemp always flogged a joke to death. Still, Will trusted comedians slightly more than tragedians. The serious actors could always convince themselves that they had been brilliant. Comedians lived or died on laughter and it was harder to lie to yourself about silence. Not that Kemp didn't try. 'They didn't laugh because they were listening so hard,' was his favourite.

'Kyd's laying low in a secret location,' said Kemp, sounding important.

'Any idea where?' asked Ann.

'If I knew that it wouldn't be a secret.' Kemp never really liked women.

A gang of boatmen clumped up the stairs, their wet clothes

steaming in the heat of the small, packed room. The fug around them made Will think of the plague and, as it drifted towards him, he backed away towards the corner of the room where fresh air came in through a hole in the wattle.

'It'll get you or it won't,' whispered Ann. She knew him too well. 'Living in fear of it doesn't keep it away.'

He rolled his eyes at her.

'What?' she said.

'I'd forgotten how annoying you were.'

She laughed briefly and he realised it was the first time he'd heard her laugh since they had met outside the town hall with Chris dead inside. One of the boatmen asked Kemp to do his Lord Cecil impersonation.

'Don't know what you're talking about,' said Kemp, following Will and Ann over to the corner. 'I'm not fucking suicidal,' he muttered and knocked back a half-finished drink he found on a table. 'So, why do you want Kyd? You want to find out if it was him who gave Chris up to the Royal Court?'

'Nothing like that.'

There was a lot of barking in the street below, and Will peered through the hole. A beast of a dog jerked on the end of its chain in a spray of spittle, as Perro and Bella passed. Perro ambled by as if she couldn't be bothered to kill it this early in the morning.

Will and Ann shared a quick look. They didn't want Bella knowing what they were doing.

'We need Kyd's expertise,' said Ann rapidly.

'Oh, poison? That what you after? It's not Kyd you need,' said Kemp, 'I know the geezer he got it off.'

'Where can we find him?' said Will, glancing at the door.

Kemp's eyes squinted cunningly. 'So this Richard III, is it one of your miserable histories or are there laughs in it?'

'There's laughs. There's a part that'll get a lot of laughs.'

'Who's that then?'

'You'll have to wait and see.'

Will wasn't going to tell him that it was Richard, and that

Kemp would never play him, though come to think of it, he'd be good.

'My contact,' said Kemp, 'knows everything there is to know about poison.'

Barking Bobby joined them. 'This the bloke who lives on the Isle of Dogs?'

Will must have groaned because Ann asked, 'What's the problem?' The Isle of Dogs was the problem. It had never left the Dark Ages. It was where London's criminals fled from the law, and where the law was too scared to follow.

'Ah yes,' said Kemp. *'Cannae Insulae, hic sunt dracones.'*

Why did everyone else know Latin?

'He's got a place hidden down in the reeds opposite Greenwich Wharf,' said Bobby. 'He's a man of God, a friar.'

'How does he survive on the Isle of Dogs?' Will asked.

'They're all fucking terrified of him, God's Poisoner they call him.'

When Will looked up, Bella was standing close by with the dog. The two of them always seemed to move so silently you never saw them arrive. She gave Barking Bobby a shilling to buy a round. Perro walked over to Ann, sniffed, and whined as she had before.

Ann pushed the dog gently away, and whispered to Will to ask Kemp about Bradley, which was good as Will didn't want to leave before that round.

'You know Thomas Watson the poet,' Will asked, 'who was with Chris when they killed Bradley. Have you seen him recently?'

'He died not long ago. Alleyn told me.'

Will felt Ann stiffen beside him. 'Do you know how?' she asked.

'He was murdered,' said Kemp, 'by someone who read his poetry.'

Will checked, 'That's a joke?'

'Yeah.'

'So he's alive?'

'No, he is dead, I just don't know how. And his poetry is shit.' Kemp hated poetry, and particularly any poetry that wasn't written for him to perform.

'You heard anything about Bradley's brother?' asked Will.

'Yeah, nasty bit of work, runs the Dutch prossies in East London.'

'So he has money?'

'Yeah, a lot of money, a lot of prossies. You think he's got something to do with this?'

'Possibly,' said Will, as Barking Bobby came over, balancing a tray theatrically above his head with half a dozen glasses of Madeira on it. Will knocked back his and hoped it would make his aching body hurt less. He was shivering and sweating at the same time.

Bella stepped over. 'If you want to find out about poison you should talk to Kyd,' she said. 'I haven't seen him since the burial. Do you know where he is?'

'He's lying low in a secret location,' said Kemp.

'Do you know where?' asked Bella.

'If we knew where, it wouldn't be secret,' said Ann.

Kemp laughed, which didn't happen often. Bella frowned. So she was looking for Kyd too; Will wondered why. It was unlikely to be for advice about poison as she seemed to know a lot about that already. Ann nudged him and he started towards the door.

'I saw the ghost of Chris last night,' said Barking Bobby out of nowhere. 'He had the knife in his eye but he didn't have the power of speech. He wanted me to follow him but I couldn't. I was too drunk. I wanted to help him but I let him down.'

Barking Bobby started to cry. Kemp put an arm around him.

'I fucking miss him and all.'

'I know,' said Bella.

Will could feel Ann's anger in the air. It was her brother who was dead, and everyone but her was in a grieving competition.

'He was going to write a play about my life,' said Barking Bobby.

Chris told everyone he was going to write a play about them. Will and Ann wove through the sailors and headed down the stairs. Will knew what was going to happen once they left the pub: Bella would buy them drinks and keep buying them drinks and if Kemp really did know where Kyd was hiding out, he'd tell her.

ANN

As they stepped into the street outside, a gang of dockers with clubs and billhooks surrounded Will. Unlike the other crowd who had recognised Will, this lot were drunk and armed.

'You a Catholic?' one of them asked Will.

'No,' said Will.

Ann exhaled and realised she'd been holding her breath. They hadn't recognised Will. They were one of the Protestant gangs roaming the city hunting for the non-existent rebels who were said to have tried to blow up Greenwich Palace.

'Say "Fuck the Pope",' said a man holding a scythe.

'Fuck the Pope,' said Will wearily.

The man reached for Will's shirt and ripped it open, looking for a crucifix. 'Dear God,' he said and stepped back.

The wound in Will's chest was red and swollen and leaking pus. Ann had no idea it had got so bad.

'I think I've caught the plague,' said Will to frighten them and they backed away and went off down Finsbury Lane to look for another victim.

'Let me see it,' said Ann.

It looked horrible. Red tentacles reached out from the gash.

'Are you feeling faint?' she asked.

He nodded. 'It's starting to hurt more than my head.'

He looked over her shoulder and sighed. She turned

around and saw that Lord Strange and his entourage had arrived on the opposite corner. Strange whispered to one of his overdressed lackeys who came over and announced: 'His Lordship would like a word if you'd be so kind.'

WILL

It always seemed so important to Lord Strange that rather than he come to you, you came to him, even if he was only five yards away.

'How's the play progressing, William?' he asked as Will and Ann approached.

'I'm very close,' lied Will.

'Our discussions on reopening the theatre went rather well. I was rather persuasive, though I say it myself. I'm putting yours in for August so we start rehearsing mid-July.'

That gave him longer than he'd expected. One of the entourage held out a snuffbox for His Lordship but he waved it away.

'Just a thought, William, the rumours that you murdered Christopher, they won't do any harm at the box office. You know, a play about a murderer by a murderer, so do keep that going.'

'He was nearly killed by a mob because of that,' said Ann.

His long neck swivelled across and down. He always seemed mildly surprised when the common folk had the audacity to speak to him. 'Killed by a mob, eh? People!' he murmured in disgust. 'I'll tell you what then, William, don't shout about it, but just don't deny it.'

One of the lackeys whispered in His Lordship's ear.

'Ah yes,' said Strange, 'so we're putting one of Christopher's on from mid-June, Alleyn wants me to revive

Tamburlaine as everyone remembers that.' Will wondered for a moment if Strange was behind 'Tamburlaine' the pamphleteer. He would do anything for publicity, and was rumoured to be a secret Catholic and despise the Protestant Dutch immigrants.

'Ideally though,' Strange continued, 'I want to put on the new Christopher one that "Rich" Spencer paid for, if anyone can find it, that is. But if it's not finished, William, I might need you to stick an ending on it. Still, old play or new play, a Marlowe play right now's going to clean up. Talk about free publicity.'

He didn't seem to feel the waves of rage coming from Ann.

'I expect you remember Chris's sister,' said Will.

'Yup, obviously, very sorry. Very, very sorry, I hear you've been to see...' He couldn't find the name. 'Plump little chap... coroner...'

'Danby,' said Ann.

'We want him to reopen the case,' said Will.

'What do you think happened?'

Will let Ann explain, as it seemed to annoy Lord Strange when she spoke.

'We think he was poisoned, but ended up dying out in the street so they called in Frizer and his gang to move him and cover it up.'

'People!' said Lord Strange again, shaking his head sadly. 'If you find out any more, William, come and tell me and we'll let it slip out just before the Marlowe opens. We're going to be able to double ticket prices, maybe triple them, and it'll still sell out.'

Lord Ferdinando Strange loved money though he despised 'trade'. In the early days when a hopeful Will hung around the theatre looking for writing work, Strange had come up to him with Alleyn at his side.

'William, I've a commission for you,' he'd said, 'do you fancy it?'

'Very much.' Will had replied.

'Then make me a nice pair of gloves,' he'd said and they'd walked off chortling.

This time he offered Will a ride in his barge if he was heading west, and when Will declined he walked off, stepping fussily between the puddles, irritated by their impudence at being in his path.

'Do you know he could have been king of England?' Will said to Ann. 'His family was named in Henry VIII's will.'

'His courtiers would have murdered him in the first week,' she said.

Kemp stuck his big head through an upstairs window and in an immaculate Strange impersonation said, 'William, a fellow here says Watson died of the plague, so it wasn't Bradley who killed him.'

Will yelled his thanks.

'People!' shouted Kemp.

LIZZIE

Lizzie had learnt to walk the streets with her eyes down for scraps. She saw a lump of bread in the gutter but as she stepped towards it a big black shape dropped past her in a rush of air and a flutter of dark feathers. It landed with a flap and folded its wings. She didn't know why the English called them red kites when they looked brown. Londoners encouraged them because they ate the filth they left in their streets. This one cocked its head and fixed her with its beady eyes. Its neck extended and its hooked beak reached forward for the bread. She felt fear in the hollow of her stomach, but that was also where she felt the hunger. She jumped forward and stamped her feet. The bird did not move. It opened its sharp beak and hissed. The crust was halfway between them and Lizzie had not eaten for two days. She reached forward with her hand at the same time it jabbed forward with its beak. They reached the crust at the same time and Lizzie held tight, and as it tore in two she came away with the larger piece. She stuffed it in her mouth as the bird, holding the bread in its beak, hopped up onto the fence post, opened its wings, wide as she was tall, and flew away.

Lizzie's stomach still felt empty. She was looking out for the dead gentleman's sister and her friend the playwright with the kind eyes, because they had said they would visit her and she felt they might help her, so when she heard a man saying, 'There goes that playwright,' she ran in the direction he was pointing. It was not the one she was looking for, but the other bent-over-sideways one. He told her to go away when she said 'hello', but her hunger made her brave, so she asked if he knew where his friend with the bruised face was.

'You're looking for Will?' he said.

'I think it is Will, yes.'

'Tell him not to come looking for me.' He hurried away in his crabbed scuttle but then stopped and turned and asked her what languages she spoke.

'Dutch and English. I can read and write both,' she said, her chin jutting high.

He got a piece of parchment out of his bag, tore off a strip and told her to lean forward. He used her back as a rest, wrote on it and then handed her the scrap. 'If you find him, give him this.'

Once she had turned a corner she looked at it. It was not written in a language she understood, but when she turned it over there was an address written in English. She would go there.

ANN

It turned out the Isle of Dogs wasn't an island and you could walk there, but even so Will had wanted to delay going there.

'At least wait until tomorrow morning,' he'd said, 'and then we can go there and back in the light.' But when she'd reminded him that she had to leave for Canterbury in six days' time to get married, he'd gone quiet and come along. He was still a man in love with her. Let's be honest, he was the only man in love with her, but he was a married man and John was waiting for her back in Canterbury. The rules, as such, meant nothing to her, but she knew what happened when you broke the rules: they broke you. There were all those people who didn't really believe in the rules either, but who couldn't stand you getting away with what they secretly wanted to do, so if you stepped out of line, then the whole weight of the town pressed down on you and crushed all the air out of you until your bones splintered.

Then there was the contract John still hadn't signed. If he didn't take over her father's debt-ridden business, then it would condemn her mother and sisters to poverty. She was just an item listed in a deal along with the shop and the stock and the loans, but without he, it would all fall apart and her mother, who rarely left the house, probably wouldn't even leave her bed.

And that was before you got on to God. She had committed

the sin of sex outside of marriage with two men. Was she already condemned to hell? Surely God wasn't that vengeful, because then He would just be like everyone else and what was the point of that? Surely He had to be better. It was always men who had decided what God wanted, how now He wanted you to be an Anglican and not a Catholic, how He wanted women to be meek and obedient. It felt like men had created God and not the other way around.

But what if she was wrong and He was counting? Had she used up her lifetime's allowance of big sins? What if she was a hair's breadth away from hell? What if the merest touch of lips with Will would condemn her to eternal torture?

'Can you slow down a bit?' said Will from behind her.

The path was narrow and they had to walk one behind the other. She had been walking faster and faster as the thoughts raced through her head. She slowed and turned around. He was sweating, pale and out of breath, and she realised that the festering wound in his chest must be slowing him down, and for a moment she felt bad that she had dragged him straight out here.

'Do you want a break?' she asked.

'Just slower,' he panted.

A confused maze of raised paths wound through the marshland, but they kept the low sun on their right to make sure they kept heading towards the southern tip of the peninsula. They couldn't see the river but they smelt its brackish reek. The tall grasses around them swayed and rustled, and she kept thinking the sound was someone stalking them and not just the wind. They reached a stretch of path covered in hundreds of small black butterflies, which didn't move, and they couldn't avoid, so their feet crushed them into the mud.

'One question,' said Will behind her. 'If we do get proof he was poisoned, where do we go from there?'

She pulled her foot loose from a bramble. 'We go back to Danby like you wanted to, get Skerries, Frizer and Pooley interrogated, find out who hired them and get them all hanged.'

She knew as she said it that it sounded naïve, but Will was naïve too, just in a different way.

Will panted as he talked. 'But if they're really Cecil's men he won't allow it.' He was puffing harder now. Hopefully it would stop him asking difficult questions... but it didn't. 'What I'm asking is what we do if we find out who's responsible and no one will arrest them.'

She wasn't going to be defeated by this. 'Then we do it my way.'

'And what's your way?'

'We kill them.'

'Us? We kill them?'

'Do you want Chris's murderers to just walk away?' she asked.

'No, but I'm not sure I want to kill a man.' He took a laboured breath between each phrase. 'Or for that matter pay someone else to kill a man. Justice and revenge are different.'

There he was thinking about it again. It was better to do something and, when it was done, that was the time to think about it. She turned her head over her shoulder towards him.

'So you're too good for revenge, you, the man who wrote a play where the hero got revenge by feeding the villain his children in a pie.'

Will sighed. 'It was a play, and Chris was right, not a very good play.'

'But why did Titus seek revenge?'

'What?' Will asked.

'Because there was no justice,' she said, 'and what are our chances of justice?'

He looked in pain, whether from his wounds or this conversation she couldn't tell. 'Revenge is just an excuse for the stronger to kill the weaker,' he said. 'One day we have to move on from a never-ending chain of slaughter.'

'But justice is just a weapon the powerful use to stop us from challenging them. And where there's no justice we have to make our own.'

She went to go on but Will said quietly, 'Look behind us.'

A short man in a flapping black coat was walking fifty yards behind them, and as she watched another one jumped out of the reeds and joined him on the path. Ahead of them, the track dropped down through a tangle of brambles and stinging nettles to a rotten plank that had once bridged a ditch. Bubbles of gas rose to the surface of the black water with a plop. On the far side stood another man blocking their path. He had long red hair, a big red beard and small red eyes.

'Lost?' he asked.

'No,' she said.

'She's a pretty lady,' said red beard, talking to Will.

Why did a man always have to speak to another man, even now, when they were probably about to rob and kill them? There was a giggle from behind them. The short man was a woman, but her companion definitely wasn't. He was big and fat and wore nothing but a leather apron.

Will spoke with his actor's voice. 'We're here to see the Friar.'

'Bout what?'

So they knew the Friar. That was a start.

'If he wants you to know, he'll tell you,' said Will, with an authority she wouldn't have imagined. In Chris's burgundy hose and yellow doublet he seemed more like a man to be obeyed, or perhaps it was the clothes that had given him that new assurance.

The red haystack glowered silently, chewing his lip.

'Will one of you be kind enough to lead us to his house?' said Will.

'Alright,' the man said finally, looking disappointed that he hadn't got to kill someone.

Ann wondered if Chris's clothes had saved them. Was he looking after them from beyond the grave? No, of course he wasn't.

Red beard pointed at the woman. 'Genghis Khan will show you.'

Ann hadn't noticed before that the woman was Asian, with high cheekbones, and red splashes of colour. Ann wondered how she had ended up here, hiding in this fetid marshland. She overtook them, jumped the ditch and led them at a dizzying pace through the marsh, her blackened bare feet squelching through the greenish mud.

'Didn't think that would work,' muttered Will, fighting for breath as they splattered along behind her.

Ann thought she would have to ask her to slow down, but the woman stopped suddenly and pointed. Fifty yards ahead of them was what looked like a pile of turf with smoke rising from a hole in the roof. She turned and sped back the way they had come.

As they got closer, there were a half-dozen empty cages in the grass, but looking more closely, Ann saw that a couple of them had the scattered bones of animal skeletons inside. She made certain she didn't meet eyes with Will as she thought that would only intensify their dread. She rapped on the upturned rowing boat that seemed to be the door. It was pushed ajar and a broad, beaming head appeared, shaved on top, but with masses of bushy grey hair on either side.

'Visitors! Enter, enter!'

'We're friends of Kemp,' said Ann.

'And Kyd,' added Will.

'If you've made the journey here then you are already friends of mine,' he said.

They squeezed through the gap. The Friar lived in what looked like a cellar with no house on top. The room had stone walls inside the turf and was crammed with glass containers that glinted in the light from an oil lamp and several large candles. The bottles and jars contained coloured liquids and dead creatures, and some creatures that still seemed to move.

'If you're friends of Kyd,' he said, 'I surmise you are also from the magical world of make-believe.'

'Yes,' said Will.

'Well, I am from God's magic theatre where we turn wine into his blood.'

Ann could see why he lived on the Isle of Dogs. If he'd stayed in London he'd have been burnt by now. He wore the white robe of a Capuchin monk and at one end of his cavern was an altar with, above it, a large crucifix carved out of ivory.

'Yes, yes,' he said, 'I'm of the Old Faith, a wicked Catholic, but here on the Isle we live harmoniously untroubled by religious strife. We tolerate all religions, Catholics, Jews, Mussulmen, atheists, cannibals.'

Yes, she had heard that.

A pot bubbled and fumed over the fire, thick juices running down the side, whether his dinner or a deadly poison, Ann didn't know.

He beamed again. 'You must be tired. An infusion to lift your spirits?'

He poured a green liquid from a metal pan into three glasses and handed one to her. She felt its warmth through the glass, but waited for the Friar to drink his before she sipped at hers. It was pleasant and refreshing and tasted like it had been sweetened with honey.

'So you're friends of Thomas Kyd,' he said. 'He was very interested in poison. Came to see me recently.'

'Why did he come to see you?' asked Ann.

'He wanted some poison,' said the Friar, tapping a large glass jar in which something with scales moved.

'Did he say what for?' asked Ann, trying to keep her voice casual.

'He was interested to find out whether very small doses could work to reduce pain. He is a scientist like myself. But tell me, how may I help you?'

Ann told him of Chris, the purple lips, the swollen fingers, how he may have escaped from where he was poisoned but then been overcome.

'Was he found near water?' asked the Friar. She nodded. 'The symptoms of several poisons include extreme thirst, and victims are often discovered at the edge of ponds or rivers. When we consider all your observations together, I would say henbane or belladonna are most likely, but I will need to see the body.'

'He's been buried,' said Will.

'We'll need to dig him up then,' said the Friar, beaming at them, the top of one cheek blackened by the stick of charcoal he kept behind his ear. Will started to object but the Friar put an arm around him and kept talking. 'Don't worry, I've done this a lot. It's not as if we all go there at midnight with a shovel. You bribe the gravedigger when he's digging a new grave. He just digs sideways and we turn up after nightfall and take a look.'

'It's quite like going there at midnight with a shovel then,' said Will.

The Friar chuckled and lifted the bubbling brown pot off the fire. The smoke was gathering under the low roof, swirling slowly around the glinting glass jars. Ann felt full of energy despite her sleepless nights.

'If you engage me,' said the Friar, 'I will be able to tell you exactly how he died. The body is a map if you just know how to read it. I'll be able to tell you if the poison was given in food, poured in his ear while he slept, or absorbed through his clothes.'

'I only have a little money,' said Ann.

'Oh, no, no, no, don't trouble yourself with that. Your interest in my humble craft is payment enough.'

A sudden movement in a jar startled them. A grey snake twisted and flailed behind the glass.

The Friar watched and smiled like a proud father. 'Have you heard of gu?'

They shook their heads.

He picked up a dog-eared and yellowed book and opened it for them. It was written in what looked like Chinese characters, and had beautiful coloured pictures of venomous creatures.

'A Genoese adventurer brought it back from Cathay. It's

a work of genius. Gu comes from a snake, that has eaten a millipede, which has eaten a venomous spider. It is the most fearful of poisons. I, of course, only create it to discover an antidote. I have experimented on some of the salt-marsh sheep. And, of course, myself.'

He put down the book next to where the snake still quivered in its jar and held up his hands, black, ulcerous and bloated.

'What I haven't been bitten by in the service of science! The giant African red ant is particularly painful.'

'Do you have any antidotes for the plague?' Will asked.

'I do,' he said. 'Staying on the Isle of Dogs.' He chuckled. 'Not that it's a hardship. What did you see when you came here? Nothing, I'll wager, except a barren salt marsh. And yet it is God's own pharmacy. I can find adder's tongue, lady's mantle, dog fennel, black spleenwort, tansy, dodder and holy rope all within fifty paces of where I stand now.' The names poured out of him. Apparently to the east there was love-lies-bleeding, poor man's treacle, nosebleed and scaldhead. Ann wondered if he was making some of these up. He finally stopped and smelt the air. 'Is that you?' he asked Will. 'The infection that is on the turn.'

'I have a cut,' said Will cautiously.

The Friar stepped over to him and opened his doublet. The wound was yellow and scabbed in the middle and the swelling looked worse. Fingers of red seemed to be reaching out across Will's chest. The Friar sniffed again.

'Yes, that is putrefying. Can you smell it? Rather like mackerel. Are you suffering from fever, light-headedness and weakness?'

Will mumbled a 'yes'.

'If you don't stop it from spreading, you will experience delirium, and unconsciousness. I will mix a salve for you. Now, will you be my guests for the night or shall I ask one of our community to guide you back to London?'

Darkness had fallen. Outside was a pitch-black bog full of

criminals and possibly cannibals. Inside venomous creatures wriggled in their jars. Will looked undecided.

'Perhaps you will be kind enough to get us a guide,' Ann said.

'Of course, of course.' He opened the door a crack and gave a piercing whistle. 'Let me know when you've spoken to the gravedigger. You can send me a message via the apothecary at Poplar.'

The same woman took them back along paths only she could see. Ann gave her a groat when they reached the oil lamps of Limehouse and she scampered back into the darkness as if the busy streets of London were the menace. Perhaps she was right. Ann took a deep breath and turned to Will.

'My heart is racing,' she said.

'Mine too. At first, I thought it was fear, but now I think it's the infusion he gave us.'

The plant names that the Friar had reeled off raced through her head, fairy egg, weasel snout, wolf's hat and beggar's buttons. 'He'd make a character in a play,' said Ann.

'Yes, yes, he would.'

Will's bruised face somehow suited him. He looked almost raffish standing there in Chris's clothes.

'You did well when we were cornered on the marshes,' she said. She put on Will's acting voice. 'If he wants you to know, he'll tell you.'

She put her arms around him and pressed her head against his shoulder. She could smell his scent and a mustardy tang beneath that must have come from the salve the Friar had put on his wound. She felt one of his hands cup the back of her neck and waited for the other and it arrived on the small of her back, resting between her top and the skirt she wore. There must have been a small hole in her shift, because one finger touched her skin, and it felt as intimate as a kiss.

'You and me, we're doing all we can,' she said. 'We're doing what Chris would do if one of us had been murdered.'

She felt the blood pumping through her as if it was a force racing around inside her. Maybe it was just the Friar's infusion.

She clung to Will and his lips weren't far away from hers and she wanted to feel their softness. Was that the infusion too? She had four days before she had to start her journey to Canterbury and become nobody. Damn God, and the people of Canterbury. Why shouldn't she cram a lifetime into those ninety-six hours? She tilted her head back and locked into Will's battered face.

'We're not really going to dig up his body, are we?' he said.

The moment cracked apart, and now her racing heart pumped only dark rage.

'Yes, of course we are.'

'We'll get hanged if we're caught,' he said. 'That won't avenge Chris.'

'Oh, so you're scared.'

'Yes. I'd be a fool to be anything else, but apart from that, how can this work? Say we dig him up. Say the crazy Friar identifies the poison. What then?'

'What do you mean? You're the one who wanted to try and get justice through the courts. Danby said to bring him evidence, so we do.'

'What? And say we went into a graveyard at midnight and dug up a body?'

Why did he keep saying midnight? Why had he spoilt everything? He kept thinking ahead, not just one step but two or three, and then everything became complicated and impossible, and by then it would always be different from how you thought it would be, so you might as well have not bothered. She jabbed him with her finger.

'Are you his friend or not?'

'I am his friend, but I'm not going into a graveyard at—'

'Don't say "at midnight",' she heard herself shouting. 'You've never wanted to find his killer.'

He tried to protest but she couldn't stop herself.

'You have all the advantages of being a man. At least act like one.' Now she was about to say things she knew she'd regret, but she knew she'd say them anyway. 'You're scared of the plague. You're scared of men in power. Or are they just excuses? Maybe the mob are right? You had the motive. You had the chance. Maybe you did kill him?'

He stared at her in disbelief.

'How did you get that cut on your chest?'

'I stabbed myself,' he said.

Now she must have been the one staring dumbly. 'What? Why? You tried to kill yourself?'

'Without conviction. It wasn't hard enough, and there's bone there. I was despairing and drunk and being dramatic. Chris said I was a shit writer.'

'Wait a moment,' said Ann. 'This was in front of Chris?'

'I saw him in the street one last time after the row in the tavern.'

'And you stabbed yourself in the chest?'

ACT THREE

WILL

He wished he had never told her. Said out loud, all this sounded even more stupid than when it was in his head.

Was she looking at him with contempt or pity or something else more complicated?

'Have you done this before?' she asked.

'No, it's not that I wanted to die.'

'So you stabbed yourself in the chest because you wanted to stay alive?'

Why did she make everything so hard? 'I was being dramatic. I mean, everyone has these dark moods that swallow them up, when... when...' He was stumbling. 'Nothingness just seems simpler.'

'No, I don't think everyone does.'

She looked wild-eyed and panicky. Perhaps this was not the time to have got on to this, with them both dosed with the potion of a mad friar who lived in a bog.

'Well, never mind that,' he heard himself say. He had to try and make sense of his own idiocy. 'Chris and I were drunk – very drunk. We were shouting at each other. He said I had no talent, and I said, "Then I might as well just stab myself," and he said, "Excellent idea," and then I couldn't go back on what I'd said, so I did. And he just laughed, and that's when I said I'd kill him.'

'You cared that much about what he thought?'

'I cared a lot. He was the only one who mattered. Well, apart from you.'

'He told me that you were twice the writer he was,' said Ann.

'Chris?'

'He said never to tell you, so I didn't.'

'Did he mean it?'

'Yes, he meant it, he was jealous of you.'

Will's chest was pulsing with throbs of pain and he felt weak and sick, whether from the wound or the Friar's potion he wasn't sure. But he also felt strangely exultant. Did Chris really think that? Had he saved the most important words he could say until after he was dead?

'Sorry I said you killed him,' said Ann, 'and all the rest. You know I just get crazy sometimes.'

He knew.

'I'll come with you and talk to the gravedigger,' he said.

'Thank you. I can't do it without you. Men like that won't talk to a woman.'

'Tomorrow then,' he said.

'No, now. He digs graves at night for the next day.'

She was a Marlowe alright. Fearless and foolhardy and dangerous to know, fierce, raging and uncrushable. No Armada would conquer England as long as it was full of Marlowes.

'Come on,' said Ann, 'I don't know what the Friar gave us, but it's not like we're going to sleep.'

He did want justice or revenge or something for Chris. The chances of getting them were low, but here he was, off to bribe a gravedigger to dig up a body. Would he be here if it wasn't for Ann with no 'e'? He wouldn't. He'd be like Kemp and Barking Bobby in some drinking den recalling Chris in all his complicated glory, telling stories as he got drunker, laughing, sobbing, stumbling home and letting the booze and the night do its work to stifle his grief. Instead, here he was walking back towards the dangerous streets of Deptford.

Ann must have known what he was thinking. 'It makes

sense what we're doing,' she said. 'What's important is that we just keep going, we keep asking questions, because whoever it is who killed him won't like it, and they'll get worried and they'll try and stop us and then we'll find out who they are.'

'Just before they kill us,' he said.

'Save you doing it yourself,' she said.

He laughed and reached for her hand without thinking, and she let him. Had she been about to kiss him before he spoiled it by telling her he wasn't going to dig up Chris? He and Ann made no sense, but then, what did? Down towards the estuary the sheet lightning of a distant storm flickered. Here, a fine drizzle was falling and a wet curl of Ann's dark hair was plastered to her cheek. Somewhere above them, a woman sang a sad song in a foreign language. Despite Chris, despite the pain of his wounds, despite the madness of what they were doing, for a moment he was happy.

'Oh, there you are,' said the unmistakable booming voice of Barking Bobby, and a short square shape loomed out of the darkness. He had a long sword tucked into his belt that nearly reached the ground. 'I was worried about you two, when Kemp said you'd gone off down the marshes.'

'How did you find us?' asked Will.

'Just been hanging around in Limehouse. There was a big blonde fellow back there who knew who you were, and saw you go by.'

'Did he have a Jerusalem tattoo?' asked Ann.

'Fuck knows,' said Bobby, scratching himself vigorously. 'But listen, Chris was a good mate of mine, and my mate's mate is my mate,' he turned to include Ann, 'and so is my mate's sister. I'm living in a place down in Hog Lane, so if you need something done, I know people, if you know what I mean.'

'Hog Lane?' said Will. 'Do you know Hal Bradley, the brother of Tom Bradley who Chris and Watson killed in that fight?'

'Yeah, Hal's a nasty bit of work, stab you as soon as talk to you.'

'He always swore he'd kill Watson and Chris. Could he have hired someone?'

'Yeah, no, he did...' said Bobby.

They all stopped walking.

'Do you know who?' Ann asked.

'Yeah, I do,' said Bobby. 'It was me.'

Will's brain took a moment to catch up.

'I found Chris, but I liked Chris so I wasn't going to kill him.'

'And Watson died of the plague,' said Ann.

'No, I did kill him. Him I didn't like. Fucking full of himself and himself was irritating. As for his poetry, "A Passionate Century of Love", my arse. Still, I was nice to him.'

Will was still struggling to catch up. 'You were nice to him?'

'Until I killed him. I told him I was an admirer of his work. I didn't want to spoil his final moments.'

'Well, that was, um, thoughtful,' said Will.

'Everyone thinks he died of the plague,' said Ann.

'Yeah, well, they took three weeks to find the body and by then everyone looks like they died of the plague.'

'So you're a hired assassin?' said Ann.

'I dabble,' said Bobby, 'that and a bit of market gardening.'

Bobby was never still even when he was standing. He was always twitching from foot to foot, ducking his head this way and that like he was listening to music no one else could hear.

He explained how Bradley's brother had paid him half upfront, and as he'd killed one of the two men, he considered they were quits. Will asked if Bradley's brother could have hired someone else to kill Chris when Bobby hadn't done it, and he said he couldn't rule that out. Then Ann asked whether you could pay to get men in prison killed.

'Which prison?' asked Bobby.

'Marshalsea.'

She saw Will shaking his head despairingly.

'I'm just asking.' she said.

'If it's down below in limbo,' said Bobby, 'there's men that'd kill a man for a lump of cheese. If they've money and live up top it's tricky. You'd have to bribe one of the wardens.'

They walked on companionably with their friend the murderer.

Out of the darkness came the sound of a church choir practising, the sweet boys' voices interspersed with the angry shouting of the choirmaster.

'Can I tell you something?' said Bobby.

He was going to, whatever they said.

'I was captured by Barbary pirates and was a galley slave for five years before I killed the pirate king and escaped. Seven years later I was King of Wapping. I ran all the bars and dressed in ermine. That was until the Kent gangs moved in and I had to hide in the marshes down Canvey. Now I'm back and rubbing along nicely. The trick is, stay alive and anything can happen.'

So they had to stay alive. Right now, that was easier said than done. They heard the baaing of a sheep and a flock came around the corner, a flurry of white ghosts in the night. The black and white sheepdog snapping at their heels appeared and disappeared in the darkness. They brought them in at night when the streets were empty, to be slaughtered in the morning. The shepherd wished them 'Godspeed'. A small child ran behind carrying a sack so he could pick up their droppings and sell them around the orchards.

'Never liked sheep, they won't look you in the eye,' said Barking Bobby, turning around and heading back the way he'd come. His voice rumbled out of the darkness. 'One thought.' They could hear him but they couldn't see him. 'You know how they reckon Chris's body was down on the mudflats and they moved it to Eleanor Bull's house? Well, the mudflats down there are just over three miles from Greenwich Palace, and her house is just under, know what I mean?'

'So they moved him into Danby's jurisdiction?' said Ann.

'Might be something, might be nothing,' said the voice, then from further away. 'Anything you need, you know where to find me.'

Will wasn't sure he did, but Barking Bobby seemed to know how to find them. Where had he come from? Was he just checking on them like he said? The moon had gone and the darkness seemed to be closing in and pressing on their faces. Ann asked if he could find Deptford graveyard and he was tempted to say, 'no', but he knew that if they went straight ahead they'd reach Deptford Strand, and from there you could see the torches that lit the bars and brothels around Candle Street.

'We should report him and Bradley's brother for the murder of Watson,' said Will.

Ann said nothing, probably because she knew he wasn't going to do it. Three days ago he would have. Then justice seemed like that choke chain restraining that lion he had seen walking through Deptford. Now it seemed more like the lion, a savage force held by the powerful to be unleashed at their whim. Ann was right, yet he held on to the notion that it existed, if only in the minds of individuals, for what else held back the bloody tide of chaos and slaughter? He should write a revenge tragedy about whether there should be revenge, not just how.

'Of course, he could have been lying,' said Ann. 'He could have killed Chris as well. And why did he come and find us? And how does he know they moved Chris's body? And what he said about how they made sure Danby was the coroner, do you think someone wants to cast suspicion on Danby so we don't go back to him with any evidence we find?' She saw Will's despairing look. 'I know, I know,' she said. 'We don't believe anything anyone says any more.'

She was right. Half of London told lies to the other half who didn't believe them. In this snarl of duplicity not even the most simple truths could survive.

ANN

The gravedigger was in a grave digging, only his head and shovel visible. On Chris's grave nearby, people had left flowers, a pipe and a couple of bottles of alcohol and Ann wondered who they were. The gravedigger turned to Will as they walked over.

'You the bloke who killed Marlowe?' he asked.

'No,' said Ann, 'he's not.'

'Makes no odds to me. Bodies are my living. Go kill some more as long as you do it in Deptford. No one seems to be dying right now.'

'Not even with the plague?' said Ann.

'Don't talk to me about the plague. I don't get to bury them, they bury 'em in pits. Get the bleeding Dutch in to do it 'cos they'll do anything for a groat.'

Ann saw she had started him off on something. His angry head peered up at her from his pit.

'They don't even know what they're doing. They dig V-shaped pits which means the bodies get wedged. It wastes space.'

'Whose grave is this?' she asked to get him off the Dutch.

'Mine,' he said. 'Cos I'm digging it. Nah, it's for that Dutch family.'

'So they're not in the common pit?'

'A woman paid for them to be buried.'

Ann looked more closely at the graves and saw two of

them were no more than three feet long. Will had put his hand to his mouth in shock.

'It's that little girl who came to find us,' he said.

'They're both boys,' said the gravedigger. 'One was a cousin staying with them.'

'So the girl's still alive?' said Ann, surprised by the magnitude of her own joy. Will was smiling too. 'We should try and find her. See if she can tell us some more about where she saw Chris's body.'

'Tomorrow,' said Will, sitting wearily on a gravestone.

'Yes, tomorrow,' said Ann.

'Their bodies looked untouched,' said the gravedigger. 'Just one little cut in the neck but dead as dead can be.' He started to complain how he only got paid half for a child, but that it was nearly as much work as an adult.

She nudged Will. He had promised to start off the talking. He stood up again.

'We've a proposal for you. We'll pay you to dig up Marlowe's body.'

She supposed there wasn't really a subtle way of asking.

'I'm a gravedigger,' he said. 'It's there in my job title. I'm not a grave-digger-upper.'

Will said nothing, like she had told him. The gravedigger filled the silence.

'They'd hang me if they caught me and I've buried hanged men and they didn't look happy. It'd have to be a king's ransom you pay me.'

So now at least they were in a negotiation.

'There's a friar, lives on the Isle of Dogs,' said Will, 'who says he's worked with you before.'

'That nutter. The mad monk of the marshes. Should have guessed it'd be something to do with him.'

They waited again. The gravedigger shoved his lantern into the grave.

'See there,' he said. He was standing up to his ankles in muddy water. 'Work in London you don't get that, but in

Deptford I hit water four foot down, but do we get paid more? No. So I do what you ask, you pay me for the risk and you pay me for the graft and you pay me 'cos I haven't felt my feet since I was twenty-five.'

'And how much would that be?' asked Will.

'Two guineas.'

Will looked at Ann.

'Oh, the little lady's the one with the money, is she?'

'I don't have two guineas,' said Ann.

The gravedigger leant on his shovel with a dirty toothless grin. 'There's other ways to pay.'

'You're not touching her,' said Will.

He shrugged. 'How about you?'

Ann almost laughed seeing Will's face. 'You're not touching him either.'

'Lovebirds,' he muttered and smashed the shovel down hard. 'You think you just dig up a bit of mud and there you are, but it's overcrowded. There's bones and rotten coffins all over.'

He reached down into the water and his hand came out holding a skull.

WILL

The gravedigger held up the skull; it looked slightly healthier than him.

Will stared at it, jawbone still intact but most of the teeth missing. 'How long's that been in the ground?'

'About ten years.' The gravedigger pointed to a small patch of something around about where the ear would have been. 'A little bit of flesh, see? Most times it falls off after seven or eight years, nine if you're a tanner.'

Will couldn't take his eyes off the hollow skull. Most people couldn't believe that when they died they just ceased to exist, but it was a lot easier to believe it about other people, and easier still when you saw their empty skulls. The gravedigger dropped it back into the water with a splash.

'You've not got two guineas,' he said.

'I've a half-guinea left,' said Ann, 'and if I sell back the cloth I bought to take home, I won't get what I paid for it, but there's also a brooch I was given. I could sell it and say I lost it. I think I could raise a guinea and a quarter.'

The gravedigger considered glumly. He had a lived-in face. A face lived in by a family of rats. 'Alright. A guinea and a quarter, because I like you. Tomorrow night there's a woman I can bury next to him so it won't look odd.'

'What time?' asked Ann.

'Midnight.'

She wouldn't look at Will.

ANN

There was a candle flickering in the Poplar apothecary's window. Will had said that he'd be asleep and it wasn't worth going there but she'd said it was worth trying and she had been right. She knocked on the door. A man instantly opened it. He had a neck that looked too thin to support his head and protruding eyes reflecting the candle he carried. He seemed thrilled to be given a message for the Friar telling him to meet them at the graveyard tomorrow night.

'Yes, yes, yes,' he said, 'will he be bringing me a little something?' His popped-out eyes were glassy and his free hand tap-tap-tapped on the door frame.

'You'll have to ask him,' she said as they walked away.

He shouted after them that he'd pay the Friar double if he came tonight.

'So we have no money left,' said Will.

'No, I had two guineas, I just didn't want to pay him that much.'

'Oh,' said Will.

It was a good thing he hadn't stayed in Stratford-upon-Avon, he would have made a useless merchant. He stumbled in a pothole. She felt sorry for him now because the Friar's salve didn't seem to have made him any better and it was still nearly an hour's walk back to his rooms.

'Shall we try and get a wherry?' she asked him.

He shook his head. 'We won't find a boatman at this hour.'

She thought she heard something behind them, and touched his sleeve to stop him walking, then raised a finger to her lips. They listened hard and he tilted his head questioningly.

'I think someone was following us,' she whispered.

'Are you sure?'

'Women who walk on their own after dark get to know,' she said, but now the only sound she could hear was a baby crying in one of the nearby houses.

The clouds had cleared and the moonlight again shone through the narrow gap between the overhanging houses and lit up the middle of the street with a slice of light, but anyone behind them could have stepped into the shadows on either side. They walked on. A dog howled and others joined in.

'The gravedigger said the Dutch family were all killed with one neat cut,' said Will. 'Imagine you wanted to kill someone.'

'I do,' she said. 'Whoever killed Chris.'

'How many times are you going to stab them?'

'Lots and lots and lots,' she said.

'Exactly. You're not going to know what it takes to kill someone, so you'll keep going. But they just used one thrust. You have to have killed people before to have the confidence to know that just one will work.'

He was right. The killers were professionals. There was the sound of footsteps running, but they were in a nearby street. She couldn't hear anyone behind them any more.

'Do you think they're the same men who searched Chris's room?' he asked. 'They did the same thing and wrote that stuff on the wall.'

Why hadn't she been asking more questions like this? Sometimes she just charged off from one place to the next. There were times Will and all his thinking had its uses.

'So they killed them to silence them,' she said. 'Who knew about her? Who was there when she told us? Was it just Bella and the Widow?'

'Yes, but we don't know who else her mother had tried talking to.'

'We must find the little girl, but we mustn't tell anyone she's alive.'

Was it Ann's fault the family had been killed? If she hadn't been going around asking questions about Christopher's murder perhaps they wouldn't have felt the need.

A large figure stepped out from an alley and blocked the street in front of them. He had long blonde hair. Ann instinctively looked around to see if their escape was cut off from behind, but no one was standing in the long streak of moonlight. Will reached for his stupid kitchen knife.

'Don't be scared,' said the blonde man, 'and please put that away.'

Will still clung to it.

'Put it away,' she said and he did.

'You're trying to find out who killed Chris, aren't you?' said the man.

Ann could just make out the Jerusalem tattoo on one wrist.

'Who are you?' said Will.

'I'm his friend.'

'I'm his friend,' said Will, 'and this is his sister, and neither of us has ever met you.'

'You've met me,' he said to Will.

WILL

Will struggled to place him.

'Remember when they brought in more actors for *Tamburlaine*?' he asked.

That was why his face looked familiar. Chris had insisted they make it more spectacular and they'd hired extras to play the soldiers.

'They got rid of me when the muskets fired into the audience, even though it wasn't my fault.'

Now it came back to Will. At the climax of Act Two of *Tamburlaine* musketeers fired over the audience, but one night the muskets were inexplicably loaded and one spectator was killed and several injured.

'Serves them right,' Chris had said, 'they didn't applaud enough at the end of Act One.'

The play went on as they dragged out the wounded and the next night, if anything, the crowds got bigger. Will suspected Lord Strange had done it deliberately as free advertising, but it was true, he had blamed the youngest of the musketeers.

'You're Rich Spencer's son,' said Will.

'Yes. Edmund. My father got Strange to fire me because he didn't want me to be an actor.'

He was the rich boy besotted with the theatre, illegitimate, but nevertheless the only son of the richest man in England.

'Why aren't you in prison?' Ann asked.

Edmund looked shamefaced.

'Because he's Rich Spencer's son,' said Will. 'Edmund Spencer, not to be confused with the poet.'

The boy nodded with an apologetic shrug of the shoulders.

'He hates me,' he said, 'but he'd never let me go to prison. It'd be bad for his reputation. Now can we talk inside?'

There wasn't any inside apparent, but he gestured up the alley from which he'd appeared. There seemed no reason not to follow him and, six feet along, there was a big nail-studded door with a knocker. Edmund knocked, two short raps, a pause, then three more and the door opened. A man in a long black coat blocked the door, his face in shadow.

'They're with me,' said Edmund and the man stepped away to let them pass.

Edmund led them down the steep stone staircase, opened another door and they stepped into a babble of voices and a fog of smoke. A lot of heads turned and stared at Ann and Will. It was an unusual mix of ages and classes, all men, apart from the barmaid. Edmund waved at her and held up three fingers and as she poured them three glasses of sack, Will saw she was a young man immaculately dressed in a red silk gown.

'Chris told me about places like this,' Ann whispered to him.

ANN

Edmund led them through the crowd. A dark-skinned man with a gold tooth and a green headscarf kissed him on both cheeks, and said how he was sorry for his loss. Another man touched his arm and he too offered condolences. Chris must have come here with Edmund, she thought. He would have been at home in this parallel world.

Edmund gestured regally at a couple of merchants to move along and they sat down beneath a gaudy painting of St Sebastian, Ann facing Edmund and Will at the end of the table.

'So what have you found out?' Edmund said as he sat. 'Do you think it was my father who had Chris killed?'

'Why would he have done that?' asked Will.

'Because he found out we were lovers.' He put on the plump voice of Sir John. 'You're so damn weak. You let these perverts corrupt you. If they just left you alone you'd be normal.'

The beautiful man in the beautiful dress put three glasses on their table. Ann liked this place. They served women alcohol.

She asked him, 'How long have you known Christopher?'

'It would have been two years this Trinity Sunday.'

She saw Will's face. He was astonished. Edmund saw it too.

'It's true. I wanted to be out with him in public, but he said he was in enough trouble already. He said he'd make it up to me, that he'd write a play for me.'

Ann thought, *This could have been me*. A secret lover kept hidden away in a room. Chris, of course, had got what he wanted.

'At least you believe me, don't you?' said Edmund, reaching to put his hand over hers.

She nodded. Edmund went to take his hand back but she held on to it. There was that tattoo on his wrist.

'The Jerusalem tattoo?' she said.

Edmund laughed and with his other arm grabbed the belt of an elderly man walking by. 'Jonno, show them,' he said, pointing at his own wrist. Jonno rolled up his sleeve and there was that same tattoo on his forearm.

'Look closely,' said Edmund.

There was the Latin cross with a smaller cross in each quadrant, but when she looked more closely she could see one of the small crosses was rotated into the X of St Peter.

'Jonno says he started it,' said Edmund, and let go of him.

'It's a sign so we know each other,' said Jonno.

'Not that anyone needs a sign with Jonno,' said Edmund.

Jonno laughed as he walked off.

'If we're arrested, then we're just good Christians.'

A drunken old man standing by the fire started to sing a song in a strange language, his face lifted to the ceiling, his eyes closed, his cracked voice full of sorrow. A red-coated constable came through the door. Was this a raid? Will had half got up, ready to run.

'Relax,' said Edmund.

The constable strolled over to the bar, ordered a drink from the man in the red dress, and she saw them joke about their matching red costumes. She recognised him as the one called Troutbeck who had charged money to let the crowd see Christopher's body, but he had at least been kind to her when he found out she was his sister.

'When did you last see Christopher?' asked Ann.

'He called in on me at about three in the morning of the day he died, though only for about five minutes.' He was fighting back emotions. 'He was upset and wouldn't say why. He had to go, but wouldn't say where. As he walked out the door he said "one day".'

So, presuming Frizer and Skerries' testimony was a lie, Edmund was the last person they knew who had seen him alive.

Edmund knocked back his drink. 'Now tell me, was it my father who had Chris killed, because if it was, I'm going to kill him.'

'That'll be one bit of trouble he won't be able to get you out of,' said Ann.

He looked at her for a moment and finally laughed.

A scrawny ginger man put his arm around the shoulder of the singer and joined in the song with an unexpected bass rumble.

Across from her, Will was gripping the edge of the table with both hands to stop himself from shivering. He was sweating and his eyes had a misty sheen.

She feared the Friar's salve wasn't working. Edmund was looking at Will too.

'You don't believe me, do you?' Edmund said.

'I do,' said Will. 'You left an Italian kidskin jerkin in Chris's room, didn't you?'

Edmund looked surprised. 'I wondered where that was.'

WILL

Everyone knew that Chris liked men and women equally. In one of those rare moments when Chris let down his guard, he had said to Will, 'It means there's twice as many people who can break your heart.'

Edmund made sense of things. Will always felt he had only half known Chris, or perhaps, more accurately, only known half of him. When Edmund had told them about Chris and him, Will, for a moment, felt an absurd pang of jealousy but, of course, one life wasn't enough for Chris, it didn't have sufficient danger or excitement. Did the secrecy add to that? He asked Edmund why Chris had told no one about the two of them.

'Why do you think?' said Edmund. 'He was reckless, but he knew there were limits, he knew there were some things you had to hide. And one of them was me.' His voice broke, but he took a breath. 'He became more careful after he killed Bradley in Hog Lane.'

'I don't think it was him who struck the fatal blow,' said Ann quickly.

'I watched as his sword went in,' said Edmund.

Ann said nothing but closed her eyes for a moment, and though Will couldn't hear it in the hubbub, he saw her sigh.

'What happened?' she asked.

'Bradley said some hateful things about Chris and me and Chris said a lot more back, then Bradley got out a knife so I took out mine, but Chris took Watson's sword. I should have tried to stop him but...' He glanced at Ann and stopped. 'Go on,' she said.

'He did it for me,' said Edmund.

The fever made the room a swirl of colour and noise. The song, in a language he thought might be Gaelic, seemed to be circling around inside his head, and he struggled to concentrate.

'I couldn't have stopped him if I'd tried. He thought of me like he always did and told me to make myself scarce before the constables arrived.'

'Bradley was a thug, a bigot and a bully,' said Will, but Ann didn't look any happier. 'Besides,' said Will, 'it's not as if you're against killing. You keep saying you're going to kill the man who killed Chris.'

'I'll kill my father if he's behind it,' said Edmund. 'He said he'd kill Chris unless I stopped seeing him.'

The room was slowly rotating and Will gripped the table with his hands to stop himself floating away with it. His body barely seemed to belong to him.

'You said the killing changed Christopher,' Ann was saying to Edmund.

'He was more careful after that. He knew he could have been hanged if Lord Strange hadn't stepped in and used his influence with the magistrate.'

Will had thought Chris escaped justice by bribing the witnesses. For every new fact they discovered they found out something that they had thought to be true was false. Ann asked Edmund if Sir John could have commissioned a Marlowe play from Lord Strange, and he said he could have, if it was before he found out Chris was his lover. She asked if Sir John owned a house in Deptford, and he laughed and said his father owned so many houses that even he couldn't remember where they all were.

In the whirling blur of the room something familiar reached out towards Will, not the music or the faces, not the sticky touch of the table or the circling smoke from the fire, but a smell he knew well.

'Do you wear the same scent as Chris?' he asked Edmund.

'Yes.'

Ann looked at Will. 'Is it the scent you smelt on the pillow in the house in Deptford?' Will nodded.

ANN

Ann took Will's arm as they headed back towards his lodging and the fresh air seemed to clear his head. In front of them, a couple of constables were sitting on upturned boxes next to a fire. Most of the doorways near them had red crosses painted on them; they'd been posted there to make sure no one left the plague houses. Will hesitated.

'Let's go down Water Lane,' he said.

You can't catch the plague from a road, she thought, but she went with him as they turned right at the crossroads down towards the river and took the parallel lane. It was utterly black and she felt ahead with each foot for potholes before she put it down.

She wasn't surprised that Christopher would have a secret lover, or that it would be a man, but she hadn't expected an Edmund.

'I can't imagine them together,' she said.

Will took a moment to answer. 'He has all these lives. He takes something different from all of us.'

He'd fallen into talking about Christopher in the present tense. She felt an ache and, for a moment, imagined Christopher walking beside them, invisible in the darkness. She wanted to reach out and take his hand, and tell him that she'd never forget him, that she'd never rest until she found out who was responsible for his murder.

'So,' she said to Will, 'we now know that Edmund had

nothing to do with getting rid of Christopher's knife at the inquest, but we can be almost certain that it was Christopher's scent on the pillow.'

'Or it could have been Edmund's,' he said. 'They used the same perfume.'

She hadn't considered that. Edmund could have been there if the house did belong to his father, but she didn't think that he'd lied. She reached for certainties.

'We do know, that if Edmund's telling the truth, Sir Rich Spencer hated Christopher and wanted him dead.'

'And we know the last words anyone heard him say,' said Will.

'What do you think Christopher meant by "one day"?' she asked.

'That one day they could truly be together.'

That's what she had thought. She wished there was a world where she could say those words to Will.

She heard the steps behind them, but didn't have time to turn her head before a big hand smacked into her mouth and jerked her head back. When she tried to scream, she could only manage a gurgling noise. The man lifted her off her feet with one arm and punched her in the stomach with the other and she gulped for air. She heard Will grunt, and footsteps moving away. She reached back for the man's face and tried to find his eyes, wishing her nails were longer, but he just changed his grip so one hand was over one of her breasts and laughed. She jerked and squirmed and kicked backwards with her feet, and clawed something soft that could have been an ear. He screamed, lifted her higher and threw her. She bounced off a wall and landed with a thump that knocked the breath out of her.

When she raised her head, the darkness was silent and the street empty. She felt sick and struggled to breathe, and it felt like when her father had broken a couple of her ribs. The thug had thrown her away, like something useless chucked out in the street for the ravens and kites. It was Will they'd wanted, and they must have wanted him alive because it would have been so easy to kill him then and there. It was just like she had said. They had tried to find out who killed Christopher and the men who didn't want them to had come for them, but it was useless because the men had come in darkness, and she had no idea who they were. Of course, of course! It was never going to work. Did she really think a Canterbury cobbler's daughter could go up against the lords and earls and dukes and sirs?

She could just about breathe again, and sat up. She had to think clearly, who would want Will and how could she get him back? The constables in the next street would be worse than useless and Danby wouldn't care. She could only think of one person who could possibly help. There was blood in her mouth and her hair was plastered across one eye and thick with stinking mud. She reached to scrape it back. There was something in her hand and she opened it to look. It was a bloodied gold earring.

WILL

They had put a sack over his head that smelt of pitch and tar, and they took an arm each and walked him along the street, holding him up when his feet stumbled. He thought of shouting for help but even if anyone heard, who would challenge a pair of thugs marching along a man with a sack on his head? They reached a slippery, muddy slope and dragged him down it. Even through the sack he could smell the rank brine stench of the river. They picked him up and heaved him in the air. He expected the cold wet of the Thames but he landed on a creaky floor. A boat, he was in a boat. They'd marched him to the river to save having to carry the body. They were going to row him out into the middle of the Thames, cut his throat, fill the sack with stones and be rid of him, or perhaps they wouldn't even bother with the knife, and he'd just be drowned like a kitten. He should kick and yell and struggle but it wouldn't make any difference. He'd feel better about it if he went down fighting, but what was the point and why was his brain bothering to have these thoughts? He should be thinking of Ann with no 'e' and his children, but when he did the sharp jolt of loss just made his panic worse.

ANN

Bella liked Will, and she knew everyone. She'd be able to help Will, but where to find her? Ann knew she lived near Will in a small house, with dried spices in bowls, and a lemon tree in a room made of glass. She would find Will's room, she thought she could do that even in the dark, and then she would hire a linkman with a torch, and they'd walk the streets, and she would perhaps recognise Bella's house and hope she was at home. She raced towards Will's lodging, running when there was moonlight, or enough candlelight through a window to see, and walking where the darkness was thickest, because if she tried to run there, she would fall over and that would slow her down. Sometimes a nightwatchman called in the distance, or a dog howled, but the streets were empty.

Ann had caused this. She knew Will had only gone ahead with all of it because it was her and somewhere among the rage and the grief she had enjoyed it. She liked still having that power, that a man wanted her, not because it was convenient and her father owned a cobbler shop, but because it was her, because she was tough and clever and in her own way beautiful. But now he'd been snatched away and they were going to hurt him and it was her fault that he was screaming in some dark basement, the one man she loved. She tried to batter these thoughts away. She must use logic. There was almost a one hundred per cent chance that she would find

Will's house, a fifty-fifty chance she could find a man with a torch, and then perhaps only a one in four chance she could find Bella's house. That was the hardest, and then there was maybe a one in three chance Bella would be in. Two times four, times three, so a one in twenty-four chance she would get hold of Bella, but then Bella still had to find Will and free him and that's if they hadn't just cut his throat with one neat slash like they had the Dutch family. The odds were preposterous, the kind of wild chance her father would take on the gaming tables. Was she just doing this to keep her mind busy so it didn't dwell on terrible things? No, because if she did nothing, the chances of finding Will were zero, and a very little chance was better than nothing.

She was only a few streets away from Will's room, but here the darkness was impenetrable and each step a lottery. The dogs started off again, one yapping and others joining in howling or barking. She tripped and slithered and then she heard it, that deep roar of a bark. Was she imagining it, or was that Bella's huge mastiff? It came from ahead of her. She tried to follow it, running, stumbling then picking herself up, with her bruised elbows and grazed knees, and running again. It was closer, it couldn't be more than a street away, but then one by one the dogs stopped, and London was silent again apart from a scream of frustration, which was hers. She ran into the blackness towards where she thought she had last heard it, tripped again, and her knee landed on a sharp stone.

There was a sliver of light where she had fallen. She reached for the stone, picked it up, stood up and hurled it hard through a window. The smashing sound started off the dogs again as she hoped, and there it was, that deep, cavernous bark really close by. What if it wasn't Perro? But what if it was? Breathless, she slowed to a walk and turned a corner towards it. She felt a jolt in her stomach. She was in the street where Will lived and Bella's house wasn't there. Yet there was that bark again.

BELLA

The men who had searched Will's room had no discernment or finesse; floorboards had been torn up and splintered, lumps of plaster hacked off the wall, parchment pages scattered and strewn. When she searched a room, she was no more than a shadow passing, and no one could tell she had been there. She looked for the strands of hair that the suspicious stuck across the gaps between their drawers and the frame of the furniture, and once she had searched she replaced them. She sometimes amused herself by adding a penny to any cash she found hidden, so when they returned and counted it, there was more rather than less.

The men who had carried out this search could easily have missed a carefully hidden package as they smashed and ripped their way through the room. She would examine it painstakingly, but for the moment she was just too weary. Bella pushed the upended bed with one boot so it fell back onto its feet. The mattress was slashed and gutted, but she lay back on it anyway and closed her eyes. She tried to work out what her aim should be. Sometimes remembering which lies she had told to whom made her giddy.

Spying paid poorly these days, for when half of London spied on the other half you had to work for at least three masters to make a living. But then they were like jealous lovers. He, of course, was jealous to start with, which made him so dangerous, scared to touch her, but obsessed that no one else should. He would never let her be with Charles.

Perro started barking again but it was just distant cannon fire at sea. Her thoughts were flimsy and her eyeballs full of smoke.

'What's happened?'

There was someone in the room. She sat up slowly. Ann stood in front of her, grazed, ragged, bespattered and panicky.

'Did you do this?' she asked Bella.

Slowly, reluctantly, she returned to the ugliness of the present. She gestured at the wreckage. 'Does this butchery look like my work? I came to see Will and found it like this. What are you doing here?'

'They've taken him away!'

'Who's taken him? Where?'

'I don't know.' Ann mopped blood off one elbow with her other torn sleeve. 'Some men dragged him off. I was looking for you. You're the only one who can help. Please.'

Oh, these two, she thought, innocents caught between the massed pikes of two advancing armies. But she liked Will, Perro liked him and she didn't want to lose him as well as Chris. The other writers were mediocre at best.

'Did they say anything?' she asked Ann.

Ann shook her head helplessly.

'And did you see faces?'

Ann reached into the small bag she carried and brought out something that glinted in the shaft of moonlight. It was a bloody earring. 'I got this off one of them.'

Bella felt herself wanting to smile. Ann was a fighter and if the earring belonged to the man she thought it did, he deserved it.

'Was he a strong man?' Bella asked.

Ann nodded eagerly. 'Do you know who it is?'

'Perhaps,' said Bella. It was not going to be easy. Still, she would fight off her lassitude and try. 'Stay here,' she said to Ann. 'Wedge the door shut and let no one in.'

Perro rose to her feet with a stretch and a yawn and together they went out the door. She would try and talk to Cecil but he would make his usual complaint that she worked for others, and ask what she could give him in exchange for Will's freedom.

LIZZIE

Lizzie watched from the shadows. She had found a piece of hessian floating in the Thames, and fished it out with a stick and hidden it in some brambles, and when it was dry she had used it to wrap around herself in the cold of the night. She found that if she sat very still, wrapped in the blackened fabric, in a dark doorway or the corner of a yard, no one saw her. It was as if she did not exist. The women with the mops and buckets of soapy water did not tell her to scram, nor the shopkeepers throw pebbles at her. Even the men who kept food in their pockets to try and be her friend passed her by. When she needed directions, she only went up to women who had children with them, as her mama had told her. She read out to them the address the crooked playwright had written on the back of the note he had given her, and mostly they were kind and helped her. That way she had found the house where his friend Will lived.

Nearly opposite was an alley with a dead end but a broken fence she could squeeze through if she needed to escape and that was where she had sat herself down. There was a swallow nest above her under the eaves, and the adult birds flashed in front of her as they swooped in and out. She counted the heads of five hungry chicks poking out of the nest, and the parents stuffed food into their wide-open beaks. Lizzie felt tears rising up, but knew she must make no noise, and forced them back.

She watched as two men hung around outside Will's door

looking suspiciously unsuspicious. She heard the sound of splintering wood, and watched them go inside. A third man came and stood in the shadows at the entrance of the alleyway where she was hiding – a big man who blocked out her view – so close she could have touched his shiny boots. She started trembling so hard she had to hold on to the wall, and for a moment she was back under that straw as they killed the others. Her heartbeat scampered in her chest and the pit-a-pat was so loud that she feared he would hear it. She wanted to dive away through that gap in the fence, but she knew she must stay as still as can be. In the end he went and she saw he was following the other two men.

Lizzie wrapped the hessian tighter around her, and tried to stay awake, but kept falling asleep. She woke from a dream of picking cherries, to see the dark-skinned woman with the huge dog turn up at Will's door, and go upstairs. She wanted to rush up the stairs after her and tell her everything, but there was something about the way she looked over her shoulder before she went through the door that made her fearful. When Will's friend, with the sad, pretty, angry face, ran to the door and up the stairs she wished she could run to her too, but the woman with the dog was still upstairs. If only she could get Will's friend on her own, she would pass on the message she had been given and say the sentence she kept practising, 'I have come a long way with this piece of paper, and I am very hungry, so please would you do me the kindness of buying me a pie.'

WILL

Will was pushed downward and his arse landed on something, and the squeak and scrape told him it was a stool. The boat had docked back on the Thames shore without them killing him. Then he'd been dragged across cobbles and up and down stone steps and through big, creaky doors with bolts and clunky locks. The sack was yanked off his head by a tough-looking man with blood running down his neck from a wound in his ear, who left, carrying the sack.

Will was at the end of a long table in a stone room lit by sconces. A guard with his breastplate and helmet glinting stood at the door. At the far end of the table was a small man twisted into a large, carved and cushioned chair.

'Do you know who I am?' he asked.

Will needed a moment to retrieve his voice from the pit of his stomach. 'I do, my lord.'

It was Cecil.

'Are you terrified that you've been brought here?'

'I'm... I'm...' Now his voice had acquired a stutter. 'I'm honoured.'

'Really?' said Cecil. 'No, you should be terrified.'

'You are trembling,' said a reedy voice from behind him. A man was sitting in the shadows.

'I do have a fever,' said Will.

'A lot of men who come here have a fever like that,' said the voice.

'Have you met Topcliffe?' asked Cecil.

Will's heart beat so furiously he was sure they could hear it. His panic rose in his stomach and chest like a physical thing trying to get out. 'I've never met him in the flesh,' Will said.

The flesh. Why had he said that?

Topcliffe the torturer spoke in his high, scratchy voice. 'I heard you based the part of the villain in *Titus Andronicus* on me.'

Will half turned to him. 'No. I swear, no.'

'I'm disappointed,' said Topcliffe. 'I'm a keen theatregoer and it would mean the world to me to be immortalised in a character.'

'I could very easily,' Will was stuttering again, 'I could easily do that for you if... erm...'

'What are you calling your new play about Richard III?' cut in Cecil.

'*Richard III*,' said Will.

Cecil had a pile of hazelnuts in front of him and a nutcracker in his hand, and he cracked one now, picked out the nut and brushed the pieces of shell onto the floor. The stone slabs were covered with them. 'Does the queen's grandfather feature in it?' he asked.

Will knew where this was leading. 'Henry VII restores peace and the rightful royal line at the end.'

'So why not write a play about him? Why write a play about a child-murdering cripple?'

Will went to speak but Cecil spoke over him.

'Why write a play about a conniving and treacherous cripple which all London will think is based on me?'

An instinct in Will told him not to deny it, for what Cecil said was true.

'Your Lordship,' said Will. 'I don't seek to get involved in politics. Theatre just sets out to entertain.'

'An utter lie, as you well know,' said Cecil. 'Are you familiar with the tragedy of *Sir Thomas More*?'

'He was in it,' chipped in Topcliffe.

'Then you'll know its hero is a Catholic traitor,' said Cecil. 'Did you know that it was originally intended to premiere on the same night as the Babington Plot?'

Will didn't.

'It was to be staged at exactly the same time as the Catholic lords slit the throat of Queen Elizabeth and installed Mary, Queen of Scots in her place. And why was that? Because the theatre is the one place you can send a message to both high society and the mob. Pamphlets are useless because most people can't read. Proclamations bore them, but the theatre is the living blood of London, so don't treat me like an idiot and tell me that it's "just for entertainment".'

'No,' said Topcliffe behind him, 'you really shouldn't treat His Lordship like an idiot.'

Possible replies formed in Will's brain, but they all sounded stupid or provocative, yet was silence even more insulting? He was shaking so much his chair was creaking. Cecil cracked another nut.

'What play is Kyd writing?'

Will remembered his ink-free hand. 'I don't think he's writing anything.' Topcliffe nodded fussily. 'That is what he claimed.'

'And what play was Marlowe working on when he died?' asked Cecil.

'I don't know,' said Will, 'he was very secretive.'

'Always or just on this occasion?'

'Just on this occasion.'

'Did Kyd know?' Cecil asked Topcliffe.

'He just said it was a history play,' said the squeaky voice from behind him and Will had a suicidal impulse to laugh but resisted.

'Would you say Kyd or you knew Marlowe better?' Cecil asked.

'Me.'

'So why would he tell Kyd and not you?'

'I don't know.'

'That again,' Cecil sighed. 'It's not a phrase we like to hear, is it, Mr Topcliffe?'

Will thought he could hear distant screaming but Topcliffe was here in the room so perhaps it was the wind.

'If I'd known what he was writing,' said Will, 'I'd have no reason not to tell you.'

'Hm,' said Cecil.

'That sounds fair enough,' said Topcliffe.

His reasonableness was terrifying. Will was telling them the truth, but what had Chris said? Always hold something back so that when they start hurting you, you have something left to tell them.

'Who commissioned it?' asked Cecil.

'I heard it was Rich Spencer.' He corrected himself. 'Sir John Spencer.'

Will felt relieved he was being asked questions to which he knew the answers.

'And where can we find this play of Marlowe's?' asked Cecil.

His guts felt liquid. He mustn't say, *I don't know*. 'In his room, perhaps.'

Cecil shook his head. 'Not there.'

Will thought of Chris's ransacked room.

'Nor is there a copy at the theatre, nor does Lord Strange have one.' Cecil turned to Topcliffe. 'Did Kyd say anything?'

There was rustling behind him and Will realised Topcliffe was consulting his notes.

'He said he didn't know. I pressed him on that point a number of times but he was most insistent.'

'It's possible he took the commission but never started it?' said Will.

'Why would he do that?' asked Cecil.

'Well, you know what writers are like.'

'I don't. Why would he not write when that was his job?'

Lord Cecil's pinched face looked in pain. Was it his bent and twisted spine, or Will's answers?

'Your Lordship will, I hope, forgive me,' said Topcliffe, 'if I say that, while you understand more about the workings of this kingdom than any other man alive, you are not of an artistic bent like Mr Shakespeare, and if I might say so, myself.'

Topcliffe got up and came and sat at the table next to Will.

'Imagination is not like a servant summoned with a snap of the fingers, is it, Mr Shakespeare? It requires inspiration to distil the poet's experience of life into a story others may enjoy.'

Will thought it was wise to agree. He wondered why Cecil tolerated all this, but then he decided it was a piece of theatre they had honed between them to unsettle those they questioned.

Topcliffe went on. 'If I may be so bold, Mr Shakespeare, in *Titus Andronicus* I fear your experience may have been inadequate.'

Now a torturer was agreeing with Marlowe.

'I'm no doctor, but if she has both her hands and her tongue cut off, she's really going to bleed to death quite rapidly. Trust me on this.'

'Right, thank you,' said Will, hearing his own absurdity.

Cecil cracked another nut. 'Where's Marlowe's play?'

He knew he was going to stammer and he did. 'I'm sorry, I have no idea.'

'That's really the same as "I don't know", isn't it?' said Cecil.

This was what horrified him. Topcliffe in his chamber asking him a question he didn't know the answer to. He'd make something up to stop the pain, but Topcliffe would know, and on it would go. 'He was quite insistent,' Topcliffe would tell Cecil.

'I'm going to let Topcliffe show you around,' said Cecil.

ANN

Ann had started clearing up the mess in Will's room just so she was doing something, but it didn't stop the terrible thoughts flailing around in her brain. Some force led her to think of the worst things she could possibly imagine, so when she knelt to pray it was just to try and get rid of them. She put her weight on her bruised and grazed knees and it was agony but she didn't move them in case God might take that suffering as an earnest of her seriousness. There was no getting around it, it was a long time since she had prayed, and she was only doing it now because she was backed into a corner, but God must be used to that, and it was worth a try because there was not a damn thing else she could think of trying. She told God that she really didn't mind if he was a Protestant or a Catholic and she begged him to save Will, but it just felt like words and, if she was God, she would pay it no attention. She told God that Will was a good man, but being good didn't save anyone. She thought about prayer and how it was just a form of bargaining and how she was good at that. If you wanted something, you should offer God something in return, so she got down to business.

'Oh God, please preserve Will. Let him come back to me. I swear on the Bible and my life and the life of any children I have, that if You do I shall never break Your commandment against adultery.' She added, 'Again.' Was it the seventh commandment? She wasn't sure. It didn't matter. 'Because,

God,' she went on, 'both You and I know that if Will and I stay together any longer we're going to.' Her bruised knees really hurt, and she wanted to stand up, but she stayed there. 'We both know I love him,' she said, 'but You demand we sacrifice something for You and I'm not sure I've got anything else.' She stopped there because she had nothing else to offer. 'Amen,' she said.

She had to roll over onto her stomach and hold on to the creaking corner of the broken coffer in order to haul herself to her feet. She didn't feel any more confident. If she had to choose between God and Bella, she'd probably take Bella, but her father had taught her you needed to hedge your bets. It hadn't even rid her of the images. Will was still bloody and screaming in her head. She tried closing her eyes, but that just turned her head into a theatre of horror. She deliberately banged one of her knees on the bedstead and for a moment the pain left no room for her imagination. There was a quiet tap-tap on the door. Well, that wasn't God. She limped over.

'Who's that?'

'Lizzie,' came the small, scared voice of the little Dutch girl. 'Are you alone?'

'Yes.'

Ann dragged Will's coffer a few inches away from the door and opened it a crack. Lizzie's face appeared, and she was small enough to edge sideways into the room. For a moment, Ann thought that perhaps God had misunderstood her and sent her the wrong one, but that was daft. The little girl had changed in a couple of days from a pink and well-scrubbed child into one of London's ragged and mud-streaked vagabond children. She pulled a scrap of paper out from under the waistband of her skirt and handed it to Ann.

'From the crooked playwright,' she said.

That would be Kyd. The piece of paper was crinkled from getting wet and drying out. On one side was Will's address and on the other side writing she didn't understand, but which she thought was Latin.

Lizzie looked up at her with her dirty brown face that made her bright blue eyes brighter and spoke. 'I have come a long way with this piece of paper and I am very hungry, so please would...' She started to cry.

Ann sat on the gutted mattress and held out her arms, and Lizzie stepped into them sobbing.

BELLA

Bella had rescued Perro from the subterranean kitchens of Alexander Farnese, general, *condottiere* and duke of Palma, Piacenza and Castro, where she was used as a spit dog. She had been kept in a raised iron cage above the roaring heat of the fire, walking endlessly on a high treadmill linked by belts and wheels to turn the massive spit, a choke chain around her neck which strangled her if she stopped or slowed. Bella, who felt her life driven forward by that same throttling choke chain around her neck, bought the dog's freedom in a moment of sentimental weakness, for she knew it would just be replaced by another. She heard they had put two children in the cage while they searched for a dog as strong as Perro but that may have been a lie. Now Perro was at least eleven years old and, though only Bella could tell, she was weakening. What would she do without her? A dangerous dog seemed to make up for some of the disadvantages of being a woman. Bella stroked Perro's nose where she liked it, and the dog made a contented rumble.

They had been standing for at least an hour outside the main gate of the Tower of London, waiting for a reply to her message. Many years earlier, when Bella's uncle was working for the Spanish ambassador, Elizabeth had been brought here through Traitors' Gate by her sister, Queen Mary. If Bella's uncle had had his way, she would never have come out, but Mary had been ill and weak and indecisive as Elizabeth was weakening now.

A man whose voice she didn't recognise called to her from one of the slit windows above the gate. 'Lord Cecil's not here.'

'Where is he then?' Bella asked.

The man laughed at her ridiculous impertinence, and disappeared. Where would Cecil be? At Greenwich Palace with the queen, or at Bridewell where Topcliffe had his chamber, or perhaps he was really there behind those stone walls and just did not want to see her. Greenwich was too far, and to stay here was pointless, so she decided to try Bridewell. That was her only hope.

ANN

Bang, bang, bang went a fist on the door and someone shoved it, pushing the coffer scraping backwards along the floor. Ann pushed back but she was too slight, and she too slid back into the room. She looked for a weapon and the best she could find was a leg that had been broken off a chair. She lifted it ready as a fat red face appeared through the crack, followed by a fat body.

'You,' said Ann.

It was her father. She stooped to put down the chair leg, then decided to hold on to it.

Her father shouldered his way into the room, dropped the travel bag he was carrying and stuck his hands on his hips.

'Of course,' he said. He wrapped his rage in disappointment. 'I should have guessed you'd be with your fancy playwright. I should have come here first. Just like you running away from the only man who'll have you.'

'I'll be back in time for the wedding.'

'Oh, that's alright then. On the morning of the wedding will that be, or will you do us the honour of getting there the night before? Why not bring your married man with you and get a quick knee-trembler in before you walk down the aisle?'

Even for her father there was something wrong here.

'Do you know Christopher is dead?' she said.

He stared at her. Word of Christopher's death and her father must have crossed somewhere on the road.

'He's dead,' she said.

'Don't think he'll thank you for pulling out of your wedding.'

She tried again. 'Christopher is dead.'

He leant back as if he'd been punched and was trying to regather his senses. 'What's he gone and done now?'

'He hasn't done anything. He's been killed.'

His puffy face stared at her, his mouth slightly open. She thought he had finally accepted the truth, but he pointed at Lizzie. 'What's she doing?'

Lizzie was cowering in the corner, scratching her forearm with small, vicious strokes.

Ann went over, put down the chair leg and took hold of the scratching hand and moved it away. Lizzie's arm was red and raw with new and old scratch marks.

'Why's this room in such a state?' said her father. 'And where's your fancy man?'

She thought for a moment that the booze had frazzled his brain far more than she had realised, but then she saw he was trying to turn his mind to anything but Christopher. For a moment she felt pity but she wasn't going to waste that on him. For once, he could look reality square in the face.

'Your son is dead,' she said. 'He was killed three days ago in Deptford, I'm not sure exactly how, but he was murdered.'

His mouth kept opening ready to speak but kept giving up. She knew him well enough to know that what he wanted right now was a drink, but she wasn't going to let him get drunk in here. He was bad enough sober.

She snatched his big leather shoulder bag before he could, but found in it only an empty bottle of sack. Why was he still adding to their debts buying expensive wine like that? She unwrapped a cloth, found a duck leg, and gave it to Lizzie, who gnawed it ravenously, as if she was going to eat the bone as well. Her father hadn't moved and was making a low groaning sound. There was a noise behind her and a man stepped through the door. It was Will.

He walked forward to embrace her, but saw her father and

stopped, and their eyes had to do what their bodies wanted to. Ann felt a great onrushing of relief and joy, that for a second seemed to lift her off her feet and render her weightless. Was his release Bella's work, and if so, was she still bound in her bargain with God? Her father had started shouting at Will.

'You,' he said, 'always you, for fuck's sake. I'm finally getting her married. You leave her alone or I'll stomp on your face so hard you'll never get a woman for the rest of your life.' He took a step towards Will, and she hastily picked up the chair leg again in case her father went for the knife he kept in his boot.

Will stood very still and spoke so quietly she had to strain to hear him. 'Touch me and I will kill you.'

It wasn't the words but the compressed fury with which he spoke them. She'd never seen it in him before, she'd not seen it in many men. Her father must have felt it too because she saw him lose confidence and the bully in him was quashed by the coward.

'Leave my house now,' said Will.

'I'm not done with you,' her dad said weakly.

She still thought he might reach for the knife, but he picked up his bag and backed out the door.

'You should be ashamed,' he said pitifully. 'My son is dead.'

'I'm sorry for that, but nothing else,' said Will.

They listened to his footsteps go down the stairs. It felt to Ann as if a different Will had returned. What had just happened? What had they done to him?

WILL

Topcliffe and a couple of guards had taken Will deep into the basement through passages with cells on either side, through which the scrawny arms of prisoners stretched out to touch them, as they begged for food. Topcliffe had known all their names and greeted them cheerfully as he had walked through this moving forest of starvation. They had gone down another flight of stone stairs into a dungeon that smelt of damp and blood. He had shown Will the rack and the Scavenger's Daughters and all the metal blades and screws and pincers and described in unending detail how he used each of them.

'I'm telling you all this because you might find it useful in one of your plays,' he'd said. Will could imagine that nasal voice chatting to you as he tore you apart. 'They call me a butcher,' Topcliffe had said sadly, as if he had read Will's mind, 'but I dismantle men delicately, tooth by tooth and fingernail by fingernail.'

Just as he had feared he might never leave that room, Topcliffe had led him back up the stairs to where Cecil was still sitting, busily annotating some papers. He had asked Will again where Marlowe's new play was and again Will had told him he didn't know. Then, just like that, they had let him go.

As he'd walked past the guards and out the gates of Bridewell, London seemed like a distant world which he had left centuries ago.

When he'd returned to his room and been faced with that swollen, red-faced bully, he felt no fear any more, only anger. Now her father was gone, he and Ann held each other.

'I thought I'd lost you,' she said.

'I didn't know you'd found me.' He held her as tight as he could without crushing her.

'Did Bella come?'

'I don't know. In the end they just let me go.'

He went to kiss her but she gestured with her head, and for the first time, he saw Lizzie. He went to say hello but there were footsteps on the stairs and her dad came back through the door.

'They won't let me leave.'

'Who?' Ann asked.

'Constables.'

What was going on now? They all walked back down the stairs. A red-coated constable stood by the front door holding a bucket of paint and a brush. He painted a big red cross on the door.

'What are you doing?' asked Will.

'Plague house,' he said, 'stand back.'

'There's no plague here,' said Will.

There were two more constables behind him who pulled out their clubs. Will recognised one of them and realised it was the huge, sinister sergeant of the guard from Greenwich Palace. Was he moonlighting as a constable? It wouldn't be surprising, it was said the royal guards hadn't been paid for months.

'Look, it's clearly a mistake,' said Will.

The big sergeant of the guard stepped forward and filled the doorway. Unlike most of London's constables he didn't have any facial features missing, though in his case it would have only improved him.

'Just check the street and house number,' said Will.

The man slammed the door shut. There was the sound of banging and the point of a nail smashed through the door, angled so it went into the door frame. Another followed, and then more. They were barricaded in, and if they left they could be buried alive in a plague pit.

'Idiots. What are you doing?' shouted Ann's dad, but no one replied.

Ann and Will left him there and went back down the corridor, where Will knocked on the doors of the two rooms downstairs, but they were still unoccupied. His fever had receded for the moment, or perhaps Topcliffe had terrified it out of him. He walked back upstairs. It was just them. He was trapped in his room with Ann and her dad for the next ten days; it was heaven and hell at once. Ann explained what was going on to Lizzie and told her that constables would guard the door and that in here they'd be safe, and it seemed to work. They could still hear her dad swearing pointlessly downstairs. Ann started picking up the broken furniture and Will helped her.

'The red cross isn't a mistaken address, is it?' she said. 'They want to keep us locked away here so we don't go looking into Christopher's murder.'

'They could have just killed us,' he said.

Ann kicked him. He saw Lizzie listening anxiously and mouthed 'sorry' to Ann, then smiled at the little girl. Lizzie didn't look very reassured, and he remembered his battered face. A smile from that wasn't going to be much help. He needed to be careful around her.

Ann silently showed him Lizzie's note from Kyd with the Latin writing. Kyd had done it for safety, but why did university men have to show off their classical learning?

'Does your dad speak Latin?' he asked.

She snorted. 'He barely speaks English.'

They walked out onto the landing to be alone and Will told her about Cecil and Topcliffe, amazed he could talk about his visit to the dungeon with words and not fall into terrified gibbering.

Ann asked him what Cecil had asked about, and he told

her that he had seemed most concerned about the whereabouts of Chris's play.

'But why?' she asked. 'Is it full of blasphemy or treason or something?'

'Then the Lord Chamberlain wouldn't pass it for performance. Could there be a secret hidden in it?' The banging downstairs got louder, though not loud enough to drown out her dad. They were making very sure no one was going to get out that door.

'Do you think it's Cecil who's behind this?' Ann asked, gesturing downstairs.

'I don't know, but it's someone who can command the constables,' said Will.

'Is Cecil behind everything?' she asked. 'We know Skerries and his lot work for him.'

'They said they do.'

Ann saw his doubts. 'So you don't think he had Christopher killed?'

'I've been thinking about what you said on that first night. Cecil summoned Chris to appear before the Queen's Court next week. Why would he kill him just before he was about to interrogate him?'

Ann's forehead clenched. You could always tell when she was considering something. 'Who's on the Queen's Court?' she asked.

'Nobles, courtiers, all the usual men.'

'What if Cecil had discovered what Christopher was going to say, and didn't want the others to hear it?'

That made sense, though he wished it didn't. He didn't want to be up against Cecil, whose influence increased as the queen's strength diminished, Cecil who sat cracking nuts with Topcliffe beside him. Will had glimpsed power in that stone room, seen only the eye of the monster but felt its massive coils behind in the darkness.

Ann's dad came stomping and wheezing back up the stairs,

pushed past them and sat down heavily. 'How are we going to get food and drink?' he asked.

Ann huffed bitterly. 'As if you care about food?'

They would be fine, he'd seen it in other plague houses. The plague vendors would come, and those barricaded in could drop them down coins from the overhanging first floor windows. The vendors would wash the coins in vinegar then throw up a weighted string tied to a basket in which they'd be able to haul up what they'd paid for. He thought again what it would be like if it was just Ann and him, the two of them tucked up for ten days in a room with everything broken but the bed. Here would be the one place where they would be safe from the plague, safe from everything except the knowledge it was going to end.

They settled down for what little was left of the night. They ignored Ann's father when he told them that they should respect their elders and that he should get the bed. He soon dropped off, propped up against a wall, and it turned out he could belch in his sleep. Lizzie curled up cat-like in the corner, while they stuffed as much horsehair as they could back into the mattress, and slept end to end in their clothes. The fever had returned and Will was hot then cold, sweating then shivering, his thoughts racing, half-heard voices hectoring him, the room blood-red, stretching and pulsing as if he was in a giant heart. He feared he had caught the plague and in his delirium became convinced he was going to die, but came round to find Ann mopping his face with a wet cloth.

'I love you,' she said, but then he thought that had only been in his head.

ANN

In the morning her father was shivering and sweating as much as Will.

'Has he the plague?' whispered Lizzie.

'No,' said Ann, 'he just needs alcohol. It's like a sickness.'

'Oh, I see.' Lizzie nodded, adding that piece of information to her file of facts about life.

'What have you done to get us locked up here?' moaned her father. 'How will we get to the wedding now? What will people say? You'll break your mother's heart.'

'You did that long ago.' Ann tensed, ready to dodge a flailing fist, but he just sat there glumly.

When the plague vendors came round, she ordered food and her father threw some coins down for a pint of sherry, but before the woman could put it in the basket, the big constable took it.

'Plague tax,' he said.

Her father raged out the window, but the constables just stood there grinning, toasted his health and necked it back. He had the shakes by midday. Will looked even worse. His body was fighting the infection, but losing. She shouted to a small boy to get a message to the vendors to bring feverfew next time they came. They'd charge a fortune, but she'd only just got him back from Cecil, and she didn't want to lose him to gangrene.

An old man lived in the room overhanging the street from the opposite side and Will got him to open his window, and persuaded him they didn't have the plague. He lent them a game of fox and geese, with the pieces made from cockle shells, that he said his son had played with back in Mary's reign.

Lizzie started to play, but Ann had to keep stopping her from furiously scratching though there didn't seem to be anything there. Ann thought it was just something in her head, like when she had found her sister Jane hacking at her arm with an awl. Will had owned a pack of cards, but they'd been thrown around the room and she gave Lizzie the job of finding them. Lizzie got them all except the queen of spades, which must have fallen down a crack. Will, despite his shivering hands, taught her how to play Pope Joan and by the fourth game Lizzie was winning. We're like a family, thought Ann, a family complete with a horrible grandfather lying in the corner.

'Let's buy your dad a couple bottles of something when the plague vendors come back,' Will said to her quietly.

'Why spend money on him?' she asked. 'Besides, the constables will just drink it.'

'Yes,' he whispered, 'then they'll be drowsy when we escape.'

She stared at him.

'We need to meet the Friar tonight,' he said, 'at midnight, wasn't it?'

'I thought after last night you'd be—'

He completed her sentence. 'Terrified. Yes, I am, but I've also had enough. I'm sick of it.'

He was whispering angry, his eyes glassy. Was this the fever talking?

'They killed my best friend, they killed an innocent family, they think they can kill anyone. I've had enough.'

Should she let his hectic brain make a decision like this?

'We're too deep in, we can't go back,' he said. 'If we do nothing they could still decide to kill us at any time. So let's escape, don't you want to?'

'Yes,' she said, 'yes, I do.'

She had to know who'd killed Christopher. Will told her the plan. First they had to break up the bed.

'My father will have a knife,' she said.

He'd fallen asleep again, so she reached down inside his right boot, and there it was, tucked into a neat leather sheath stitched into the lining, probably the last bit of shoemaking in which he'd taken pride. He woke up as she took it.

'We need to borrow this,' she said.

A week ago he'd have tried to grab it back, but he just sat there glaring. He had never mentioned Christopher's death again after she first told him, and she thought it had hollowed him out.

'We're going to buy you a couple bottles of something,' she told him.

'The bastard constables will just drink it,' he said.

'Oh well, worth a try, eh?'

The plague vendors came back after dark, but the boy hadn't passed on the message, so there was nothing for Will's fever. They paid for two bottles of Dutch gin and the constables took them and drank them, unable to believe their luck. Soon they were singing soldier songs down below. Will and Ann took turns hacking the bed apart until they had two long boards about six inches wide. Her father asked what they were doing.

'We're taking the bed apart,' she said and he went back to muttering threats at the constables.

Down below they were singing a jolly song about Dutch prostitutes. A smart couple, dressed in matching red and green capes, came around the corner into the street but, seeing the drunken men, turned back to avoid trouble.

'Now?' she whispered.

'Might as well.'

She hadn't seen Lizzie below her.

'Take me with you,' Lizzie whispered.

'She has to come,' said Ann, remembering her sister Jane's words not long before she died.

What were they going to do about her father while they made their escape? She and Will hadn't talked that through. If they left him behind, he'd go and tell the constables what they were doing.

'Lizzie, have one more look for that missing card, would you?' she said brightly. 'Try in that corner.'

Ann picked up the chair leg, walked across to her father and smashed him across the head.

'Nothing to worry about,' she said to Lizzie, who had turned around and was staring open-mouthed.

She hadn't been sure how hard to hit someone in order to knock them out without killing them, but her father was slumped on the ground, though still breathing, so she'd done alright.

Will too was staring at her, his face stiff with surprise.

'We don't want him shouting when we go,' she said.

He still looked shocked.

'He got my little sister pregnant,' she whispered, and had to stop herself from hitting him again. 'Come on then,' she said to Will.

They opened their window and the old man opposite opened his. The constables were still singing below. Will pushed the first plank across. It scraped and creaked as it reached the far window ledge, and they looked down, but the constables didn't look up. They lifted the second plank, and the old man beckoned and pointed unhelpfully as they placed it next to the first one.

'You'll need to pay him a half-guinea when we're across,' said Will.

That would leave her short when she came to pay the gravedigger, but one thing at a time.

'I'll go first,' said Lizzie, and before they had time to think about it, she skipped up onto the planks, and with her arms held wide like a tightrope walker, she scooted gracefully across to the far side, jumped down silently and took hold of the plank to steady it for them. Ann felt strangely proud of her and, looking across at Will, saw in his face something of the same. Ann's father had started making grunting noises so they had to hurry.

'You go,' said Will.

Lizzie had made it look so easy, but the window was small and she had to step up on what was left of the bed and reach one foot onto the plank. Will steadied her as she got her other foot out. She'd intended to walk across like Lizzie, but she found herself on all fours so kept going that way. The plank on the left creaked when she put her weight on it, but the constables still didn't look up. There was a crack in that plank which they hadn't seen, so she tried to shift her weight to the right. Every time she moved her bad knee forward it hurt a lot, but she inched her way to the far end where the only way to get into the room was to tip forward and use her hands to catch herself. She tumbled in with a thump and, again, waited for the constables to start shouting. Nothing happened. She gave the old man his money and he went to bite it to check it was gold, then seemed to remember he had no teeth, and put it in a purse hanging from his belt.

WILL

Will was already half out of the window and he threw the cloth bag over to Ann. Even back in the room he'd been dizzy and shaking with the fever, but now the arms and legs which were saving him from dropping to his death felt vague and formless and barely attached to his body. He forced himself to creep forward. The constables below looked like they had got hold of some more booze and were singing 'Let the Canakin Clink'. The big one, who was also a sergeant of the guard, had a fine baritone voice and the other two stopped to let him sing.

'A soldier's a man.

A life's but a span.

Why then let a soldier drink.'

He had a sweet, melodious voice, but there was something demonic about him, a capacity for cruelty Will couldn't pin down, but which made him fear falling into his hands. Will edged forward as Ann and Lizzie steadied the far end. There was a sudden loud creak and the left plank split. Will slewed sideways and felt a sickening lurch in the pit of his stomach but got both hands on the good board and held on. He was sure the constables had heard but the mellow baritone voice still sang. The board on the left had bent into a dog-leg, with one end dangling into the street, but there was still enough splintered wood to hold it together.

Ann slid it slowly, inch by inch, towards her until she

could grab the dangling half, and haul it inside. Now though, Will was stuck lying on a plank only four or five inches wide and he was barely halfway across. He knew he mustn't look down again but that thought somehow drew his eyes inexorably towards the street below, and as he glanced down a wave of dread and nausea sent his world into a spin. He had to cling on until once again it became still. He pushed up with his arms until he was able to raise himself onto his knees again. Strangely the words of the man who'd sold him the second-hand bed came into his head. 'Good English oak,' he'd said. He had to hope that at least this plank was. He started to creep forward, concentrating hard on each movement, and how to make it, as securely and quietly as he could. He moved only one limb at a time, keeping the other three fixed. Right knee, left hand, left knee, right hand. Ann's face was almost in touching distance, but then her encouraging smile suddenly turned to panic. She was looking down the street.

The stylish couple who had gone the long way around to avoid the drunken constables were coming down the street from the opposite direction. The plank wasn't directly above them like it was with the constables; from where they were, thirty yards away, they had to see it between the windows. Will froze. Behind him, the groans of Ann's father got louder, and Will could hear him stir.

The woman saw him first, and he saw how she nudged her husband who looked up too. Will tried to catch their eyes and plead with his face but they were probably too far away. They whispered as they walked and he thought that the man was all for telling the constables and the woman against. They stopped as they reached their front door, still quietly arguing.

The big constable shouted, 'Here, love, ditch your ugly husband and come and have a drink with us.'

That might have saved him.

'Later,' she shouted back, not wanting to provoke them, and as they hurried into their house she gave Will the smallest of smiles.

Ann's father had moved on from groaning to swearing and there was the sound of furniture being knocked over. Was he coming for the window? Will tried not to rush as he crept the last few inches along the narrow plank. He stretched out his right hand. Ann grabbed it and he collapsed forward into the room. Ann slid the piece of plank over to their side then reached in the bag. In it were a few pieces of costume and make-up Will had forgotten to return to the theatre. Ann put on the hooded cloak, while Will donned the beard and a baggy jerkin that made him look fatter. They were going to have to come out the door opposite their own and right next to the constables.

'You know what you have to do,' Will said to the old man, handing him a small pork pie from the food they'd bought. 'You go up and offer them this, but you do it so the constables are facing away from us as we come out the door!'

He shook his head. 'I've changed my mind.'

'Too late,' said Will, but the old boy shook his head again.

'When the constables find out, they'll beat me half to death.'

'If you don't do it,' said Ann, 'we'll beat you half to death.'

He assessed them. 'Don't reckon you will.'

He was right, of course. Ann had just smashed her father over the head with a chair leg but there she had a motive. 'Give us our money back then,' said Ann.

'I earned that,' he said, 'you came through my window, didn't you?'

She reached for the purse hanging from his waist and tried to yank it away from him, but he dodged backward and made a noise like a cat hissing.

'I'll do it,' said Lizzie. 'I'll take them the pie.'

They'd forgotten she was there.

'They never saw me so I could live here for all they know.'

Christ, she was quick-witted. Her small, serious face with its wrinkle of concentration broke his heart. Ann let go of the old man and looked at Will questioningly.

'I don't think it puts her in danger,' he said.

They went through it with her, and told her to run if anything went wrong, then Will opened the front door. She actually skipped out the door and over to the singing constables. 'My mum said to give you this,' they could hear her say.

'Oh, thanks, love,' said one of them.

Now was the time to go. They hurried out the door wrapped in their disguises. The constables had their backs to them. There was a shout from above and they looked up to see Ann's dad leaning out the window.

'They've escaped!' he yelled in a slurred roar.

Ann and Will knew him well enough to make out his words but the constables only heard his garbled anger, and laughed at him and shouted.

Will took Ann's hand and they walked swiftly along the street towards the corner. Ann's dad yelled with renewed rage but with everyone shouting no one could make out what he was saying. Will glanced behind and saw one of the constables prise a lump of stone from the mud and hurl it at the window.

All three of them were looking up. By trying to betray them he had helped them escape. They made it around the corner and Lizzie came pelting after them on her light feet. The constables would realise soon enough, but by then they'd be on the boat to Deptford, to dig up a body.

ACT FOUR

BELLA

How kings and queens loved lines drawn on a map, though they might as well have been drawn by a child. The forests did not suddenly change where a line had been inked along the edge of a ruler. The deer did not stop and turn back, the rivers continued to flow. Yet because of disputes about those lines, armies slaughtered each other with abandon. Then there was religion. Did the wine and bread really turn into Christ's blood and Christ's flesh at the moment of sacrament or not? For this distinction, how many millions had died? How many women had been raped, children butchered, towns burnt and families starved, because popes and archbishops disagreed about the details of how that gentle and forgiving Christ appeared to them? The black beast of war had crawled across Europe for a century and only little grey England had escaped it. Yet now, these men around her wanted to join in. They were gamblers and plotters, with time on their hands. They were rich, bored men who would roll a dice for power or death, just to pass the time. If only they had to spend their days finding enough money for a loaf of bread, everything would be different. Yet here she was helping them.

She had been waiting for three hours. Hesketh, who hated her, had summoned her to see his master and this time they had taken away Perro. As she sat outside in the cold, she heard the dog howling from time to time. When she had asked for a drink of water and been refused, she considered shouting out the command that would make Perro turn on her custodians. Then there would be blood, but they were just servants like her, told to do a job. Finally she was shown through, and as usual he sat at the end of the long table ignoring her. This time he was making a tower of the dominoes an Italian explorer had brought him back from Cathay.

'So, Bella, where have you hidden your poison today?'

'I have none.'

'I thought you always hid some away when they searched you.' He painstakingly stacked another domino on top of his tower. 'Take off your dress.'

So today it was going to be this. He did it when he was angry though she knew he would never touch her. He had always seemed both revolted by her and insanely jealous of men like Chris or Alleyn whom he thought were her lovers. It had become worse after someone told him that Helen of Troy, in Chris's *Doctor Faustus*, had been inspired by her, that it was her face that 'launched a thousand ships, and burnt the topless towers of Ilium'. That was when these time-consuming routines had started. She took off her dress, trying to hide her weariness at this ritual.

'The poison's in here,' she said, indicating her corset, and she started to unhook it.

'No, no, no,' he said. 'Keep it on, I don't want to see your ageing flesh wobble.'

He knew she was numbed to his cruelty and sought new ways to cause her pain.

'Just give it to me,' he said.

She took out the tiny bottle and placed it on the table. He put another domino on top, and his tower teetered but did not fall.

'So, Bella,' he said. 'You've brought me poison. Anything else? Any more of your clever ideas?'

'No.'

'Because your last one didn't work out very well. You said we could let them be. You said nail them up in a plague house and it will all be over by the time they're out. Well, now they've escaped.' The fools, she thought. Did Will and Ann want to die? You try to help people, but they will not be helped. Well, now they were on their own, and must accept the consequences. 'Find them and find it,' he said.

'Yes, my lord.'

'Because if you don't, I'll send word and they'll chuck him out a window into the sea.'

'I'll do it,' she said and picked up her dress.

'Don't put it on here,' he said. 'Go!'

She scooped up her dress, walked out the door and closed it quietly, but still the vibration must have been enough because behind her she heard the clatter of the domino tower collapse. At least now she knew that they were keeping Charles somewhere on the coast.

ANN

Ann seemed to be spending a lot of time in Deptford graveyard – mind you, if the authorities caught her, she'd be spending even more time there as one of the permanent residents. The gravedigger had his lantern hung on a stick and as she and Will walked in he was in a hole heaving out soggy shovelfuls of clay that landed with a wet slap. They couldn't see the Friar but as they reached the grave edge his big, beaming bald head loomed out of the darkness.

'This will be interesting,' he said.

The gravedigger looked up. 'Got a little boost for a working man, father?'

The Friar pulled a small glass vial out of his bulging leather bag and handed it to him. He necked it, and either it worked at once, or the thought of it cheered him, for the shovelfuls came out faster.

'Can I get you a pick-me-up too?' the Friar asked them, pulling out another of his small bottles and filling three small glasses. He drank one, sniffing it and savouring it in his mouth as if it was fine wine. The excitement of the escape had worn off and the many sleepless nights were dragging her down. The tincture had worked last time, so she drank the proffered glass of the honeyed liquid and Will did the same.

'Best not mix it with alcohol,' said the Friar.

He sniffed the air and peered at Will's chest.

'The corruption's still spreading then,' he said.

Will looked anxious. 'I've been using your salve.'

'Hm, yes, that was somewhat experimental and I fear the experiment has failed.'

'You were trying it out on him?' said Ann.

'Thus medicine advances,' he said and reached again into his bag and brought out a small pot and a bandage. 'Now, though, I will give him a tried-and-tested remedy.'

Something was moving in the pot.

'Lucillia sericata,' he declared. 'Known to the less educated as maggots. They should feel at home in a cemetery.'

Will stared at the wriggling creatures in disgust and took a step backwards.

'Do you want to die?' the Friar said amiably. 'If not let them eat the corrupted flesh.'

Ann had known a woman in Canterbury with a septic leg wound that she claimed was a goblin bite. Her sepsis, though, was real enough and she'd recovered when maggots had been left on it to eat away the rotten flesh.

'Try them,' she said to Will.

Will hesitated.

'He'll try them,' she said.

Lizzie came over and watched in fascination as the Friar lifted up Chris's doublet that Will was wearing, and with a pair of tweezers introduced the maggots one by one. He bound them in with a bandage.

'They are your guests and you are the banquet,' said the Friar. 'As the rich feast off corruption and grow fatter so will they.'

Ann gave Lizzie the crust of bread she had been saving and the little girl went off and sat on a gravestone to eat it. Ann felt like curling up on a gravestone and going to sleep herself, this infusion wasn't working as fast as the last one. Will nudged her and pointed at Lizzie.

'You know she's sitting on her mother's grave?'

She was, sitting there chewing the bread slowly to make it last. They shouldn't have brought her here but what else was there to do? To have a little girl like her, thought Ann. She wouldn't let anything bad happen to her. She'd keep her safe and far away from reality for as long as she could, tuck her away in a bright-painted room with toys and dolls, and tell her lies about the outside world.

'Ann?' said Will.

She had drifted away with her vision. 'Leave her be,' she said. 'She doesn't know.'

Will was still looking at her expectantly and she realised she had thought the words and not said them. She said them again and this time he heard. Her sleepiness had gone but the world seemed a little blurred. It must be the infusion but it was different from last time. The thoughts she was having felt like they had a physical substance, as if they were walking through her head. The gravedigger was waving at her. Her legs were like smoke, but they still carried her over to him.

'You'll need to pay me now,' he said. His burst of energy now seemed tinged with irritation.

'No,' she said, 'when you're done.'

'No, the coffin stays here until you pay me.'

She'd given the old man half the money she had promised the gravedigger. 'I'll tell you what, I'll pay you a half-guinea now and the rest when we see the body.'

She held up her last half-sovereign and the sight of the gold glinting in the lamplight seemed to convince him, and he took it. She was surprised that she could still haggle despite the effects of the potion. What would they do when he asked for the rest of the money? Oh well, that wasn't now. Will had come over too. And the Friar. He tapped on the coffin that sat on a wooden trestle ready to be buried the next day.

'People say my medicines are the "work of the devil",' said the Friar, his face not beaming for once.

'Do they?' she said.

'But you know what is the true work of the devil? Alcohol. Kills thousands.' He tapped the coffin. 'In there is a drunk woman who fell out of a window in Oxestalls Road and broke her neck. Her cousin's a lady in waiting.'

'Was she called Eleanor Bull?' asked Will.

'That's right,' said the gravedigger. 'Now less chit-chat if you don't want to bring the law down on us. Everyone knows I work here at night, but I don't talk to the corpses.'

Ann looked at Will; she wanted to say something, but then again she didn't need to because they understood exactly what had happened. Everyone who knew anything was being killed.

WILL

Will first saw the horses watching them over the wall of the graveyard when the moon came out from behind the clouds. He turned to Ann, but she seemed lost in her thoughts, and when he looked again the horses were in the graveyard, three, four, five of them standing, watching, ears flicking, pawing the ground as if ready to run. They're not real, he told himself, but they stubbornly remained. What was in the brown potion the Friar had given them? He went to ask him but the gravedigger hissed, 'I need help.'

He, Ann and Lizzie stepped forward.

'The infusion,' he whispered to Ann. 'It's different.'

'I know,' she said.

Her pupils were black and huge, dark tunnels leading to her soul.

'I can talk to the dead,' she said.

He looked around, but could only see the horses, more of them now. They raised their heads high to the night sky, the white vapour of their breath curling in changing shapes towards the moon.

'Down here,' said the gravedigger, jabbing Will's ankle. Ann held one of his arms as he slithered down into the water and mud.

He was unshocked by the murder of Eleanor Bull. Soldiers said you soon became accustomed to violent death and felt nothing. Had that happened to him already? He wished he'd become equally hardened to the thought of his own sudden end for, in truth, that still terrified him, its finality, a candle blown out, darkness, but not even darkness, just nothing, nothing ever again, the world going on without you for centuries and centuries.

These thoughts seemed to have happened in only a second of real time for the gravedigger was standing exactly as he had when Will first joined him. He pointed at the handles of Chris's coffin which he had exposed. They were going to do what the Friar had described and pull it sideways into the new grave. They heaved together. His chest hurt but with a dull, distant pain. He thought he could feel the maggots nibbling at his flesh, their little jaws working busily.

'Harder,' said the gravedigger.

Will braced his feet against the muddy side of the grave as best as he could, and took a deep breath, and gritted his teeth, and groaned and heaved, and finally the coffin came free with a slurp and fell at their feet with a loud, sloshy splash.

'Stay there,' said the gravedigger and he clambered out of their pit.

Will watched him over the lip of the grave. At least the horses had gone. The gravedigger took two iron stakes with a loop at the top, banged them into the ground and attached two ropes. Will's breathing was rapid. His heart seemed to be knocking at his ribs, asking to be let out of his body. The maggots sang a little shanty as they went about their work. What in God's name had the Friar given them?

The gravedigger slid back down and lifted one end of the casket and then the other, so he could drag the two ropes under Chris's coffin. Then they had to get out of the grave. Ann took Will's arm as he slithered and slipped on the wet clay. The horses were back. More of them now, their huge, crazy eyes glinting, their snorts of breath a thousand different colours.

'We'll need all of us on the ropes,' said the gravedigger.

Lizzie stepped forward, and he was going to tell her to go

and sit down, but Ann whispered, 'She's happiest when she's helping.'

The Friar was sitting down making notes in a notebook.

'You too, please,' said the gravedigger, and the Friar stepped forward still holding his book and making notes until the last minute.

'What was in the infusion?' Anna asked him.

'Yes, it's interesting, isn't it? Stronger than I expected.'

'But what is it?' Will heard himself say.

'*Hyoscyamus niger*, also called black henbane or stinking nightshade mixed with a pinch of mandrake.'

'Doesn't henbane kill you?' said Ann.

The gravedigger hushed them as he prepared the ropes.

'Only in a higher dosage,' whispered the Friar. He seemed to be allowed to talk. 'Diogenes recommended it as an analgesic and the Phoenicians used it to achieve the sensation of flight. Tonight I just thought it would be relaxing, but I'm experiencing some hallucinations so possibly I used too high a dose. I do have a tendency to do that'

Well, that explained the horses.

'I was dead for nearly five minutes once,' said the Friar

'All pull together,' said the gravedigger, handing Will and Ann one of the ropes.

The Friar took the stick of charcoal from behind his ear and ate it before he took hold of the other rope. 'It absorbs the liquids, lessens the effect,' he said.

'Now,' said the gravedigger before Will could ask if he had any more of the sticks for him.

They pulled on the ropes, and the coffin rose up steadily. For a moment, Will felt as if Chris was coming back to them, that he would step out of the coffin, and they would embrace and say they were sorry for what they had said, and everything would be alright. When the coffin was level with the surface, the gravedigger let go of his rope and hurried over to it. Left on his own, the Friar struggled to hold the rope and his feet started to slide in the mud, but Lizzie ran over to help and it was enough to hold it firm. The gravedigger grabbed the coffin, now at ground level and slid it endways onto the grass. He picked up a crowbar.

Ann asked Lizzie to please go and keep an eye on her bag to get her away from the coffin so she wouldn't have to see the body.

A sharp sliver of moon sliced open a black sky and beneath it the horses were eating each other. The metal bar slammed into the gap between the coffin and the lid and Ann grabbed Will's hand. The gravedigger stomped on the crowbar with one of his feet. The lid resisted for a moment and then sprung up with a splintering crack. The Friar stepped forward, actually rubbing his hands in anticipation.

He rested the lantern inside the coffin at the foot end, then walked around, reached inside from behind the head end, put his arms under Chris's shoulders, pulled them towards him and raised up his head. They could see his face, and shockingly it was still him, his hair, his lips, still Chris. Ann held Will's hand tightly and it felt as if her hand was inside his chest squeezing his heart.

'He still looks so handsome,' she said in a small voice.

The Friar turned to them. 'I'm going to check mouth, throat and ears first, then look at his fingernails and stomach.'

Chris turned his head towards Will, the white lightless orbs of his eyes staring at him, his purple lips open wide.

'Avenge me!' he cried.

Everything inside Will turned to ice. He took a step backwards, jerking his hand out of Ann's.

'What?' she asked.

He went to tell her but Chris was a corpse again, a dead thing rotting in his coffin.

'I'm seeing things,' said Will.

'Me too,' she said. 'Men with the faces of beasts. Has he poisoned us?'

'Avenge my death,' hissed Chris in a whisper, and for a moment he was looking at Will with pleading eyes.

Will could barely speak, barely breathe. 'Come closer,' said the Friar. 'They didn't pour poison in his ear when he was asleep or there would be blistering.'

He instructed them to hold the lamp above Chris's face. Lizzie, ever helpful, went to pick it up, but Ann took it off her and told her to sit back on the gravestone. The Friar lifted Chris's tongue with a flat stick. There was a sweet, rotten smell.

'It is poison,' said the Friar, 'but a slow poison administered orally. It's probably too late to cut his stomach open and examine its contents.'

Chris still fixed Will with his dead and sightless eyes.

'Avenge me!' he cried. 'Soon I will be dragged back down into the sulphurous pits of hell, so swear now, you will avenge me.'

Most of him knew that it was only Chris's dead body there, knew that his heart's hammering and the ice in his blood and the dread panic squeezing the breath out of him was his body's natural reaction to this hallucination. But as much as he knew that, his dead friend was talking to him.

'I promise,' said Will.

Ann stared at him. The Friar was still talking.

'It's most likely cantarella, a poison much favoured by the Borgias but hard to obtain in England.'

Will still stared at Chris's face, lit garishly in the lamplight.

'It would have been administered twelve to fifteen hours before he died.'

Will closed his eyes, and when he opened them Chris was dead again but more animals had gathered at the edge of the light: horses, wild boar, antelopes and strange beasts Will didn't recognise. Behind them were a million more, their eyes glinting in the darkness like all the stars in the sky. They parted and two men walked between them holding torches that flamed wildly in red and white, blue, yellow and colours previously unseen by man.

'We're constables,' they said.

Ann ran to Lizzie and took her hand.

'Stay with me,' she said and they ran away. 'Will, come on!' she shouted.

The men must be real and he must run too. As he turned to go, he heard Chris shout again, 'Avenge me.'

The sound ran after him in a long-echoing scream and the beasts running alongside him picked it up.

'Avenge him!' they all shouted. 'Avenge his unnatural murder!'

Giant steps, that he thought must be his, ran through the darkness, splattering one after the other into the mud. He left a trail of light behind him like a comet, which surely the constables could follow, but there was no sign of them. Two lions were walking through the streets, and when he passed a church door a man who looked like Kemp was nailing something up with a hammer. He started to shout 'hello', until he realised that Kemp must surely be a hallucination too. He ran and ran until he realised he couldn't breathe and when he stopped, the animals were gone and he was alone. He called 'Ann!' but his voice was tiny and the night huge. A man coughed inside a house, but then it was silent again.

The maggots were eating his flesh under the bandage burrowing between his ribs to eat his heart, to eat his lungs and leave him hollow, but no, that was the brown potion making him think that. He had to escape this witch's whirlpool of madness and hold on to what he needed to do. He had to find Ann again, and together they must find a place to hide until whatever it was pumping around in his blood could subside and desist.

Ann would head to his rooms and he could meet her there. No, he couldn't because Ann wouldn't go to a plague house with a blood-red cross on the door, and her father trapped inside. Where else would Ann think to go? Deptford Town Hall was near but that was too risky. There were public places like St Paul's Cathedral, but that was across the river and at night there were guards on London Bridge. She too would be fighting off the draught the Friar had given them and its strange hallucinations and trying to find somewhere to hide away so she could think straight. And then he knew. She'd be at the Rose Theatre in Southwark, where they had first kissed in the costume store, where they knew where the key to the back door was hidden outside, where they had snuck in to meet secretly when everyone else had gone home.

'She'll be there,' he muttered to himself and one of wild boar nodded in agreement. Was it the Friar's drug that made him so certain she would be there? It didn't matter. He had nowhere else to go.

His head hurt less but his chest hurt more and he could feel the sole of one foot rubbing against the ground, where all his walking around London had worn a hole in his shoe. The streets were empty of people, and mercifully, hallucinations, and there he was, on the run, walking at three in the morning, walking, walking, walking, looking for a murderer and looking for love.

'A murderer and love,' he said out loud. If he was saying it out loud then the cocktail of henbane must still be sloshing around in his brain. 'A murderer and love.'

He took the shortcut through the market garden, and there he was in that alley behind the Rose that smelt of piss and smoke, but made him think of Ann's kisses. He found the rotten beam with the hole where the key was hidden. She would need it to open the door, so if it was there she couldn't be inside. His hand reached in among the rotting splinters hoping to feel nothing, and felt the cold of metal. His heart lurched with disappointment, but he took the key anyway, and reached for the lock, and opened the narrow door that didn't look like a door, and pushed his way in.

BELLA

Her lord had been angry when he had discovered that Will and Ann had escaped again, but she had seen so many angry men. The Dominican abbot had been angry, when he discovered that she was a girl who had shaved her head so she could pretend to be a boy and get an education. Men raged and roared, but eventually they stopped. The Genoese lawyer who had tried to rape her had been angry when she stabbed him with her blade in the thigh, but had ceased to be angry when she had cut his throat.

The Friar, who the constables had arrested, talked so fast that they had to slow him down. Some of what he said seemed only to be in his head, but she didn't think he had held anything back. Hesketh had taken him away to squeeze him just in case.

A distant boom rattled the shutters of her room. What was blowing up now? London, with its unstable explosives and its shifting clay and collapsing houses, felt like some sleeping monster that shuddered and stirred as it lay. She thought of the sea captain who had told her of the island they had unexpectedly come across. They had rowed ashore to refill their water casks only to find it was an enormous sea beast, which awoke to throw them off its back and churn the sea into huge waves at it dived back down into the deep. London was a great monster too, ready to wake and hurl its citizens into war and chaos.

She lay back on her bed and closed her eyes. They had the

power to keep her here in England, but they could not stop her escaping in her head to the warm south, to the smell of figs and the hum of cicadas and a glass of red wine raised against a blue-green sea.

Perro lifted her head and her hair bristled and stood on end. A half-second later she heard the creak of a footstep on the stairs outside her room. A carpenter had tried to fix the loose board. She had stopped him. A creaky stair could save your life. There was someone outside the door, but no one knocked. Perro rose silently to her feet, her massive head bent forward. Bella had her knife in her hand. There was a moment of silence, and then a slip of paper was pushed under the door, and the footsteps went back down the stairs. She went and picked it up and her life changed. It was a note from Charles.

She had persuaded the malleable Throckmorton to send Charles a note from her, but not expected an answer. Her son was now eight years old and they kept him somewhere secret and he was safe as long as she continued to help them. She had tried to keep him a secret when he was born because she knew her lord's jealousy was extreme and unpredictable, but later he had found out. He claimed she favoured the others over him and used that as an excuse to take Charles as a hostage. She read the note still standing by the door. He was well. He was learning Latin and Greek and they were teaching him how to fence. It was a note written with someone looking over his shoulder, but when she saw how it was awkwardly expressed and unevenly spaced, she knew. She had taught him simple codes as a game as soon as he could read and write, and she was sure he had used one. The first letter of each line spelt out a message, but she could not make it out. *I m g s t m a w e s*, it read. She remembered she had told him that for a code to be safe, you should not start the message until the fourth line, but even then she could not make it out: *stmawes*, it read. Then she saw it. *St Mawes*. She remembered the threat to throw him out of a window into the sea. They were keeping him in St Mawes Castle.

She had imagined a Scottish Island or a Baltic port, so Cornwall was nearer than she had hoped. Could she feign illness and get there before her absence was discovered? And how would she free him? *I take exercise outdoors every day at four*, he had written near the end. He had sent her a clue. He left the castle walls then, but, of course, he would be guarded. What were the chances of freeing him? Fifty-fifty at best. Heaven or hell. She would flip that coin in a trice for herself, but did she have the right to do it for a child? Whatever else, she must be assiduous in her dedication and obedience from now on to allay any doubts about her loyalty, but then again not too eager, for that too would cause suspicion. She must give Throckmorton hope to keep him as her ally, and not go out of her way to antagonise Hesketh. She must do nothing to tilt these odds against her.

She reached in her purse and picked out a gold sovereign: on one side, Elizabeth severe and queenly, facing sideways; the royal coat of arms on the other. *Heads is death and tails life*, she told herself. She flipped the coin in the air and it seemed to spin forever. She caught it in one hand and covered it with the other. Would it be the coat of arms meaning freedom, or Elizabeth looking at her to pronounce a death sentence for her and her child? One hand stayed clenched tight on top of the other. She was unable to look. She closed her fist over it and put the coin away in her purse.

One thing was certain, that from now on she would only be looking after herself and Charles. Any others were on their own. They could, as the English said, go whistle.

ANN

Ann hoped she had guessed right. She pushed open the door and stepped into the darkness. Will leapt forward and put his arms around her and then they were kissing. She hadn't promised God that they wouldn't do that. Will flinched and she realised the wound on his chest was hurting him, but he came back and kissed her more, and she kissed him back and held him gently so as not to hurt him. The Friar's potion was still in her blood, and for a moment they seemed suspended in time, the only two people in the world.

'I must tell you something,' said Lizzie, who had come through the door into the theatre behind her, and they stepped apart hastily as if caught in an illicit act.

Ann had forgotten that the child was with her for a moment. That must be the Friar's brew as well. 'What must you tell us?' she asked Lizzie, as Will fumbled for the fire steel they kept in the wings. Lizzie went to speak but nothing came out.

Will struck a spark and lit one of the torches at the lip of the stage. He walked around lighting one torch from another, until they stood in a half-circle of flame and light. Now Ann could see how upset Lizzie looked. She wished they hadn't taken her to the graveyard but what else could they have done?

Lizzie struggled to speak again but started to cry.

'What's the matter?' said Ann, putting her arms around her.

She sobbed in gulps and gasps, and Ann thought, that's

a stupid question, everything's the matter. Her mother and brother had been murdered. Her father was probably dead. She was eight years old and alone in a strange country. It was extraordinary that she didn't sob like this all the time. Ann sat down on the edge of the stage, Will beside her, the torches around her, the crescent moon above her, and she held Lizzie curled up on her lap until her crying became quieter. 'Sorry,' Lizzie said.

'You don't need to be sorry for anything,' said Will.

'I must tell you,' Lizzie managed to get out.

'Whatever it is,' Ann said, 'just tell us in the morning.'

They wrapped her in some cloaks Will had found in the costume store, and almost instantly she went to sleep at their feet.

Ann too longed for sleep, but she and Will had so much to talk about.

'So the Friar...' she started to say, but it was hard to think with the henbane still swirling in her brain.

'What do we know that's new?' asked Will, and she could see he too was grappling with his thoughts.

'He said the poison would have taken twelve to fifteen hours to kill him,' she said.

'Yes, so if she's right about when she saw him dead down by the river,' he pointed down at Lizzie, 'and I do believe her.'

Ann nodded. She was certain Lizzie had told them the truth. Of all the people they'd spoken to she was probably the only one. Will struggled on.

'So that means he was given the poison early in the morning, when we were drinking in Deptford.'

'Who was there?'

'Kyd was there,' said Will. 'Kyd, who we now know went to get poison from the Friar.'

'But why would he want to kill my brother? Wasn't it Christopher who was angry at him?'

She supposed it was possible that there was bad blood between Kyd and Christopher, but the growing list of murders didn't fit with a private grudge.

'Who else was there?' she asked.

'Barking Bobby, the Widow and Bella, but she left well before midnight so I don't think it could be her. But then some of the actors turned up, definitely Kemp and Alleyn, but a couple of others I can't remember.'

'That's about seven people,' said Ann, 'it's one of them.'

'Not necessarily. Everywhere Chris went men would buy him drinks.'

'But they would have to have known he was going to Deptford.'

Will considered this carefully.

'They could have just followed us.'

They kept finding out new information, but rather than helping, it just seemed to complicate the mystery.

'What do we do now?' Will asked her. 'Do we get the play?'

'We go see Danby,' she said.

'What, and tell him we dug up a grave?'

'The constables have probably told him by now. I don't think he'll care. We can tell him Chris was definitely poisoned which means Skerries and his gang just cleared things up. You heard him, he said if that was the case he'd hang them.'

Will nodded slowly, but she could see he wasn't convinced. He got up and stood centre stage, brightly lit, in Alleyn's spot, where he never got to stand during a performance.

'He's a curmudgeon, but I think he cares about the truth,' she said.

Will was still hesitant. In the time he took to make a decision, you could have done the damn thing he was trying to decide.

'Have you a better idea?' she asked.

He didn't answer.

'So we'll go and find him in the morning,' she said.

He nodded. The only sound was the hissing of the torches. He still stood centre stage and he turned to the empty seats of the theatre, and started to speak the final monologue from *Doctor Faustus*.

'Ah, Faustus.
Now hast thou but one bare hour to live,
And then thou must be damn'd perpetually!
Stand still, you ever-moving spheres of heaven,
That time may cease, and midnight never come.'

The verse unsettled and uplifted her as the best dramas always did. Will spoke with a power she hadn't seen in him before. Her brother's words went out into the darkness.

'Mountains and hills, come, come, and fall on me,
And hide me from the heavy wrath of God'

His memory failed him for a moment, but then he picked it up again.

'You stars that reign'd at my nativity,
Whose influence hath allotted death and hell,
Now draw up Faustus, like a foggy mist.
Into the entrails of yon labouring cloud.
That, when you vomit forth into the air,
My limbs may issue from your smoky mouths,
So that my soul may but ascend to heaven!'

He stopped and tears were rolling down his cheeks.

'He's dead,' he said quietly. 'He used to say he didn't want to grow old, joked he didn't want to live longer than Jesus. And he didn't.'

Ann remembered Will's wild words after they had opened the coffin. 'In the graveyard, was he speaking to you?' she asked.

She saw him shiver at the memory.

'He was calling for revenge.'

She felt triumphant. 'See.'

'What?'

'He wants revenge just as I do.'

'It wasn't really him. It was in my head.'

Of course she knew that, but so much of what you really thought was hidden and you only glimpsed it in the dark corners of your head.

'No,' she said. 'It wasn't him. But it was you.'

Will opened his mouth to argue but she saw his exhaustion win out, and he came over and sat down next to her. Distant thunder rumbled and the church bells all around London started to strike three o'clock, one after another, overlapping, near and distant, deep and high. Will checked to see if Lizzie was still asleep.

'You said about your father and your sister,' he said.

Why did he want to talk about this now?

'She told you?' he asked.

'When she was dying in childbirth, yes.'

Will hesitated. She could see that he wanted to ask more, but couldn't find the right words.

'She was in a fever, and some of what she was saying made no sense, but I think it was true. When he found out she was pregnant, he was barely angry, he just went off and found some useless carter's son to marry her.'

'And you?' asked Will. 'Did he ever try to—'

She cut him off. 'Never me. Men like him know to stay clear of the strong ones.'

'But you're still going back to Canterbury?'

His question pleaded with her to answer 'no'.

'Yes,' she said. 'That's one reason why, to look after the others.'

'You should have hit him harder and killed him,' said Will.

She wished she had. She wished she had years ago. In one way, she was glad the conversation had taken this turn and the mood darkened. Now she and Will would curl up in the costume store and sleep, but nothing else. She had worried she would betray her vow to God. She didn't really think God had saved Will because of her promise, but what if He had? What if she broke her word and an angry God destroyed Will? She didn't imagine He'd strike him down with a thunderbolt, but there were so many ways to die in this city, by plague or poison, with a knife beneath your ribs or a noose around your neck. She wouldn't risk God's wrath. It wasn't long until she left for Canterbury, before she walked into her cage and shut the door behind her, so she just had to remain firm for a couple more nights. She had decided, and now it was safe to do so, she put her head on Will's shoulder.

'I love you,' he said.

Her legs felt weak and her heart too big for her chest. She was shocked at the effect it had on her. It wasn't as if she didn't know it already. Should she tell him she loved him too?

'It's not possible,' she said.

'I didn't say it was possible.'

Lizzie, wrapped in the cloaks, stirred in her sleep, and far away the bells of one last, late church chimed three.

WILL

They wrapped themselves in some squirrel furs which had been costumes for *Edmund Ironside*, abandoned since the play had been banned for the scene where two archbishops traded punches. The furs were riddled with moths, which fluttered silently around them as they went to sleep, Lizzie curled up between them.

Will dreamt henbane-tinged dreams of a red-faced God sitting on a cloud with a rod, fishing for devils using live wriggling cherubs impaled on hooks for bait. He was woken by the toe of a boot poked into his midriff. He jolted upright and reached for his useless bread knife, but it was only the theatre's nightwatchman, who must have been there all the time, fast asleep in his own corner. They had slept almost to midday.

The watchman recognised Will, and there was, at once, an unspoken understanding that Will would say nothing about him sleeping through his watch, and he wouldn't say anything about them breaking into the theatre. The Rose had been dark since the start of the plague, but the old man had been told to get it ready again, though he didn't know for which plays. He told them that they should leave as a new stage manager was coming in to take a look around.

Mobs were looking for Will Shakespeare who had killed Marlowe, and constables were searching for a man and woman who had broken out of a plague house and robbed a grave. No one was looking for a puritan mother and father and their eight-year-old daughter who were taking the boat from the jetty at Southwark to Greenwich. The costume store had come in useful once again, and Ann had even found some make-up to mask the bruise on his face. Their story would be that, fearful of the plague, they were leaving London to stay with relatives at Blackheath.

Will was wrapped in layers of disguise, the puritan coat over the theatre jerkin from his room over Chris's gaudy doublet, and beneath it all, the maggots chewed on his decaying flesh. He only felt them when he thought about them, but then their writhing and wriggling seemed utterly real. It seemed too soon for them to have helped, but, for the moment, his fever had receded. His body, though, seemed to have spent all its strength on battling the infection, and he had to concentrate, and drag each leg forward with every step he took.

It was raining again when they reached Greenwich Palace, but despite that and the plague, there were still a few onlookers in their Sunday best, peering at the gates behind which the queen of England was sequestered. A man in a ragged uniform, whose large, pale face had no eyebrows, had set up his medicine show, selling Colonel Parrot's Famous Purgatives. He lifted a handful of squirming tapeworms from a bucket and held them aloft.

'All from one dose,' he boasted.

No one paid the colonel much attention. Will looked over to the guards at the gate. He told Lizzie that if they were arrested, she should run away and find Kemp. He had drawn her a map.

'Kemp? Really?' Ann whispered.

'I trust him more than the others,' Will said.

The vision of Kemp at the church door flashed into his head. Could it have been real? He told Ann about what he might have seen.

'Do you think he's "Tamburlaine" the pamphleteer?' she asked. 'Does he hate the Dutch?'

'Well, everyone.'

And yet Kemp as a pamphleteer didn't quite sit right; it involved Kemp believing in something. Perhaps he had been conjured up by the henbane like the animals and the ghost of Chris.

The guard in charge had most of his nose missing. What was it with London's soldiery? You could make a new one from all the body parts they had lost. At least the terrifying one, who took night shifts as a constable and had been guarding the plague house, wasn't there. Will walked over, his heart racing; it had been kept busy over the last couple of days. He told no-nose his name, and that the queen's coroner William Danby was expecting him. He waited to be seized.

'Wait here,' said the man, and walked off into the palace.

They hadn't even been sent to the back gate. Was Danby really going to see them? A servant chucked a bucket of leftover food from a high window. Beggars limped over, and clawed and scrabbled for the bones of jugged hare and honeyed quail. Two of them fought over a pig's head, though it had already been picked clean.

'Oh, oh, oh!' said Lizzie suddenly. 'The Friar!'

Will had forgotten how the night before she had wanted to tell them something.

'I asked him if he spoke Latin and he said "yes", so I told him what the Latin was on the note.'

'But you don't have it.'

'I remembered the words. Do you want to know what it says?'

'Yes, please,' said Ann and Will at the same time.

'The Widow has the play. Destroy it.'

'You're a very clever girl,' said Ann, and Lizzie beamed.

So it really existed. Despite everything, Will felt something close to joy. Chris had been butchered at the pinnacle of his powers, but there was one more play. It could be another *Faustus*. It could be the greatest drama ever written in the English language.

'Do we go and find it?' he asked Ann.

'We speak to Danby first.'

'But we don't mention it,' he said.

He was fearful for its safety, for everyone from Cecil downwards seemed obsessed with it. He wondered why Chris had hidden it with the Widow. Was he using it as a bargaining chip? Did it have a message hidden in its poetry?

The rain got heavier and the three of them went to take cover under a couple of plum trees. The fruit was rotting on the ground and the air humming with wasps.

'Why did no one pick them?' asked Lizzie.

'It's forbidden. They're the queen's trees,' said a voice behind them. A gangly teenage boy stood there. 'Mr Danby had another inquest in Deptford this morning. He left word that if you turned up, I was to take you to him.'

His face was covered in red and yellow spots, and the rain dripping from his hair ran in small rivulets in the runnels between them. He must have seen Will looking.

'It's not the plague, I always look like this,' he said brightly, 'I'm not allowed to take messages to Lord Cecil because I turn his stomach. Follow me.'

Will expected him to turn west towards Deptford, but he walked north towards the river and the Royal Pier. Half a dozen gold and red painted barges were moored there, the liveried oarsmen sitting in the boats, playing dice beneath the canopies. The boy handed what looked like a token to a hugely fat official who filled a small hut, and the man shouted at the royal bargemen. Eight of them seized an oar from where they had left them in a pyramid and ran to one of the barges. The boy jumped in.

'Deptford Creek,' he said, sticking out his chest, enjoying his moment of authority.

'Your Majesty,' whispered Will as he handed Ann aboard and they sat back among fat cushions.

They'd travelled against the tide on the way to Greenwich but now, powered by eight oarsmen, they sliced down the

Thames, overtaking wallowing dung boats and overcrowded wherries. Their boy captain swore as a sloop-rigged hoy, about to sail from Masthouse Pier, swung at its anchor, and nearly cut across them. Its captain swore back with a broadside of filth, until he saw it was a royal barge and stuttered an apology. Lizzie, sitting next to them, trailed her fingers in the water.

'Make sure the fish don't bite,' said Ann, and Lizzie grinned. There were moments when the dark horrors lifted and she was, for a moment, a happy little girl.

'Are you and Will going to get married?' she said.

After his unrequited declaration last night, he was going to keep quiet, but perhaps Ann felt it was her turn.

'We want to,' she said. 'But we can't.'

'Why not?' asked Lizzie.

They both hesitated.

'Because,' said Will, 'Ann comes from the Land of Fairies and is only visiting this world.'

Lizzie scoffed. They weren't going to catch her out with that. Will smiled at Ann. Perhaps this was as close as they'd get to being a happy family, her engaged, him married to someone else and a little girl who'd seen things no child should see.

It had been still, but there was a sudden breeze, and all over the river, boatmen who had been relying on their oars heaved on the ropes and soon the water was dotted with their cream and maroon sails. The boy had found a trumpet, and standing in the stern blasted away on it to clear their passage.

Ann nudged Will. In a carved walnut box beside them were two delicate, long-stemmed glasses and several small bottles of wine. The cobbler's daughter and the glovemaker's son were travelling in style.

When they reached the jetty at Deptford, the chief bargeman said he hoped they had enjoyed their journey. He was clearly expecting a tip, but Will had nothing and he knew that

Ann had only two gold coins in her purse and they couldn't give him those. The boy led them to a street of tall houses.

'Mr Danby isn't in court until ten o'clock,' he said as he knocked on the door of the first one and gestured for Will and Ann to walk up the stone steps.

Will stumbled. One of the steps was an odd height. He felt a cold chill start in his chest and reach to the tip of his limbs. This was the same house Bella had brought them the night before the inquest, where the master hadn't got out of bed, where he had smelt Chris's perfume on the pillow. The door opened and standing there was the blonde Dutch servant they had woken up. She gestured for them to walk inside and shut the door behind them.

The rings under the woman's eyes were deeper than before and her cheeks blotched red. She saw Lizzie and gasped and exclaimed something in Dutch. Lizzie ran over to hug her, but the woman put her hands out to stop her and shook her head. She was visibly terrified. She shoved them into a room, different from the one in which they had talked before, and hurried out.

'It's my aunt,' said Lizzie. 'She's Tom's mother, well, she was.'

Lizzie was trembling. The servant was the woman whose child had been murdered along with Lizzie's family, the woman whose son had been mistaken for Lizzie. She was probably the woman who had paid for their burial.

The room they'd been put in was windowless, and some wooden crates piled along one wall were giving off a strong spicy odour. There was one black stained wooden bench, but they remained standing, too perturbed to sit. Will was troubled by many things but he couldn't quite order them. Was this Danby's house? Had Chris stayed here? Was this a trap? The door opened and Perro padded in and walked over to Ann and sniffed her as she always did, then sat back on her haunches and looked around as if expecting a reward. Bella followed her in and said something to the dog in a foreign language, and it slumped down in the middle of the room, head down, jowls draped over the floor. Was he imagining it or were the dog's eyes watching him? 'I hear you caught the plague but recovered,' said Bella. 'Not many manage that.'

'We came to see Danby. Does he live here?' Ann asked.

'I believe he sometimes stays here when he has business in Deptford.'

'And was it him upstairs when we stayed the night before the inquest?' said Ann.

'You would have to ask him that.'

As ever, Bella's face was unreadable, but her voice seemed to have lost its smoky insouciance and have a harder edge.

'When will we see him?' asked Will.

'He'll come down in a moment,' said Bella and she left the room, speaking again in some strange tongue to the dog who stayed.

'We might as well sit then,' said Will, but they didn't, and Ann began to pace back and forth nervously. The spice was sweet and citrusy, but so strong it sickened the air with its suffocating fragrance.

'It's bergamot, isn't it?' said Ann.

She was right. It was one of the reputed plague preventatives that Sir John 'Rich' Spencer had bought up before the plague crossed the channel. Perhaps he did own this house. Lizzie's aunt came back in with a jug of something and three glasses on a tray. She put it down with a rattle, whispered something in Dutch to Lizzie and hastily left.

Lizzie beckoned Will and Ann to come closer and whispered, 'She said to run away now.'

Everything they had done had been so they could tell Danby and get justice. They had come all this way. Should they really run? Will looked at Ann and she gestured her head towards the door. She was in no doubt. He nodded and they stepped quietly towards the exit. The dog raised its huge, wrinkled head and bared its teeth. Ann tried to edge around it but the dog heaved itself to its feet, and took a couple of steps to block her way. Will tried to step the other way around it but it swung her massive head his way, showed its teeth and let out a low rumble of a growl that seemed to rattle the furniture. Was a dog their gaoler?

Apart from at the cemetery, Will had only seen Bella give the kill command once, when a couple of footpads tried to rob them on the way home from the theatre. The two men stepped out with kerchiefs over the lower half of their faces and knives in their hands. Bella threw a small stone at their feet so Perro knew who to attack and spoke some low, guttural words. The mastiff knocked over the first one faster than the man could raise his knife, then it was on to the second, dragging him down, before he could choose to run or fight. Its power was fearful. It straddled its screaming victim and had half torn his throat apart before Bella gave the command to stop. Then it trotted back to its mistress, wagging its tail, ready to be praised, and Bella gave it a morsel of the smoked lamb she kept in her purse, while the man tried to hold what was left of his throat together with his bloody hands.

Now the dog stood, front legs apart, its mottled pink jowls drawn back enough to show its yellow teeth, a line of drool dripping onto the floorboards.

'Good girl,' said Will, feeling foolish, but when he inched one foot forward it let out another warning growl.

Lizzie walked past him up to the dog, raised her finger and said what sounded like, '*Lignear meisjay.*' Perro cocked her big lump of a head to one side, Lizzie said it again and the dog lay down on the floor with a loud clump. Lizzie walked to the door and amazingly Perro did nothing to stop her. Ann and Will followed. Will almost had to step over her big, panting body. He could smell her wet, meaty dog smell and he waited for her giant jaws to clamp on to his leg, but she remained where she was. Ann opened the door and they went out into an empty hall.

Lizzie whispered, 'She commands her in Limburgish. It's the dialect my grandad spoke.'

A door opened upstairs and they looked up to see Danby coming down the staircase. He saw them and gave them a huge smile. Will didn't think that he'd seen him smile before.

'You did the right thing to come and talk to me,' he said, trotting down the stairs.

The smile was still there, lasting for longer than a smile should. It was a smile that said, even more clearly than his servant's whispered message, *Run like hell*.

They sprinted out the front door and turned left down the street but two men were walking side by side down the middle of the road towards them. He and Ann turned back, dodged Danby coming down the steps, but another man, a big man, blocked the other way down the street. Lizzie ran past him and he made no effort to catch her. Ann went one side of him, and Will the other. He went for Will and grabbed hold of his wrist. Will saw Ann hesitate but he shouted to her to keep running. He struggled and swung a punch at the man holding him, but missed and the big man, laughing, pulled him in, as the other two arrived and grabbed him. They were Pooley, Frizer and Skerries.

'What the fuck are you wearing?' said Skerries, as they dragged him up the steps and inside.

Will started to ask what the hell they were doing out of Marshalsea, then didn't bother, because he knew the answer. Danby had ordered their release. Were they there for him? Was he about to get caught up in a drunken brawl, where they – purely in self-defence, mind – would stab him to death? No, they were too clever to try that for a third time. Maybe they would take him back to Topcliffe's dungeon, or just slit his throat and leave him out for the kites and rats and ravens.

Bella came out into the corridor with the dog, and started whispering with Danby and a man Will thought was called Hesketh. He was up against all of them, Bella, Danby, Cecil, Topcliffe, Skerries and his gang. What chance had he ever had against the most powerful and ruthless men in England?

Bella walked over to him.

'Come with me,' she said, opening a door off the corridor. Danby nodded to Pooley to go with her, but Bella told him, 'Just me,' and shut the door behind them.

It was the room they had talked in that first night. It reeked of salt and sewage and Will saw the windows looking on to Deptford Creek were open. A hunched heron waited on a post, ready to spear a fish.

'We can both go out that window,' he said, 'make a run for it.'

She looked at him wearily, and didn't bother to answer. Her face never gave much away. *She allows men to create the woman they want*, he thought. Who had he created? A schemer and a plotter, but one who cared for him. Was that an illusion?

'Will,' she said, 'they have reluctantly given me two minutes, because I've told them you will tell me who has the play.'

'And why will I do that?' he asked.

There was an ornate brass candlestick on the table that he could use as a weapon. She must have seen his eyes flick over to it.

'That could work on me, but it certainly won't work on the dog,' she said. 'And to answer your question, if you tell me where the play is, no one will hurt Ann.'

He felt a flicker of rage. 'You mean you'll hurt Ann if I don't?'

'Not me, but yes, Hesketh, Skerries, the others, they will find her and hurt her.'

It was too late to save himself, but perhaps, if he made the right decision, he could save Ann.

Someone started banging on the thick oak door, which made it hard to think.

'Soon our two minutes will be up,' she said, 'and Hesketh will get it out of you, but offer you nothing.'

'How do I know you won't hurt her?'

'You'll have to trust me because my promise is better than the certainty that they will kill her.'

'Kill?' Now it was kill. He had nothing to bargain with. He knew they could get it out of him with sufficient pain. 'Swear you'll make sure no one hurts her,' he said.

'I swear on the life of my child. Yes, I have a child,' she said before he could say anything.

Someone banged on the door again, and a voice he thought was Hesketh shouted, 'Your time's up.'

'He's just about to tell me,' she shouted back and looked at him, expectantly.

'You mustn't hurt the Widow either,' he said.

'Why her?'

'Because she has the play. Say you won't hurt her and I'll tell you where she lives.'

Hesketh shouted something again, and the handle turned and rattled but the door wouldn't open. He hadn't seen her lock it.

'We've no reason to hurt her. Now tell me.'

'She lives near the Rose Theatre in an attic in one of the streets off Three Ways.'

Pooley's face appeared at a window. He must have gone around the back to check on them. Perro sat up on her haunches to look at him. 'Ask around and you'll find her easily enough,' he said.

She nodded and stepped over to the door to unlock it.

'And what about me?' he asked.

She shrugged. 'I tried.'

BELLA

Danby and Hesketh were arguing over who should go and find the play.

'They're idiots,' said Danby, pointing at Skerries and his gang. 'Let her go get it.'

'One of them should go with her, I don't trust her,' said Hesketh, and they went back to arguing.

It made no odds to her whether they found the play or not. What she needed was money and time. She would need to spread some gold around to get to Cornwall and reach St Mawes Castle quickly. By land it was too slow and too dangerous. Outside of London, they thought her dark skin meant she was a Spanish spy. West of Southampton they would just think she was a witch. She would need to take a ship to Portsmouth and, from there, find one of the small boats that traded west along the coast, but they were old and slow and rotten. She needed to get to St Mawes before they sent a message ordering the death of her son. She would be up against a slick system of men on horseback who galloped for half a day, then passed their message on to a fresh man on a fresh mount. What she really needed was one of the sleek smuggling vessels that sped between France and the small coves of the south coast but those men would take your gold and throw you overboard.

'We haven't got all day,' said Danby, and she realised she hadn't been listening.

The new dutiful Bella apologised. He pointed at the three thugs he'd released from Bridewell.

'The three graces, who do you want to take with you, Beauty, Mirth or Charm?'

'I'm Beauty,' said the one with the yellow eye. 'Take me and we'll have some fun.'

So, not him. That left the square one and the talkative one, who today was wearing bright green breeches and a striped purple and yellow doublet. The square one would think he was in charge, so she chose the one who dressed like a washing line.

WILL

Pooley and Skerries took him back to the room that smelt of bergamot. With them in it, it smelt of bergamot, cheap wine and sweat.

There was a knock on the door and in walked the huge constable who had been in charge of guarding them in the plague house. This was the man who was also a sergeant of the guard at Greenwich Palace, the man who scared Will more than the three murderers. Was this royal business, or was he being hired by someone in power to be a constable, or had he never really been a true constable? Probably the answer didn't matter because Danby was going to kill him anyway.

'That was very funny escaping like that,' said the big man.

Will looked into his face, then looked away because there was something not quite human in his eyes.

'I hate all these bastard writers,' said Skerries, 'sitting on their fat arses putting words on paper like it's a proper job.'

'Yeah,' said the constable, 'crawling out of windows getting working men into trouble.'

Will tensed himself for the punch he knew was coming, but when the big man hit him in the stomach it still bent him double and left him nauseous and sucking for air. He was going to get a beating. Then Pooley saw the festering wound on his chest under Chris's ripped doublet.

'What's that?' Will was still hunched over. 'It's probably

not the plague,' he gasped and they all stepped back. His putrefying chest was turning out to be useful.

Danby came in. The room was getting crowded.

'Should have put you in prison at the inquest when I had the chance,' said Danby.

Will wished he had. Bridewell seemed cosy compared to this. 'So,' said Will, 'you poisoned him, then he slept here, then what? He worked out what was going on, and made it out of here and you lost him, so you called in the clean-up men who found him down by the creek.'

Danby looked mildly amused. 'Too much exposition, just like in *Henry VI*,' he said.

'Shall I shut him up?' asked Skerries, clearly keen to do so.

'Who was it that gave him the poison?' asked Will.

'If only you knew,' said Danby impatiently, and started speaking fast. 'I'm convening a Court of Convenience by the power invested in me. You're charged with grave robbery and I find you guilty and sentence you to be hanged by the neck until dead, Lord have mercy on your soul. I think they're doing a batch of pirates at Execution Dock on Monday, so we'll fit you in there.'

Pooley coughed, trying to get Danby's attention.

'What? Spit it out.'

'If you'll forgive a suggestion, sir, we don't have to wait that long.' He whispered something in Danby's ear.

Faunt, the lawyer, stuck his long neck around the door. 'Does he require legal representation?' He laughed at his own joke and disappeared.

Behind him, Will saw Bella and Frizer putting on their cloaks.

THE WIDOW

The Widow sat on her bed staring at a quarter of a potato pie. She'd decided to make it last two days so she had eaten half of it for lunch, but then she was hungry, and had split the remaining bit in half, and eaten that. Now she was considering slicing the quarter in half and eating that. Or was she deluding herself? Was it better just to eat it in one go now, because whatever she told herself it wasn't going to last the night. There was a buttery brown crumb on the edge of the knife and as she considered, she pressed it onto the end of her finger and licked it. There was banging on the door downstairs.

She jumped to her feet. There was a muffled conversation at the door and footsteps on the stairs. She stuffed the last piece of pie into her mouth. If they were going to take her away, she wasn't leaving it behind.

'It's Ann,' said a voice outside her door.

She tried to answer, but her mouth was full of pastry.

'Please open the door,' said Ann.

'I'm going to,' she said, spraying out precious crumbs, and lifted the latch.

Everyone around her seemed to look scared these days but Ann looked terrified. 'You have to give me the play,' said Ann, gasping for breath.

'The what?'

'Chris's play. I know you've got it. Please.'

What was Ann talking about? But then she put it together. 'Do you mean the package Chris gave me?'

'Didn't you look at it?'

'He told me not to.'

'Then, yes,' said Ann, 'the package. I ran here as fast as I could. They've got Will, I might be able to trade it for him.'

She reached under the mattress, pulled it out and gave it to Ann. She was glad to be rid of it, like pulling a splinter out of her skin. 'Who's got Will?' she asked.

'Danby, Bella, Frizer, Pooley and Skerries.'

That was a lot of people. None of this made sense.

'You need to come with me,' said Ann, 'they could come here anytime. Grab your things.'

'Very well,' said the Widow and picked up her calico bag with her one change of clothes.

'Is that it?' asked Ann.

She felt ashamed that she had so little. 'I'll leave the rest and come back for it later.'

ANN

The Widow followed Ann out of the door. It was getting dark and there was a flicker of a lantern and the sound of voices at the far end of the street, so they hurried in the other direction hugging the wall with the darker shadows. Ann was a good haggler, but she was used to negotiating for leather and cloth, not a man's life, the life of the man she loved. Should she go to Danby or try Bella? Was Bella any less ruthless? Probably not. If she just turned up with the play, they'd simply take it off her. She would have to make sure Will was released before she gave it to them. But if she turned up without it, they'd just beat her until she told them where it was.

Could she call on God again? She'd kept her side of their bargain and stayed away from Will. Only just, but God seemed to judge you on results. The problem was what else did she have to offer? That she'd be a good wife to John? That was probably just a minimum requirement. That she would respect her father? She had just smashed him over the head with a chair leg. She decided there was no time for God and she would have to do this alone, but in her head she quickly said, 'O Lord, please help me,' just in case, because there was no point annoying Him unnecessarily.

'I think those men went into my house,' said the Widow, looking over her shoulder. Ann stopped where a glimmer of candlelight from inside a house glowed through a window.

There was screaming from close by and Ann hoped it was just cats mating. She ripped open the parcel and the Widow gasped as if she had committed sacrilege. Inside was a thick sheaf of papers and Ann angled the first page so the lights flickering through the uneven glass panes illuminated it. She could just make out what looked like Christopher's writing. *Edward II* was written in big letters and below it was Christopher's name. So this was it. Why did everyone want it so much? It was supper time, and as they hurried on their way, they smelt the baked bread and roast meat and fish stews coming from houses where families were eating meals and not running away from sudden death. Passing a side alley, Ann heard a burst of shouting and the clink of glasses, and then a single man laughed a deep, booming laugh. She knew who it was straight away.

BELLA

Bella wished she had brought along the big bossy one, or even the lascivious yellow-eyed one. Frizer not only looked like a rainbow in hell, but he would not stop talking. She kept asking him to be silent and he would be but then thirty seconds later he seemed to forget, and started babbling again, his Adam's apple bobbing up and down in his scrawny neck. She had known a man like him before, a sailor on a voyage to the Indies. When they had become becalmed on the oily seas of the doldrums, where men longed for wind and the awful heat shortened their tempers, he chattered incessantly. He had mysteriously gone missing on a night watch.

'There's no one here,' said Frizer as they looked around the Widow's empty room. 'It's empty.'

She put her gloved finger to her lips.

'Looks like she had pie for dinner,' said Frizer, licking some crumbs off his finger. 'Potato, I reckon.'

She signalled him to be silent once again, and pointed at the door. She had caught a glimpse of a shadow beneath it. Frizer finally caught on, drew his knife and took a step so he would be behind it if it opened. She tugged Perro's lead but the dog had sensed something already.

'Gone quiet in there,' said a voice she recognised from outside the door. 'Now don't set that big fucker of a dog on me when I walk in, how about that?'

The door opened and Barking Bobby cautiously stuck

his head around it. Frizer was still crouched behind the door.
'Alright there, Ingram, mate,' said Bobby, 'I can see a reflection in the window and you're the only fucker that would dress like that.'

Frizer stepped out and Bobby pretended to be blinded.

Bella wondered how a black man like him had survived among the deep prejudices of the English, a nation which had a visceral hatred, even of the French from whom they had descended. She, at least, possessed beauty which distracted men from her colour. Barking Bobby did not. Standing there, short, bald and toothless, he was not to be underestimated.

'Now listen,' he said, 'I'm just the messenger, alright?'

He handed Bella the front page of Chris's play.

'I dunno what that is because I can't read, I dunno why you want it for or where the rest of it is hidden, if it is hidden or who hid it, but...' He took a deep breath. 'But,' he repeated, 'whoever it was who hid it will send it to Mr Danby's house as soon as you set Will Shakespeare free.'

She was ready to agree when Frizer chirped up. 'Bit too late for that.'

WILL

Skerries, Pooley and the brutish constable prodded Will ahead of them. His hands were tied behind his back so there was no chance of running away. They had kept him in a cellar where he had ended up so thirsty he had licked the green water seeping out of the bricks and running down the wall. Now it was dark, they were taking him somewhere to kill him. Would Bella keep her promise and not let them hurt Ann? He'd never know.

He heard Skerries ask the constable, 'Was it you who did the Dutch family?'

'I was there, but in a supervisory role.'

'Nice,' said Frizer.

They turned a corner and Pooley gave him such a big shove that he stumbled and fell heavily. He couldn't get up with his hands tied behind his back, so the constable hoisted him to his feet. He'd panicked in the cellar, and thought of that nothingness again, to be gone forever, never to think or feel for all eternity. He'd been unable to stand, unable to breathe, heard himself gasping like a man being hanged, but now he was surprised how calm he was. Maybe he was getting used to terror. They'd smash his skull open or slit his throat, but whatever it was, he told himself, it would be quick.

They shoved him through an iron gate. Ahead of him, some men stood around a two-wheel ox-cart piled with sacks. They were joking with each other as they unhitched the oxen. The slim moon came out from behind some clouds and then he saw. They weren't sacks, they were human bodies, lolling cadavers piled high on the cart, the corpses of plague victims, and next to the cart was a pit and a pile of earth. They were going to kill him and bury him at the bottom of a plague pit, where no one would ever find his body. Men prayed at times like this, but his lips couldn't find the words. Men screamed and fought, but his arms were tied. Men sobbed, but he wasn't going to give them the satisfaction. Men thought of their wives and children, but it was Ann's face he saw.

The men were talking Dutch as they heaved the cart into position at the edge of the pit. The gravedigger had been right, it was the desperate Dutch refugees who did this, who knocked on the doors with the red crosses after ten days, and when there was no reply, smashed them down and went in and dragged out the bodies to stack on the carts and bring them here.

The constable was humming cheerily to himself as they walked him to the edge of the hole. Skerries pronounced his sentence in a fast mumble. Will didn't know why he bothered.

'Found guilty of leaving a plague house,' he was saying, 'and duly sentenced by the queen's coroner to be buried alive with the bodies of plague victims.'

Oh God, oh Jesus, now cold panic tore through him, buried alive, suffocating slowly amongst the filth and decay. He tried to run sideways away from the lip of the pit, but Pooley shoved him in the back, and he tottered forward and just stopped himself, and for a moment teetered on the edge. A big shove sent him into the pit and, without the use of his arms, he landed heavily in the mud. He twisted his body and raised his face.

'Just kill me,' he shouted.

'We are killing you,' said the constable.

Skerries chuckled. 'Do you know, when work is this enjoyable it's not really work at all.'

The Dutch were tipping up the cart and the bodies started to tumble. He glimpsed the big constable grinning down at him, waving goodbye. The first couple of bodies just thumped down beside him, but then there was a heavy whack as one fell across his legs. He tried to twist to free himself, but then the rest of the cadavers all fell at once and smashed down on him and knocked the breath out of him and it went dark. A tangle of torsos and limbs on top of him, a terrible, sweet, rotten stink choking him, a panic seizing him, pinioned, unable to move, suffocating. And yet, he found he could breathe. He was in a crevice at the bottom of the pit so the other bodies were partly supported by the earth, and there were enough gaps between them that he could suck in the filthy air. He was going to take a long time to die.

Something was crawling across his face and he writhed furiously but the rope behind him held his arms tight, and he could barely move from where he lay, crushed on his back. The effort had left him struggling for air and he tried to hold his breath to hurry death along, but his body wouldn't let him and he ended up taking a huge gasp that sucked in air and filth. He was drowning slowly in rotten flesh.

There must have been some light creeping in, for he began to make out something in front of him. It was a face. It was Chris. It started to talk. 'Is that you, Will?' it asked.

'I'm sorry,' said Will, 'for all the things I said.'

'It's alright, I know you didn't mean it.'

The knife was still in Chris's eye.

'Do you still want revenge?' Will asked.

'I want everything. vengeance, mercy, love, heartbreak, fame, obscurity, pain and happiness. Everything I can't have.'

Why had Will stabbed himself in the chest? Had the gods been angry that he valued so little the life they had given him? Was this their response? Was he unconscious now, slipping into endless darkness? Chris reached out a hand to him.

'Where are you?' asked Will. 'Where will I go when I die? Are we ghosts? Do we sleep? Do we burn?'

Something was burning him. Chris had vanished and he was choking and his chest was on fire. And one leg. Was hellfire reaching its flames up for him? The pain sharpened his mind. It was the quicklime they shovelled into the plague pits seeping down. The weight was still crushing the breath out of him. He was going to drown and burn at the same time.

ANN

How many times must Ann run through these dark and treacherous streets of South London? Frizer had told Barking Bobby that Will had been buried alive in the Deptford plague pits. It was twenty minutes' walk but Ann had made it in ten, the Widow running behind, doing her best to keep up. The pits were by the creek, next to a beached ship that had burnt down, the remaining curved black timbers like the ribcage of a long-dead animal. The cart had been left next to the pit it had filled and one of the workers sat propped up against a wheel, eyes open, perhaps just too exhausted to leave. The moon was just a sliver but a dim wash of light picked out the white of the quicklime they had shovelled over the bodies.

'This one?' shouted Ann, pointing at it.

The Dutchman's glazed eyes stared at her, and she wondered for a moment if he was dead, but then he nodded.

There were shovels by the cart and Ann took one and was surprised at its weight. The Widow dragged another one over to the mass grave. This was pointless, a voice was telling her. Will was unreachable, beyond help beneath the quicklime and the dead, but the voice sounded like her father. She ignored it and took a shovelful of quicklime. She could barely lift it but she heaved it aside. The Widow struggled alongside her. She dug down again and her shovel hit something, a body. The corpses were barely covered and, when she bent down, she could see hands and limbs and pieces of clothing sticking up through the claggy white paste. That had been one of the gravedigger's many complaints, that the Dutch didn't use enough quicklime. She reached for what looked like an arm and tugged. It turned out to be a leg. She got her hands around the ankle and it shifted a little. She called the Widow to help. Together they pulled, and the body shifted more and another leg came loose, and taking one each they heaved. It wouldn't move any more. They caught their breath, then braced their feet against the other bodies and Ann shouted 'Now!' and screaming with the effort, pulling with a kind of wild rage, heaving and straining, it suddenly came free. They dragged it aside. Ann was breathing heavily, her back wet with cold sweat, and she had to bend over and take some deep breaths before they moved on to the next one.

'Thank you!' she gasped to the Widow.

'Don't worry,' said the girl, 'the plague doesn't seem to affect me.'

She hadn't been worrying, but she probably should have. Was she risking both their lives for no purpose? Too late now. She walked back into the sludge of dead flesh, and looked for the most exposed body. How many were there? Twenty? Twenty-five? Would they manage to move that many? It would get harder as they got deeper, and had to haul them up over the edge, but she just had to get on with it. Pulling out the first body had revealed another one and she found an arm and grabbed and pulled and it came loose from the torso with a sucking noise and Ann stumbled backwards. She chucked the arm away and looked for a body they could move. Her hands were burning, it was the quicklime of course, that's what it did, it dissolved flesh. Oh well, too late for that now.

'In for a penny, in for a pound,' she muttered to herself and scrabbled and clawed at another body. The Widow stuck the handle of a shovel underneath it, and together they used it as a lever to heave up the top half, but it was a big man and they still couldn't pull it aside. She heard wheezing behind them and turned and it was Barking Bobby. She hadn't even known he had followed them, but he stepped up alongside them and helped them roll the body away.

'Well, this is mucky work,' he said.

Now there was more of a hole.

'Will!' screamed Ann into the pit. There was no reply.

Ann thought, *This is hopeless*, but then she remembered the game the apprentices played in Canterbury at Lammastide, the great piles of them, five or six deep, and the ones at the bottom of that came out alive.

Her fingers were quivering with pain from the quicklime, so she took off her apron and tore it in two and wrapped a piece around each hand. She reached for the shovel and stepped into the hole. From below she could lever another body loose. Barking Bobby stepped in beside her with a squelch holding the other shovel. 'Bodies are heavier than people think,' he said.

The smell seemed to be seeping deeper into her nose and throat and made her want to gag, but they dragged another body free and together threw it out of the pit.

'Heave-ho,' said Barking Bobby and turned around and started to urinate into the pit. She thought nothing could shock her right now, but that did. 'It counters the quicklime,' he said, 'stops it burning so much. This lot won't mind.' Now one of Ann's feet was hurting too. The quicklime must have seeped through the hole in her shoe, and she cursed in rage and pain at her cheapskate father.

'Language,' chuckled Bobby as he threw something that might have been a child out of the pit.

A crescent moon, sharp enough to cut throats, came out from behind the clouds again and Ann saw a fourth figure beyond the edge of the pit, a tall, pale shape walking towards them. For a moment, she thought it was the ghost of Chris coming to help them, but then she saw it was the Dutch plague worker, a tottering wraith of a man, but he too stepped in to help, bent down and worked with the Widow to pull another body free. The hole was getting bigger.

'Will!' she yelled again. 'Will, Will, Will.'

A distant voice replied. She looked at Bobby and the Widow, thinking she must have imagined it but they had heard it too. 'Well, I'll be damned,' said Bobby, 'down there, I reckon.'

He pointed further along the pit.

Now they worked with fresh fury and Ann forgot the pain in her hands and feet and back and head, and she tore and ripped at the bodies, not caring if they came away whole or in chunks.

'Will,' she shouted again and again and the voice came back louder, guiding them towards him. She thrust her arm between the corpses and reached for him but could feel nothing that felt alive, but then his shout came back louder.

'Ann!' She stretched her arm deeper and her fingertip touched the warmth of living human flesh. And it moved, only a quiver, but it was him. She didn't want to let go, but she shouted, 'We're coming,' and the four of them hauled more bodies away and there was his head, his face turned upwards, his eyes huge, red-rimmed, staring and terrible, but alive, definitely alive. Bobby got out his knife, reached under him and cut the rope that tied his hands.

WILL

They helped him from the pit, his teeth chattering, his body shaking, his hands blindly grasping, his eyes unable to believe what he saw, a place where people were alive. He breathed in the filthy smell of decay like it was a rose garden. He hugged Ann, and holding her seemed to steady the shaking. She had come for him, reached into hell and dragged him back into the world.

When he had first heard her voice, he had thought it was just another illusion that his brain had dreamt up to torture him, but then it had grown closer and more real, and though he had told himself he mustn't hope, hope he had. Then her hand had touched his face and a breath of cold air had reached him.

Now he wanted to hold on to her forever, but as he came back to life, the quicklime burnt more and more, and he tore himself away and ran down a muddy slope and hurled himself into the black waters of Deptford Creek. Ann followed him in, scrubbing at her arms and hands. The quicklime was chewing at his scalp, and he took a breath and ducked his head under the water, and ran his fingers through his hair. When he surfaced, Ann was in front of him, up to her shoulders in the water, strands of her dark hair plastered across her face, the moon a long stripe of light on the dark waters behind her. Big tears were rolling down her face. He took a step forward, heaving his feet out of the sucking mud, and put his arms around her again.

'Will you look at that?' said Barking Bobby, watching from the shore. 'First time any fucker's gone into Deptford Creek to get clean,' and he turned and walked off into the darkness.

'Thank you,' yelled Will after him. 'And you,' he said to the Widow. 'I don't know your name.'

'I'm Agnes,' she shouted.

He shouted thanks to the Dutchman too, then looked back into Ann's face. 'Thank you,' he said.

Never had words seemed so inadequate.

The clouds blocked out the moon again and there was only darkness in front of Will, but he knew she was there.

ANN

When they got to Kemp's place, they found him sitting next to Lizzie telling her a story.

'She couldn't sleep,' he told them.

Lizzie wanted to know how it ended. From her questions it seemed to involve wolves, monsters, a lot of violence and have an unappreciated jester as its hero.

'This writing game, it's easier than you'd think,' said Kemp.

When they told him what had happened he dug out a bottle of spirits, the posh French liquorice stuff Will had said they'd been drinking on the Deptford trip.

The Widow, Agnes, helped Ann heat water on the fire, while Kemp sat Lizzie down by the open window at the far end of the room. He was worried that she would catch the plague off them. Will saw what Kemp was doing.

'I suppose I've a couple days before I start showing symptoms,' he whispered to her.

'You may not catch it,' she said.

He gave her a too quick smile, to thank her for lying to him.

'No,' she said, 'I talked to the Friar. He thinks it's an invisible spirit that dies soon after its victims die, and those bodies were long dead. He thinks it leaps from one person to another because it's the only way it can survive.'

He still looked doubtful. The water was getting hot.

'Take your clothes off,' Ann said to Will.

He glanced across at Agnes.

'Don't worry, I've seen naked men before,' she said. 'Though only dead ones.'

'Eh?' said Kemp.

'I had to prepare my husband's body. He'd kept his nightshirt on up till then.'

'There you go,' Ann said to Will. 'There's people like her who the plague doesn't touch. Everyone in her house died, but she didn't get it.'

She was arguing with herself as much as Will, for if he was going to die, so would she. She wouldn't have cared that much a couple of months ago, but now she had to live.

Kemp took Lizzie outside to help him make a fire in the courtyard.

'Chuck your clothes out the window and we'll burn them,' he said.

Will started to take off his clothes and Agnes, though she had seen naked men, went downstairs to join Kemp.

Will threw the clothes he had taken from Chris's room out the window and the fine burgundy silk pantaloons wafted this way and that and Kemp had to stop Lizzie from trying to catch them. He went back to teaching her how to do a pratfall.

'They have no power over me,' said Will.

'Who?'

'Danby, Cecil, all of them. If I'm going to die anyway what can they do?' He knocked back a slug of Kemp's liquor, and the liquorice tang filled the room. 'If I catch the plague they can't even come near me.' He spread his arms wide. 'I'm coming for them. I'm invincible because I don't fear death any more.'

'Can you shut up about dying?' Ann heard herself shouting. 'I didn't wade through a bog of corpses for nothing. If you're just going to die anyway, I might as well have left you at the bottom of the fucking pit.'

He looked shamefaced. 'Sorry,' he said. His arms were still spread wide and he lowered them self-consciously. 'Sorry, I went a bit mad there.'

'It's fine.' She could forgive him. He'd had a difficult day. 'What you did, there's probably no one else in the world who'd have done that.'

'Well,' she said, 'there's Agnes and Barking Bobby... And that Dutch bloke.'

'Only because of you.'

'Alright, shut up now,' she said. 'Take off the rest.'

Will took off his undergarments and the bandage that had held the maggots. Unsurprisingly, they had left for richer pickings. He stepped naked into the cauldron of hot water. He was thinner than she remembered him, but more muscular. Maybe these last few days had stripped any fat off him. She threw his remaining clothes out of the window, and managed to get the stockings and bandage straight into the fire. Kemp picked up the undershirt that had missed with a stick and dropped it into the flames. 'I'm taking these two for breakfast,' he shouted.

She realised he was leaving them to be alone with each other. 'Have you any soap?' she asked Kemp.

He laughed at the thought, but Agnes told them to look in her bag and there was indeed a small bar. Kemp offered each of the girls an arm, and walked off into the pale morning light. Lizzie waved goodbye.

Will was slopping the warm water over himself with a big iron ladle. She handed him the soap and he scrubbed furiously to try and rub away the horror. His eyes were hollow, his face still bruised on one side of his forehead and down one cheek, his chest around its old wound pitted with raw craters where the quicklime had eaten into him.

'You're a mess,' she said, as she took off her shredded apron and lifted her smock over her head.

She remembered to take the buttons she'd picked up in Chris's room out of the bag at her belt, before she threw that away too.

'They've left us alone,' she said as she stepped out of her underwear. She felt no embarrassment. Too much had happened. Next to murder and betrayal it was nothing.

'Your hands,' said Will.

The quicklime had made a mess of them too.

Will scrubbed and scrubbed until he was clean, stepped out of the tub and offered her his place. When she got in, the hot water stung her raw foot and she gritted her teeth until it subsided. He was still holding the ladle and he unclasped her hair and poured warm water over her head. Her bracelets rattled as she lifted her arms over her head and she felt his hand on the small of her back as he rubbed away with the soap at some stain. Her hands and his worked away until finally she felt cleansed.

She'd promised God that if He gave her Will back, she would cease her sinning and be a good wife and mother, and God had delivered him twice. But… had He? Hadn't it been her who had saved him? She had bargained with Bella and run across London and scrabbled in a plague pit with her bare hands. What had God done? He'd had his chance. Besides, she was a Marlowe and God was only God.

She turned to face Will and God went out the window like their clothes. She held him gently because so much of him was bruised or raw. One thought still nagged away at her. Should she tell him now or could it wait a little longer? But they kissed and then there was only room for that. She did wonder for a moment as they fell back on Kemp's mattress if it was unsanitary, but then she remembered they had just come out of a plague pit and laughed, and after that, everything was easy. Fear and hate and murder and injustice faded away. Pain and worry disappeared. London crumbled away around them until it was just them and the room and finally not even that.

ACT FIVE

ANN

When Ann woke the sun was bright and she prodded Will awake because there were things to do. She watched as he took a moment to remember where he was and the happiness in his face when he did was wonderful to see. They couldn't have slept for that long because the water in the metal tub was still tepid. Her hands and wrists hurt a lot and in the worst places clear liquid was seeping to the surface, but she washed herself again and wrapped herself in a blanket. Will's wounds too looked worse in the light, all except the septic gash in his chest that had scabbed over and looked much better. Was it thanks to the maggots or the quicklime?

'I feel like Lazarus,' he said. 'I came back and all the things I took for granted are miracles.'

Ann knew she had to do it then to stop his thoughts from running away with themselves. 'I'm pregnant,' she said.

Will didn't understand. 'You can't know that soon, can you?'

'No,' she said. 'I was pregnant already.'

'But who's the father?'

She looked at him, expecting the answer to dawn on him, but it didn't. 'John, the man I'm going to marry,' she said.

He sat down on Kemp's bed. For once she couldn't read those brown eyes.

'He knows about you and me,' she said, 'well, all of

Canterbury does. I'm not much of a catch as a wife and John's saving the family from bankruptcy.'

Will said nothing so she went on.

'So when he asked, I thought I've decided to marry him so why not get on with it, then I can't change my mind.'

'Why didn't you tell me before?' he asked.

Why hadn't she? Because she thought he would despise her for risking her baby in their reckless enterprise, for treating the life of an unborn child so lightly. Because he wouldn't understand that she had valued her own life with the same careless abandon.

'There wasn't a good time,' she said.

'Who knows apart from John?' he asked.

'He doesn't know. Just you. And Bella's dog, so probably Bella?'

'The dog?'

'I know from the way she sniffs me and sits on her haunches. My aunt had a bloodhound that could tell and she did the same.'

Her aunt had hired the dog out around all of Canterbury, but now wasn't the time to tell him about that. Ann sat on the bed next to him, wanting to put her arms around him but knowing she mustn't.

'Don't go back to Canterbury,' he said. 'I could say it was mine.'

Oh no, here we go, she thought. 'Haven't you got enough children already?' she said.

Now she could read the deep hurt in his face clearly enough. She had to be cruel to stop this now. She shouldn't have slept with him. She should have known he'd think it meant they had a future. He got up and walked to the window.

'You'd get what you want. You'd live your life but I'd be left looking after a baby in some attic.'

God knows, she wanted to say that it would all work out fine, she wanted to stop thinking ahead and to walk up behind him and put her head on his shoulder, but she remembered the cage they had built at Buttermarket in Canterbury for 'talkative women', and she saw her mum behind those bars mocked and caged for two days, her mum who was never the same again and now hid indoors in a cage of her own making.

'My mum and dad loved each other once,' she said. 'They really did. It wasn't a marriage of convenience. And now look at them. They say love will conquer all, but it won't. It gets old and tired and gives up conquering and lies down in a corner and dies.'

Will looked like she'd hit him and she turned away so she didn't have to see his distress and walked to the window.

'You know you feel the same as me,' he said. 'If you can dig me out of a plague pit you can make this work. There must be a way.'

'And what is it?' He couldn't answer.

She swatted at some flying insect on the windowsill and crushed it and wished she hadn't. 'There hasn't been a way since you got your Anne pregnant,' she said.

He looked so sad and hopeless. She'd made him miserable, but she could because she'd saved his life.

WILL

Will was good with words but words never worked on Ann once she had made up her mind. He felt he knew her better than anyone else in the world, but there was a part of her that she kept private, that he'd never see into or understand. He thought he must be too battered and burnt and exhausted to have space for heartache, but he was wrong. He felt like a baited bear in a pit. You swatted away the dogs that came at you, you killed or maimed them one after another, but there were always more dogs. You never won.

There was a knock on the door and Will covered his nakedness up with a cloak. It was Agnes, the Widow. She offered Ann the one spare change of clothes she carried in her bag. Ann put them on and Will saw her tuck Chris's buttons in the top of her hose. Kemp came in carrying the sleeping Lizzie, and gave Will a huge lewd wink; his expressions were all designed to be visible from the back row of the theatre.

'I expect you want some of my clothes,' Kemp said to Will. 'You're not getting any of the silk or fur though, and if they chuck you in another plague pit make sure you take them off first.'

This was Kemp being kind so it seemed harsh to ask him now, but Will had been buried with the dead and didn't really care. 'I saw you at a church door tacking up a pamphlet. Are you "Tamburlaine"?'

'No,' said Kemp very quickly.

Will didn't believe him.

'Come off it,' said Kemp, 'can you really see me writing that shit poetry of his?'

Will couldn't. 'Were you putting it up there for someone else?' he asked.

'Can you fuck off about fucking "Tamburlaine".'

Will glanced at Ann, and saw instantly that she didn't believe him either.

Kemp threw some clothes at Will. 'Do you want them or not?'

He muttered angrily as Will put them on.

This was Will's second costume change, and if Chris's clothes had made him more like the hero, these were far too short and wide and he looked like the fool.

'We should read Chris's play,' said Ann. She had hidden it in the costume store of the Rose Theatre while the nightwatchman as usual watched only the dreams in his head.

'Are you sure it's *Edward II*?' Will asked Ann.

'That's what it said on the front page.'

'So was Edward II a king?' asked Agnes.

'No, he was a fucking window cleaner,' said Kemp, who was still angry.

Ann gave him an admonishing look.

'Yes, he was a king,' said Kemp, 'but not a very good one.'

Edward II didn't seem a very dramatic king to Will. He and Chris had talked about which historical figures were worth turning into plays and neither of them had considered Edward. Will wondered whether this really was a Marlowe play.

A couple of flying ants came in through the window and Will knocked one away and peered outside. They were rising, fluttering in their hundreds. It was the day they all emerged; it would be the same all over London, all over the world for all he knew. How did they all know to come out on the same day? It was things like this that made him think there might be something like a God. The Bible with its brilliance and idiocy felt like it was created by man, but in these moments nature seemed to have a coherent power.

Kemp was changing into a summer doublet. 'Did Edward have a jester?' he asked. 'At least three,' said Will.

Lizzie had woken up and Kemp put his hands over her ears as he turned to Will and told him to get fucked. Will caught a flash of blue on his shoulder, a cross, a Jerusalem cross. He thought it had the X in one corner but he wasn't sure. He looked across to Ann but she hadn't seen. Was Kemp one of the men who met in those underground bars? If he was, then Will was certain he'd be the opposite of Chris and do anything to keep it a secret. Had someone got a hold on him? Was that why he nailed that pamphlet to a door, and what else would he have been capable of doing to ensure silence? He was glaring at Will but then he did that a lot so Will wasn't sure if Kemp had seen him spot the tattoo. All he knew for sure was that Kemp hadn't been on a pilgrimage to Jerusalem.

THE WIDOW

Ann had told her she could stay at Kemp's because it could be dangerous, but her husband and parents and Margarite had stayed at home and look what happened to them. Her dad had told her once, 'God decides everyone's fate on the day they are born and we cannot change it.'

Agnes liked that idea because you didn't have to be afraid. Why be fearful or frightened when it was all decided? She could be stabbed in the heart by a madman now as they all walked to the theatre, or she could find another Margarite and they could both live to a hundred and die in their bed.

Some red-coated constables had set up a checkpoint ahead. Will and Ann hesitated but the constables had seen them. Kemp strode ahead.

'Leave this to me,' he said.

'It's the one called Quinn who wouldn't let me into Deptford Town Hall,' said Ann. 'He'll recognise us.'

'We'll be fine,' said Kemp.

He shouted 'Morning, lads' to the constables. 'You know who I am, don't you?' The one called Quinn didn't look that impressed. He was staring at Will with his one good eye. 'I know you, don't I?'

'I don't know myself,' said Will, 'so I don't see how you can.' Will was acting oddly.

'Where are you coming from and where are you going?'

asked one of the other constables, swatting away a couple of flying ants.

'I'm coming from my mother's womb and going to my grave,' said Will. 'It's a short journey.'

'He's lost his wits,' said Ann, shaking her head sadly.

So that was what he was playing at.

'I have lost my wits,' said Will, getting down onto his knees. 'Will you help me find them? I'm sure they're here somewhere.'

The baggy, ill-fitting clothes helped his ploy. He looked like a doll dressed by a child.

'He's wanted for breaking out of a plague house,' said Quinn to the other two.

One of them, a pink-scrubbed, viciously shaven man with clumps of ginger hair around his ears and Adam's apple, said, 'Didn't he murder Marlowe?'

'No, that was Alleyn,' said Will. 'Did you see how much he overacted in the final scene of *Tamburlaine*?'

Kemp laughed.

'I heard they buried him alive in a plague pit,' said Quinn.

'They did,' said Agnes. 'That's what drove him mad.'

'He went in a man like you,' said Ann, 'and he crawled out a lunatic. We're going to put him on a cart back to Stratford.'

'We should arrest him,' said Quinn's mate.

'I'll tell you what drove him mad,' said Agnes. 'He's sure he's caught the plague from the bodies in the pit.'

They took a step backwards.

'We're trying to get him on the cart before he starts showing the symptoms, otherwise they won't take him,' said Ann. 'If you want him, he's yours. It doesn't make a blind bit of difference to him where he is, so have him.' Quinn and his mate considered. Will doubled up, wheezing and coughing and spluttering.

'My coughin' will lead to my coffin,' he said.

Ann swore under her breath and gave him a shove towards the red-jacketed constables. 'Please take him.'

'I'm not going near him,' said the one who hadn't yet spoken.

Will snapped at a flying ant, trying to eat it.

'Yeah, get lost,' said Quinn. 'We never saw him, alright, lads?'

Ann gave Agnes's hand a little squeeze as they walked off. She had done well. She'd done better than Kemp who'd been rude to her because she knew nothing about history. She smiled at Ann, as they turned around the corner.

'You're not mad, are you? Just checking,' said Ann to Will.

'No,' said Will. 'I'm sane. It's the rest of London that's mad.' Agnes saw a flicker of worry on Ann's face before Will put an arm on her shoulder and said, 'I'm fine.'

Ann punched him. It was quite hard for a playful punch. 'You're not such a shit actor as I thought,' she said, and he smiled as he rubbed his shoulder.

Agnes was glad she'd come along. If her dad was right and God had truly mapped out her life He'd gone to a lot of trouble. Perhaps, having killed everyone she knew, He was giving her something to keep her busy and stop her from grieving all the time. Here she was involved in what Ann called a 'conspiracy'. Not long ago she'd had a family and a husband and a girl she loved. A lot had happened in – how long was it? She'd been married on May Day.

'What month is it?' she asked.

'June,' said Ann.

'What day?'

'The fifth.'

'Oh,' said Agnes, 'it's my birthday. I'm fourteen.'

WILL

'So, fuck me, is this it?' said Kemp. 'Not a laugh in sight.'

They passed the pages of *Edward II* from one to another, reading mostly in silence, only interrupted by Kemp grumbling. Will read ferociously, for he felt his friend was speaking to him for one last time. It wasn't the crowning masterpiece he had hoped for, but there was no doubt it was Chris's work. As ever, his characteristics struggled with power and desire, and there were moments of poetry that made Will's heart race. There was only one problem. The play could never be staged. *Edward II* was a weak monarch who had misgoverned England and placed his favourite, Gaveston, above the lords of the land.

'They'll think Elizabeth is Edward and Essex is Gaveston,' said Will, 'and what happens, they're both killed. The rightful king is murdered and replaced.'

It wasn't surprising Cecil wanted to get hold of it and suppress it.

'Do you think this is why Christopher was summoned to appear before the Queen's Court?' asked Ann.

That made sense. Kyd had told Cecil and Topcliffe about it under interrogation and they had asked him where they could find it.

Will thought back to the cold stone room in the Tower of London where Lord Cecil had questioned him and remembered the rustle behind him as Topcliffe consulted his notes on Kyd's interrogation. Kyd had not known where the play was. 'I pressed him on that point a number of times,' Topcliffe had said.

Those words made him shiver, but there was logic here. He and Ann talked it through. Kyd told them about Marlowe's seditious new play, but he didn't yet know where it was. Cecil ordered Marlowe's arrest to follow the trail.

'But then,' said Ann, 'why would Cecil have him killed before he gets a chance to question him?'

They were back to this.

'Perhaps someone else had him killed so they could put the play on before Cecil was able to find out about it.'

As Will said it he realised that all this was based on endless surmise, and that nothing in this snake pit of entangled lies wholly made sense.

'So you think someone paid him to write a subversive play? Hardly sounds like Sir Rich Spencer.'

'No,' said Will, though he thought back to how Chris had suddenly had a lot of money.

'If he was commissioned he didn't just write what they wanted, did he?' said Ann. 'He put in a love story. He really did write Edmund the play he promised him.'

It was true. The poetry was at its purest when Edward and Gaveston spoke of their love.

'So apart from being seditious and a love story between a couple of blokes, it's fine,' said Kemp. 'Shall we burn it?' For a moment Will's outrage made it hard for him to speak. 'Burn it?' He heard a quaver in his voice. 'It's the last thing Chris will ever write.'

'If you give it to Cecil he might leave you alone,' said Kemp.

Ann said nothing. For a moment her ferocious energy was depleted and she seemed utterly exhausted. Was she tempted by the idea?

Will started to read the Mortimer speech aloud.

'There is a point, to which when men aspire,
They tumble headlong down: that point I touched,
And, seeing there was no place to mount up higher,
Why shall I grieve at my declining fall?
Farewell, fair queen. Weep not for Mortimer,
That scorns the World, and, as a traveller,
Goes to discover countries yet unknown.'

'Do you think he knew he was going to die?' said Ann. 'It's like this epitaph.'

'Fuck it,' said Kemp. 'We can't destroy it, can we? I'll tell you what we can do though.'

ANN

Ann was never sure where Chris's poetry came from. He was clever and remarkable and fearless and fun, but the sheer beauty of his words always shocked her. These men, like him and Will, didn't come from the leisured nobles who strolled through their fine libraries and exquisite gardens but from the sons of tradesmen in grubby backwaters, outsiders who could never match the wealth and breeding and martial skills of the aristocrats, but who found in words a currency where all men were equal, whose imaginations lit a fuse that fired an explosion of language that held all London in its thrall, whose very existence was a kind of revolution. They couldn't let his final words be destroyed.

Most of the boys who played the women onstage were housed in a building just behind the theatre and Kemp sent them out to gather the actors, Strange's Men, the Admiral's Men and what was left of Pembroke's and Sussex's. They came in ones and twos, sleepy, hung-over, confused by mangled messages, but they came. They all had questions but Will just kept saying that Chris's last play was going to be destroyed and that learning and keeping it safe in their heads was the only way to save it. Ann handed out the parts, splitting up the larger ones so a different actor learnt each act. She organised the chairs into a circle and tried to get them to pass the pages only one way, but they didn't listen to her, and they all seemed to need the same page at the same time.

Tom Kyd limped in, his face pale and clenched in pain. He looked slightly less healthy than one of the severed heads on spikes by London Bridge. Will and Ann saw him at the same time and hurried over to join him.

'Oh, both of you,' he said, grasping a table to help support himself.

'You knew Agnes had the play,' said Will.

He looked blank for a moment. 'Oh, is she the Widow? Yes, I knew.'

'When did she tell you?' asked Ann.

Since his arrest, Kyd had always looked frightened and in pain but now he looked angry too. 'She told me the night we went to Deptford that Chris had given her a package to hide so I guessed that was the play.' That at least chimed with their theory. 'Why did you tell us to destroy it?' asked Will.

'Oh, you're not. I told you to destroy it because I didn't want anyone else to die for it.'

He looked around him at the hubbub of actors.

'Lovely to see you've acted on my advice.'

A flying ant had landed on his forehead but he didn't seem to notice it. He pulled his body upright and turned away from them.

'Why did you go to the Friar and get the poison?' Ann asked.

'Oh, for fuck's sake! Let's all interrogate Tom Kyd because he hasn't been interrogated enough. Is that the new game?'

Ann said nothing and waited.

'I got the poison,' he said, 'so, if they came to take me back to Topcliffe's torture chamber, I could kill myself first, a course of action I'd strongly recommend should they come for you. Now, I'm going.'

'Aren't you going to read Chris's play?' asked Will.

'I'm sick of plays,' he said. Will's eyes flicked to his right hand, still free of ink stains, and Kyd saw his glance. 'I haven't been able to write a damn word since *The Spanish Tragedy* was such a hit.'

He was struggling to walk out but his warped body wouldn't obey him.

'Pray to God you never have a big success.'

He lurched away into a bunch of drunk actors who had come straight from a pub and bought with them three prostitutes and a cat. It was a mess. Some learnt their lines by walking around performing them, while others rehearsed the scenes in pairs, and they all raised their voices so they could be heard over the noise in the room that then got louder. The theatre was full of Chris's words, but they were being shouted over each other until none of them could be heard. The nightwatchman came over to Ann to complain about something or other but she saw Lizzie sitting in a corner scratching furiously at her arms and ran over and held her hands and tried to calm her. Will was trying to separate two actors who'd come to blows fighting over a page. A drunk actor was trying to grab Agnes. The theatre was full of men arguing and shouting in the midst of filmy swarms of flying ants rising into the fug of tobacco smoke.

'Silence,' shouted a booming voice and amazingly it went quiet. Ann turned to see Alleyn on the lip of the stage, his big black cape billowing, his great, hewn face frowning. He raised his arms wide and there was complete silence. 'Is it true?' he asked. 'Is there indeed one last Marlowe?' He raised a hand to silence the many answers.

'Will, where are you? What have you found?'

Will stepped forward.

'Jesus, God Almighty, what are you wearing?' said Alleyn. 'No, don't answer that. Tell me what's going on.'

Will did.

'Then we indeed need to learn it,' said Alleyn.

'Ann has worked out a system,' said Will.

'Ann who?' said Alleyn.

'Ann Marlowe.'

He looked blank for a moment and then remembered. 'Oh, Miss Marlowe is here,' he said. 'I'm profoundly sorry for your loss. The only alchemy that has ever worked was what Chris did with words.'

As he repeated himself from before, it dawned on Ann that Alleyn was drunk. She started to speak but Alleyn spoke over her.

'Everyone listen to Ann Marlowe. Do exactly what she says.'

Everyone did.

When Ann had finished explaining, Alleyn announced, 'I shall be Edward II. Fortunately my powers of learning are prodigious.' She knew this was true. Drunk or sober, Alleyn only seemed to have to look at a page for it to be fixed in his memory.

Lizzie was propped on a bench with her eyes closed, seemingly asleep, but when Ann sat next to her she reached for her hand and lay down with her head on Ann's lap. Ann closed her eyes too for a moment but then felt a presence in front of her. When she opened them, Chris's lover Edmund was standing there, his handsome face even more hollowed and drained than the last time she saw him. Was this Chris's true legacy, all these haggard faces walking around London, in grief and fear and anger?

'They found you?' said Ann.

She'd asked Kemp to send a boy to fetch him but he'd told her that no one knew his address.

'A boy came with a message,' said Edmund.

Had Kemp known where he lived all along? Will had told her about the tattoo that he thought he'd seen. Were Edmund and Kemp part of that same hidden world? It didn't really matter, she was glad he could be here. He held a page of the manuscript.

'How much have you read?' she asked.

'Enough,' he said, and read out loud.

'The sight of London to my exiled eyes,
Is as Elysium to a new-come soul;
Not that I love the city, or the men,

But that it harbours him I hold so dear.'

'He did write you that play,' said Ann.

'I'd rather have him than a play,' said Edmund. 'All day long I can think of nothing but him.'

She could have told him that she did think of things other than Chris, that she was pregnant and about to marry a man she didn't care for, and leave a man she loved, that she was fighting for her life against the most powerful men in England, that these things sometimes drove her grief for Chris out of her mind, but she said nothing and just touched his hand.

'I think a lot about those last words of his,' said Edmund.

'One day?'

He nodded. 'Do you think he meant in heaven? I know everyone says he was an atheist but I'm not sure. I've watched him tear pages from the Bible to roll tobacco, but I've seen him on his knees praying. What do you think?' Before Ann could say anything he went on. 'Do you think he knew he was going to be killed?'

'Maybe.' She realised she was too exhausted to complete a sentence.

An actor she didn't know hurried over and asked Edmund if it was page twelve he was holding, and when he said 'yes' scurried back to the circle with it.

'So did my father kill him?' said Edmund.

Ann's exhaustion was a fog that blurred thought and sense, but she did her best to explain what they knew, and how there was no clear connection to Sir John.

Edmund interrupted. 'My father's paying you to say it wasn't him, isn't he?'

Ann took a moment to understand. She looked at Edmund, the staring, red-rimmed eyes in the sunken face, and saw a man who hadn't eaten or slept for days, whose thoughts whirled around in his head until the only place they had left to go were into the crazy cracks and corners.

'I'll kill anyone who helped kill Chris,' he said. 'It's the only way I'll ever sleep again.'

Ann wanted to say something kind to him as he walked away but she was so tired that no words would come.

Will came and sat beside her. He held her hand beneath a discarded cloak so no one could see.

'They can burn a manuscript,' he said, 'but they can't burn all the actors in London.'

'No, they can,' said Kemp.

She hadn't seen him standing beside them.

'But it is less likely,' he conceded.

BELLA

This time they made Bella leave Perro outside the door as well as her small dagger. He was sitting at his usual place at the far end of the long table. Bella went to sit at the opposite end.

'Did I say you could sit?' he said without looking up.

He was so different in private. Was his public face make-believe or just another part of him that he chose to let people see? She waited. It was quiet inside these thick stone walls. She could hear Hesketh's wheezy breathing from behind her where he had posted himself at the door. She had once made the long sea voyage south from Spain to Argentina. It had been winter when she left, winter when she arrived, and when she returned, winter again. These cold walls made her think of that long, bleak journey.

Finally, he put the pen down and dabbed the ink dry with powdered cuttlefish bone. 'All I wanted was the play,' he said. 'Was that too much to ask for?'

'I was the one who found out who had it,' she said.

'Look at the table.'

She did. There was a tiny hole between the inlaid shells and a fine powder around it. It had woodworm.

'Is there a play on it?' he asked. 'Because, if there is, I can't see it.'

'I advised we should have it in our hands long before you decided to kill Marlowe.'

She felt rage in his stillness. Nothing moved but then one long hand started tapping on the table. It had been a mistake to defend herself, and now was not the time to make mistakes. She must cower in front of him. She must roll on her back and expose her throat. She started to apologise but he raised the hand that wasn't tapping to silence her.

'You strut around London like royalty,' he said, 'but I know where you come from. How dare a whore like you treat me like an equal? You're more of a mongrel bitch than that horrid hound you walk around with.'

He slammed his hand down on the table and the fine powder from the woodworm disappeared. She needed to look scared or he would never stop. She must shiver and fawn while she racked her brains for the best way to kill him. She dropped to her knees, her hands clasped in supplication as he ranted.

'You've nothing but a concoction of foreign sewage in your veins. I have the blood of kings.'

Perro was barking outside. There was a knock on the door and she heard Hesketh whisper with another man, and then he stepped past her with a scrap of paper and bowed.

'There's a message for her,' Hesketh said. 'Someone knows where it is.'

He took it, and turned to Bella. 'This time you do exactly what I say, no more, no less, do you understand?'

'Yes, Lord Strange,' she said.

ANN

The actors had left for the Cross Keys, which opened early. Lizzie's terrors had passed for now and Kemp took her with him. Being in a pub full of drunks was probably safer for her than being near Will and Ann right now. Agnes had promised to keep an eye on her.

'So what now?' said Ann. Her own voice sounded to her like it came from a cellar far away. She had barely slept last night, and not much the night before. Though which was the night before? Her thoughts were blurred and heavy.

'We need to trade the manuscript for our lives,' said Will. What a sight he was, gaunt-eyed, bruised and unshaven.

She must think clearly if they were going to survive and yet she would almost trade her life for a short sleep curled up amongst the furs in the costume store. 'We can't go out on the streets,' she said. 'There's too many people looking for us. We should send Cecil a message saying we've found it and he can have it.'

She wished they'd thought of that before Agnes and Kemp had gone.

'Did you see Kemp before they all left for the pub?' Will asked her. 'He was following Alleyn around whispering something angrily, and it looked like Alleyn was trying to get away from him.'

She hadn't, but a thought blundered its way through the fog of tiredness.

'Could Alleyn be "Tamburlaine" the pamphleteer? Could Kemp have been tacking up the posters for him, and now you know about it, he wants to stop?'

WILL

Will considered. It made so much sense. Alleyn's political delusions, his self-importance, his reported secret Catholicism and his scorn for Protestant refugees. And, of course, the awful, awful verse.

'I think you're right,' he said.

He wondered why he hadn't seen it sooner. Alleyn taking the name "Tamburlaine" from his greatest triumph. After he had played Tamburlaine, he had never really gone back to being Alleyn. Perhaps he had a hold over Kemp because he knew Kemp was one of the men with the Jerusalem tattoos who met in those underground bars.

'But does it matter?' said Ann.

It probably didn't.

'What we need to do now,' she said, 'is get a message to Cecil.'

But at once there was a loud banging at the bolted main door. They froze.

'I know you're in there,' boomed the voice of Ann's father. 'I'm not going away until you let me in.' Ann stifled a scream of rage and frustration. Her dad kept up the banging.

'Open the bloody door, Ann!' She opened her mouth to yell at him but Will took her by the arm.

'We have to let him in or he'll tell the whole world we're here.'

She nodded reluctantly and Will walked fast to the door

and unbolted it. He blustered in with a rolling walk that meant that somewhere between Will's room and the theatre he'd found alcohol. His expensive coat with its rabbit fur collar was smeared with grease and there was dirt in the lines on his face.

Will didn't have time for this. He grabbed him by the throat and shoved him backwards. Ann's father was twice Will's weight but he wasn't expecting it and once he started going backwards, his legs lost confidence and he took a few increasingly wobbly steps and sat down on his arse. His mouth opened to speak but Will got in first.

'Shut up and stay shut up.'

The small bloodshot eyes in the large bloodshot face flickered in confusion. He tried to save face. 'I've got mates who'll make a mess of you.'

'That's not true,' said Ann, 'you haven't got any mates.'

He stared at her as if he hadn't understood. 'I'm hungry,' he said finally.

Ann ignored him. 'We could send the nightwatchman to the pub with a message,' she said to Will.

They split up to look for him.

Will checked the dressing and make-up area and the costume cupboard, but he wasn't there. He was about to try upstairs when Ann called from where she was looking in the props store. 'It's full of muskets in here.'

'They'll be the replacements for the faulty ones that fired into the audience.'

'How many were there?' she asked.

'Four or five. Chris wanted ten, of course.'

Will walked over to look. There was a window that cast a bright square of sunlight into the room. There wouldn't have been space for the nightwatchman in there, because it was packed from ceiling to floor with guns.

'There's between sixty and seventy,' said Ann.

He looked at the oiled wood stocks and shiny barrels.

'They're snaphaunces,' he said. 'Chris taught me. You know how he loved guns.'

She knew – she'd been there when Chris had taken Will and Tom Kyd out to a field near Newington Butts, where they had fired pistols at targets and, as they got drunker, at each other's hats.

They stared at them for a moment. These were the most modern weapons in Europe that ignited the powder with a spark not a match. Even the queen's guards still had the old matchlocks.

'So, not for a play,' she said.

Will broke open the door of the next store along. It was packed with halberds, breastplates and helmets. Ann had opened a cupboard full of wooden boxes. She opened one, reached inside and came out with a handful of musket balls.

'Whoever has bought all this has a lot of money,' he said.

There was a voice behind them.

'We could take some of this stuff and sell it on,' said Ann's dad. 'A couple of breastplates and a box of gunpowder and they'd never notice.'

'Gunpowder?' said Ann.

'It's somewhere close. I can smell it.'

They heard the creak of the main theatre door open. Will had forgotten to rebolt it after Ann's dad came in. They hastily closed up the various stores. Ann picked up the manuscript and they walked out onto the stage.

Lord Strange stood there with his retinue.

'William,' he said. 'I hear there's joyous news. You've found Chris's lost masterpiece.' His eyes fixed on to the manuscript in Ann's hand. 'Is that indeed it?'

'It is,' said Will.

Lord Strange rubbed his hands gleefully. 'We're going to rake it in. Murdered Marlowe speaks from beyond the grave. I've greased a few palms and they'll let us reopen to perform it to an invited audience. Top people, top prices. I'll cut you in as you found it.'

'I don't think we can put it on,' said Will. 'Not while Elizabeth is on the throne. It would be seen as sedition.'

Lord Strange laughed humourlessly and the other three behind him aped their master. 'Oh tush, it's only a little-bitty play.' He stepped forward with his hand out.

'I'm sorry we can't give it to you,' said Will. 'We're going to give it to Cecil.'

'Why ever would you do that?'

'So he doesn't kill us,' said Ann.

'Well, I rather think I'm going to take it,' said Strange, 'because I fucking paid for it.'

The change was sudden and ferocious. For the first time ever the voice matched those dead eyes.

'I thought you said Sir Rich Spencer paid for it,' said Will.

'Of course he didn't. I just told people that. Give me my play.'

'You commissioned a seditious play?' He glanced at Ann and guessed they had worked it out at the same time. Lord Strange was leading a rebellion to depose Elizabeth. The rumours of rebels moving into London were for once true, and he was using the theatre as an arsenal to arm his men. Will tried to muster his weary thoughts to see if finally this explanation added up. Strange had commissioned Chris to write a play, Chris who owed him his life after Strange had intervened to save him from a murder charge for killing Bradley. He would stage the play on the night of the coup as propaganda to show that the English had always deposed weak monarchs. His plan had gone wrong when Chris was summoned to appear before Cecil and the Royal Court. He felt he was close to the truth, or at least closer, but right now, he must stop trying to pick his way through this tangle of duplicity. Right now, time was what they needed.'

Who will you replace Elizabeth with?' Will asked Strange.

'Who do you think?'

Will saw that Danby and Hesketh were with him too.

Hesketh moved to stop Strange but he went on. 'I have more royal blood than anyone alive in England. I am related to Henry VII through my mother and Henry VIII through my father. Elizabeth is the illegitimate daughter of a whore. Henry isn't even her father. She dyes her hair red to make fools think he was.'

That's a new one, thought Will.

He looked at Ann and her eyes gave the slightest flick towards the secret back door. That's what Will was thinking. Strange and Hesketh had swords, but if they moved fast they stood a chance.

Strange was still ranting. 'The Pope has absolved me in advance for any sin in killing Elizabeth.'

Hesketh had given up trying to restrain him, and instead put his fingers in his mouth and whistled. Will heard the secret back door behind them open and, as they turned, Skerries, Frizer and Pooley walked through it. So it wasn't that much of a secret.

Skerries grinned and gave an elaborate mock bow. More armed men came into the theatre through the main door. Among them, the great lump of a palace guard turned constable who had helped bury Will alive. So Strange had at least one palace guard on his side and, of course, Danby. That would get his force into Greenwich Palace so he could seize or murder the queen. The last one to arrive was Bella with the dog. Strange turned to her.

'Well, at least you got one thing right.'

'Thank you, my lord,' she said in a small voice. 'What's going on?' said Ann's father.

Will had forgotten he was there. Strange ignored him, and stared at Will.

'Looks like there's going to be a shortage of good playwrights during my reign. Oh well.'

'You think you're going to become king but you won't,' said Will.

'Why's that?' said Strange.

'Because you'd be King Ferdinando the First and that's just too ridiculous.'

He could have sworn Bella, standing alongside him, suppressed a laugh.

'Who wants to kill these two?' asked Strange.

Frizer put his hand up, but Skerries shook his head and said, 'Sorry, Ingram, mate, but I'm having this one.'

Will was about to die. Again.

'Kill me,' he said to Strange, 'but not her, she's with child. The Pope wouldn't want you to kill a pregnant woman.'

Behind him he heard her dad shouting abuse at Ann, but someone hit him to shut him up. 'You can put her back in my room with a red cross on the door, and this time she'll stay there for ten days and then you'll be done.' He couldn't bear to look at Ann as he said, 'Killing an unborn child, it's the one thing God won't forgive.'

Strange flicked a long aristocratic wrist towards Skerries. 'Is that a problem for you?'

'Nah, done it before.'

He hadn't supposed it would work. For them her death was a droplet of blood in an ocean. Strange held out a dagger for Skerries to take, and Ann gasped and grabbed Will's arm.

'Look,' she said, gesturing at the knife. 'That's Chris's.'

'Yes,' Hesketh said rapidly, 'Marlowe gave it to His Lordship shortly before his death.' Strange's face contorted into a laugh. 'You're such an arse, Hesketh, we don't need to lie any more.' He held up the knife. 'I rather imagine the story about the female pirate was invented, but I've always liked this chap.'

In the new Lord Strange, there was still an element of the foppish fool he had pretended to be. Of course, thought Will, that indulged popinjay was no threat to anyone. That was how a nobleman with a genuine claim to the throne had survived for thirty years without being murdered.

Strange read the inscription on the blade. '*Pro me amico.*' The future Ferdinando the First turned to Will. 'Rather appropriate.' He grinned. 'If only you spoke Latin you'd know why.'

Danby and the others laughed obediently. 'Why did you kill him?' asked Ann. 'He wrote you the play you'd asked for.'

'I think even you two can work that out.'

'Because he'd have told Topcliffe about it under interrogation and Cecil would have discovered the conspiracy,' said Will, trying to keep him talking.

'You seem to have grasped the plot,' said Strange.

'And who was it who poisoned him?' asked Ann.

Strange ignored her and handed Chris's knife to Skerries. 'If you'll do the honours. I'm sure your companions will assist.'

Ann whispered in Will's ear.

'A final "I love you", is it?' said Strange mockingly. 'No, it wasn't,' said Will.

What she had whispered was, 'Clap your hand over Bella's mouth,' and he did.

Ann shouted what sounded like '*Doodslang*' and made the signal for Perro to attack by throwing something at the feet of Skerries, Frizer and Pooley – not the small stones Bella used but the buttons she had taken from Chris's room. Perro leapt forward and knocked Skerries off his feet. Bella tried to speak but Will jerked her head backwards. Skerries made the mistake of trying to wrestle with the dog. He lost. It was all so quick that Frizer was still standing frozen with his mouth slightly open, when Perro leapt at his throat. The mauve and yellow outfit he'd chosen that day was instantly splattered in red. Bella bit Will's hand, but he wrenched it free and leapt back as she sliced at him with a small knife that was suddenly in her hand.

He and Ann pelted for the small back door that Skerries, Frizer and Pooley had been blocking. They leapt sideways through the narrow opening into the alleyway. It was empty. Ann's dad followed them and flung himself through the door but he was too fat to fit and got stuck. They could hear the men who were trying to chase them shouting and smashing at him but he was like a cork in a bottle and no one could get past. Will and Ann threw themselves over the low wall that led to the market gardens and ran between the runner beans and asparagus and rhubarb, glass cloches shattering beneath their feet. The flying ants rose around them in a flutter of gauzy wings.

ANN

Lord Cecil had seen them as soon as the guards at the Tower gates took him their message. Now they sat in a stone-floored room, that was cold even in June. Many more had walked through the gates of the Tower than ever walked out but, inside these thick stone walls, Ann felt safe for the first time in days.

They told Cecil everything, and as they spoke lords and captains gathered in the room, and Cecil gave orders for troops to be sent to secure bridges, confiscate weapons and make arrests. Cecil stood, his hands braced on the oak table, his body twisted and skewed, his mind precise, incisive and calm. Word came that Strange had been seized, and they heard his indignant protests as he was dragged past them down the corridor to the dungeons below. After him, the one they most wanted was Hesketh who they thought was the link to Spain. They seemed to have forgotten that Will and Ann were there.

She felt someone sidle up behind her and turned to see Topcliffe smiling over her shoulder.

'I'm going to be busy downstairs for the next few days. Will, you'd be most welcome to observe and, of course, bring your lovely lady friend.' She found her dread made her mirror his smile. Will thanked Topcliffe but said that he hadn't slept for three days. 'Are you sure? I've a new toy I've never tried before,' said Topcliffe.

'Oh, leave them alone,' said Cecil, shaking his head

indulgently. They were, in some ways, like an old married couple. 'He does love an audience,' Cecil said to Will.

Topcliffe sighed. 'My only regret is not following my dream of a career onstage.'

'It's the theatre's loss,' said Cecil, his expression deadpan.

A boy ran in, bowed, whispered in his ear and ran out, and Cecil turned to them.

'I think we're done with you two. Mr Shakespeare, you were right to come to me, but let what happened today be proof of the theatre's power, and the consequences for those who abuse it.'

Will bowed.

'So,' Cecil went on, '*Richard II* is a cripple who all London is going to think is based on me.'

Will went to speak but Cecil hushed him. 'Make him clever.'

The red cross was still painted on the door below Will's room, but they didn't care, and she thought no one else would any more. They slept, woke to use the chamber pot and slept some more. She was aware of Will next to her, his smell, his quiet breathing, an arm that had fallen across her as they lay on his narrow bed. It was light when she finally got up, and it must have been near midday because the sun shone directly into the narrow street. London had become hot and it smelt like summer. Will woke too, and his battered face smiled. His chest wound was healing and neither of them showed any symptoms of the plague. They washed in cold water, spent her last few coins on some bread and cheese, ate it and made love. They didn't know what day of the week it was, and felt no desire to find out.

They might have stayed there, but they ran out of money, so Will headed to the theatre in Shoreditch to try to get an advance, though they didn't even know if Lord Strange's theatre company still existed. There were armed patrols in the street and gangs of men looking for Catholics. They heard fragments of conversation about plots and murders. A butcher proclaimed that Elizabeth herself had struck down a rebel who had broken into her bedroom.

When they walked into the theatre, Kemp and Lizzie were up onstage trying to outdo each other with their pratfalls. The little girl was giggling. Ann had never heard her laugh and it was a lovely noise.

A voice shouted, 'William.' They turned around. Standing there was Lord Ferdinando Strange.

WILL

Will stared at him. He was dressed magnificently even for him, a green silk doublet trimmed at the cuffs with pearls, scarlet breeches, a white ermine cape, a piratical cocked hat topped with ostrich feathers. He smiled smugly. For an instant, Will thought someone had slipped him some more henbane, and it was all in his head, but when he saw Ann's face taut with twisted hatred, he knew he was really there. He was eating a fresh, crisp apple. How had he got it, a month before the earliest apples were ripe, and seven months after the last crop of the year?

'Come and talk to me,' he said, gesturing at the room he used as an office. 'You too, Marlowe's sister.'

They didn't move. Will looked across at Kemp, who wouldn't meet his gaze.

'Come along,' said Lord Strange. 'Don't you want to know what happened to Chris?' Ann moved, so Will followed her into the room. It was dark and stuffy and smelt of Strange's cloying perfume. Strange seemed to have adopted a manner somewhere in between the gleeful killer they'd last seen and the fumbling fop with which he'd disguised it for years. Had he spent so much of his life dissembling that he had no true personality?

'Rather a good malmsey,' he said as he poured them all a glass of wine. He sat on the desk, his shiny black shoes dangling. 'Now, I know our relationship had a bit of a snag—'

'Would that be when you murdered my brother?' said Ann.

'Oh, that,' he said, wafting his hand as if that was now all done with. 'William, you and I still need each other.'

Will said nothing.

'We need to work together, because I'm here to stay,' he said. 'I've reached an accommodation with Robbie.' He saw their bafflement. 'Cecil, Lord Robert Cecil.' He beamed. 'It seems that history will tell how Hesketh came to me with a plot to install me as king but I, like the loyal subject I am, went straight to Cecil and reported it.' He was enjoying this. 'It seems that Hesketh, if he ever emerges from Topcliffe's little room of fun, will be hanged, drawn and quartered. Oh, and I don't think we'll be seeing Mr Danby again. Perhaps, William, you can write a play about it all.'

Will and Ann just sat there staring. Strange's smug superiority made him tell them more.

'Lord Cecil's opposed to bringing James of Scotland down to succeed Elizabeth so he's keeping me up his sleeve, so you'll be wise to work with me as I may yet be your king. I think you're right, by the way, King Ferdinando may be a little rich for the masses. I'm thinking, "Henry the Ninth".'

Their silence seemed to irritate him.

'Are you just going to sit there?' he asked. 'I thought words were your speciality.'

Will remained silent and went to leave, but Strange stood up and blocked his way.

'You can go when you desire but first you will want to hear this. Lord Cecil has agreed that I can stage *Edward II*, if it is rewritten to be less...' He looked for the right word. 'Inflammatory. I'll pay you to do that and then the public, bless them, can see your friend's final play.'

'No,' said Will.

'It speaks,' said Strange. 'I tell you what, if you do as I ask, I'll tell you who killed Christopher.'

He was grinning from ear to ear.

'I'm going to be sick,' said Ann.

'Good God, not in here,' said Strange, but she bent double in the corner and retched.

Will put a hand on her back.

'Is it the plague?' asked Strange.

'No, just you,' said Ann, between spasms.

'People,' he muttered as he came over to look. 'Oh, Holy Mother of God, that's my cloak.' For the first time, he seemed to feel something. 'You've been sick on my cloak.' He came over and picked it up. There were only a few small streaks of bile on the fine merino wool, but it seemed to utterly revolt him.

'Are you alright?' Will asked Ann.

She nodded. 'It's just pregnancy sickness.'

Will took her arm and helped her out the door.

'You'll be back,' Lord Strange shouted after them.

BELLA

It was the worst news in the world. Why had they released Lord Strange? When the conspiracy had been discovered, she had at once told Cecil everything she knew. He had asked her why she hadn't told him before, and she told him the truth, that Strange held her son prisoner and threatened to kill him.

'Well, well,' he had said, 'I've underestimated him,' and he had let her go. She had set out thinking that with Strange in the Tower she would have a few days head start to reach St Mawes and her son.

But now they had released him. Why?

The news overtook her at Dover, where she was stranded by a stubborn south-westerly wind blowing up the Channel. No ships were setting sail west to Portsmouth, let alone Cornwall. She restlessly walked the quay, cursing the wind that whipped her cloak around her face, watching as a couple of grubby coastal schooners from Zeebrugge unloaded grey-faced Dutch refugees. A privateer returning from the Spanish Indies docked, and its gold-toothed captain said that he hadn't seen a woman for six months and hadn't expected the first one he saw to be so beautiful. He reached inside his leather coat, held out a handful of semi-precious stones and told her to take her pick, but he laughed at the suggestion he might put back to sea.

The wind was shifting to the west and ever-darker clouds

piled up on the horizon. Old sailors muttered that their wounds had not ached like this since the great August gale of 1588, which had destroyed the Armada. They stashed away sails, double-roped their vessels to the dock and headed for the taverns.

No ship moved, not a brigantine nor a barque, not a fishing boat nor a wherry left the harbour. Time passed, each second like the ratchet of a rack tightening.

WILL

When he first escaped the tight-lipped hypocrisy of the provinces, Will had loved the brash, big-mouthed ferocity of London, but now he saw that this too was a kind of disguise, and he could see the city's septic heart beneath it, the hidden chambers where powerful men who upheld religion and morality by day whispered, plotted and murdered in the dark. No rules applied to them. They could kill, torture or fuck whomever they wanted, for no other reason than they always had. Lord Ferdinando Strange could walk free because he was related to kings.

There was a contagion stranger than the plague gripping the city, and Will felt it eating away at him from the inside. It had always been there and it always would.

Ann had two days left before she had to leave for Canterbury to get married, but their time together was poisoned by the knowledge that Strange was walking around London a free man. Her father turned up in the afternoon, unfortunately still alive. He'd been pummelled black and blue, and he claimed they owed him their lives as he had fought off their pursuers and given them time to escape, when they knew all he had done was plug the doorway like a giant slug in a spout. He wanted money for drink.

'I just want to toast the memory of my son,' he'd said. Ann kicked him out.

It was difficult with Ann. Talking about the storm that had

blown in from the west, or the first cherries on sale, seemed too trivial, and talking about him and her too huge. They didn't make love because it would have been the last time and too sad. The wind rattled the windowpanes, and rain poured through the cracks in the ceiling and puddled on the floor. He could see there was something gnawing at her and a couple of times she started to say something and stopped.

'Tell me,' he said finally. 'You might as well.'

'I want you to go back to Strange and accept his offer,' she said. 'You can lie to him, say you'll rewrite the play, and then never do it, but I need to know who killed Chris. I know Strange ordered it, but I want to know who carried it out.'

'Very well,' said Will.

'Really?'

'Why not? I'll grovel and wheedle, and fawn and flatter. I'll be like everyone else in London. Let's send him a message now.'

LIZZIE

Lizzie had tried to hold on to the memory of her papa's face, but after nearly two years there was very little there, only really his white scar above one eye, and you could not make a face from that. Yet, as soon as he walked into Kemp's rooms, she knew it was him, and when he called her, she knew his voice too. She ran to him, and he picked her up in those big, hairy arms.

'I thought I'd lost you all,' he said.

So he knew about her mama and Henry, but when he looked at her, his face had a sort of painful happiness. He looked at the scrapes and gouges on her arms, but he said nothing. He told them he had caught the last ship from Zeebrugge before the storm, and bought a horse with the last of his money and rode day and night for London. She asked if she could meet this horse and he promised her she would. Perhaps, now her papa was here, she could be Yolente again. Her papa thanked Kemp for looking after her in his terrible English. She would have to teach him quickly or the Londoners would laugh at him.

'It'll be nice to have a bit of time to myself again,' Kemp said to her papa. 'She's a nice girl, but looking after a child is no job for an artist.'

Papa didn't understand and nodded politely.

'I suppose I better give you a hug before you go,' Kemp said to her, rubbing hard at his eyes. He held her tight for a long time. 'Go on then, get out of here,' he said.

She walked with her papa towards the door, and to try and make Kemp less sad, did one of the pratfalls he had taught her.

'Perfect,' he said.

WILL

They walked to Shoreditch to meet Strange. The stalls selling herring, cod and mackerel lined the streets, fish scales glinting in the sun beneath them. Elizabeth had decreed that, on certain days, the English had to eat fish to support the fishermen. The fish stalls had lined the road when Will first ran to Eleanor Bull's house. It was only one week since Chris had been found dead. That day felt like it was in another century, another country, another world.

Strange was waiting for them in the room put aside for him at the theatre. Since they had last spoken to him, the walls had been hung with rich materials, damask and linen in reds and purples. Strange stood wearing an ocelot cape, hands clutching the edge of the desk, his face pale and sweaty. There was a disgusting smell.

'So you'll rewrite the play,' he said to Will, his lips twisted into something between a smirk and a grimace.

'I shall, my lord, and for no payment.'

Strange was shivering despite the cloak, and Will realised he was gripping the table to try and stop the shaking as Will himself had done not long ago. Had the plague come for him? He had never feared it. He seemed to think that no disease would have the temerity to enter his royal bloodstream. Ann jogged Will's foot with hers and he went on.

'I'm sorry I was short with you the last time we met, but I've considered, and Chris would want audiences to watch it, even if it was changed a little, and I'd rather craft it lovingly then let it be butchered.'

'Now we're getting somewhere,' said Strange, 'and I, naturally, will keep my side of the bargain.'

'Thank you, my lord.'

'We need to work together so I will be completely honest with you. I did give my assent to the unfortunate events that led to your friend's demise. Sometimes you must sacrifice a pawn to save a king.'

Will nodded as if he appreciated this honesty. Rage tautened his performance.

'It was thought wise to get him to Deptford, where they are more relaxed about sudden death and where Danby could run the inquest, and Bella convinced him to go.'

'She knew he'd be killed?' said Ann.

'She didn't. She was absurdly sentimental about the late Mr Marlowe,' said Strange. 'Do you have any idea where she has gone?'

'We don't,' said Will.

'I heard a rumour she took a ship for Dover. Do you know anything about that?'

'We don't,' Will repeated, struggling to keep an even tone. 'So you had Christopher poisoned in Deptford.'

'It seemed best, yes. But unfortunately after his little tiff with you he ran off in a bit of a state. My chaps found him collapsed outside the room where he kept Spencer's bastard. They took him to Danby's and put him to bed, but he proved stronger than anyone imagined and made it out of the house and as far as the river before he died.'

He sighed at how unhelpful people being murdered could be.

'Anyhow, I brought in Skerries and his lads, at considerable cost, to find him and do their "killed in a brawl" thing.'

Strange went to speak some more, stopped, shuddered and made choking noises. A liveried servant ran into the room and thrust a large Venetian glass bowl beneath his head. Strange put his hands over his mouth, making horrid retching sounds, and a torrent of black vomit spewed between his fingers. It missed the bowl and spurted over the servant's golden livery. There was a terrible stink of rotting human matter. This was what they'd smelt when they first entered the room. The servant hovered, black slime dripping from his tabard onto the floor.

'Go change your clothes,' said Strange. 'Go!'

'My lord, I've no more...' he started to say.

'Change!' shouted Strange. 'I won't have my servants dressed in filth.'

He hurled the bowl at the servant as he backed out of the room but it missed him and shattered against the door frame. He saw Will and Ann staring.

'I'm fine, it's nothing.'

His legs seemed to give way and he sat down suddenly in his chair.

'I've never been ill in my life and I'm not going to start now.'

He really thought he was so exalted that disease dared not touch him. Will looked at Ann. Her face was fixed in a grim stare.

'Who killed my brother?' she asked. 'Who gave him the poison?'

'Patience, patience,' said Strange, retching again. His body convulsed horribly but nothing came out. He paused, regathered himself and spoke as if nothing had happened. 'Now, where were we?'

His one pleasure seemed to be stringing this out to make them wait.

'Bella had told Kyd to get some slow-acting poison from the Friar. She told Kyd he'd be taken back to Topcliffe's dungeon if he didn't.'

'And she still didn't know?' asked Will.

'Whatever you offered her, she wouldn't kill Christopher,'

said Strange, his lip curled bitterly. 'No, she just gave it to Alleyn like she was told.'

'Alleyn?' said Will in disbelief.

'Amusing, isn't it?' said Strange. 'The puppet killing his puppeteer.'

It came to Will. 'Of course, you knew he was "Tamburlaine" the pamphleteer, and you threatened to reveal that.'

Strange applauded sarcastically. 'Well done, William. I forget that you possess a certain shopkeeper cunning. It was a little more subtle than that.'

They could hear his stomach gurgling obscenely.

'He thought he was emperor of London and could do anything. We told him Chris knew he was "Tamburlaine" and that, once Topcliffe got hold of Chris, he'd blab and Alleyn would be the next one in there.'

He vomited another filthy torrent of clotted black sludge.

'Bowl,' he yelled, but no servant came. Perhaps the valet was changing his livery. Strange's body convulsed and more vomit splattered onto the desk. Will wanted a complete explanation before he collapsed.

'So you're saying that Alleyn gave Chris the poison?' he said.

'No,' said Strange. 'He couldn't go through with it, typical actor.'

Despite his torment, he exalted in making them wait. Now something dark was coming out of his nose. It was blood and he licked it with his tongue to clear it from his lips.

Will was almost shouting. 'Who gave Chris the poison? Tell me!' Strange smiled through bloody lips.

'It was you, William!'

Will knew at once it was true. He was back in that crowded pub and it was more real than the stinking room in which he now stood. It was before the quarrel turned vicious. Alleyn reached across to him, handing him the tumbler with the yellow swirl of pastis.

'That's for Chris.'

He could smell the aniseed in it, strong enough to mask the taste of any poison. He could feel Chris's hand touch his as he handed him the glass, see Chris wink as he knocked it back, and from that moment on he'd been dying slowly of poison, all the time they cursed each other, even as Will had shouted his final words to him, 'I'm going to kill you.' He had killed him.

Strange spluttered a chuckle as he choked on his own royal blood.

'You wanted to know,' he got out before he retched again, yet more black liquid spewing across the room. A fleck of it went into Will's eye but he was too stunned to wipe it away. Strange's face was stretched tight with pain and yet gleeful as he turned to Ann. 'Didn't you say you were going to kill your brother's killer?' Will had been trying not to look at her but now he had to. She had no anger for him, only pity.

'Let's leave,' was all she said.

Strange tried to stand, but his legs buckled and he slumped against the wall behind him, clawing to hold himself up.

'Help me!' he roared to his servants. 'Your master is indisposed.'

No one came.

Ann took Will's hand and led him from the room as Strange slowly slid down the wall.

'People,' he muttered.

BELLA

Bella had found a ship's captain so desperate for gold that he had set sail in his leaking and lopsided schooner, and headed west into the rising storm. One of the crew jumped overboard as they rounded the harbour wall, and swam for the beach rather than come with them. Bella watched from the deck as a huge man in high black boots fished him out of the waves, lifted him off the ground, apparently asking him some questions, then dropped him, and stared at the departing ship. It was the murderous constable who Strange employed. There was a time when she would have done nothing to antagonise him, but now she knew that the cruelty of men like him required no motivation. She waved.

Once they left the shelter of the bay, the wind grew steadily stronger. There was an eerie, sunless light and the ship looked tiny in the vast sea as huge, smooth waves rolled towards them a hundred yards apart. As each struck the ship, it teetered skyward, and plunged back down into the deep trough as if it would never rise. Then the storm broke in its black fury so she could see nothing and only hear its howling and screaming and feel its savagery. The captain lashed himself to the tiller. The mizzen mast snapped and fell overboard, threatening to drag the whole ship under. As the sailors tried to hack it away with axes, a huge crack of lightning struck the deck and a tongue of flame flickered crazily past her feet. The captain was dead, still lashed to the tiller, a thin plume of smoke rising from his head, and another man took his place.

Bella had to go below for fear of being swept away. She and Perro crouched in her cabin, as the ship creaked, groaned and splintered, and freezing sea water fell on her from above and rose around her feet. She grabbed her pistol for fear the seamen would think her an evil spirit, and throw her overboard as an offering to calm the sea, as a crew had once tried in the South Atlantic.

Yet they survived. Now as she walked on the shore, the land seemed to heave and pitch under each unsteady step. The sun had come out but the wind was still brisk and the scudding clouds reflected in the rock pools as she walked along the beach towards the small boy running wildly in circles around the two guards who accompanied him. She hoped the gold she had left would be enough to persuade them to let him go, but if not she had the dog and the gun. Now she was close enough to see the boy's face and she gasped out loud. Already he looked like Chris.

WILL

Strange died that evening. The rumour was that he had been poisoned by Hesketh's friends for betraying him, but that sounded like the sort of rumour Cecil would put about. Will thought it was more likely that Cecil had double-crossed him, preferring to dispose of him quietly, rather than risk putting a man with so much royal blood on trial.

He died in agony vomiting up his own stomach. His last words were reported to be, '*Sans changer*,' the family motto.

'Pretentious to the last,' said Ann.

At least revenge was now pointless. Skerries, Pooley and Frizer had been torn apart by Perro, Strange was dead, Danby and Hesketh were doomed, and the hand that had poisoned Chris was his own.

'It wasn't your fault,' Ann kept telling him and he knew it wasn't, and yet anytime he closed his eyes, he saw that glass being passed, felt the cold of it in his hand, watched Chris drain it.

He knew what he would do once Ann had left. He would drink until he was ill, and then sleep for a couple of days and then he would work. He would finish *Romeo and Juliet*. *Richard II* would be part Cecil and part Strange, and he had a new play in his head based loosely on Kyd's story that he would write when he was ready. And he was ready to write. Now murder, treachery and revenge weren't just things that happened to other people. He could write of evil having stared into its eyes. He could speak of death knowing he had only just wriggled free from its jaws. 'You've nothing to write about,' Chris had told him. Well, perhaps now he did. Had the horror of the last week been his friend's final gift to him? And, of course, without Chris dying he wouldn't have seen Ann again before she disappeared into the dark house of a loveless marriage. At least they knew that they still loved each other, though perhaps they had always known that. They had spent the night before in the sudden heat that had followed the storm, unsleeping and unspeaking, lying in each other's arms. Would he truly never see her again? He looked across at this woman who had saved his life and wished she could save his life once more. Endings were always hard.

ANN

One day of sunshine and everyone forgot the plague. The streets were full as she and Will walked to Southwark Cross where the carts left for Canterbury. He had wanted to carry her bag, but she had said 'no'. Now she asked if he would, just to break the silence. She couldn't think of anything else to say to the one man she could talk to. She thought she glimpsed a man walking with a lion on a chain as they reached the busy junction where the cart stood waiting with the oxen already between the shafts.

She tried to remember all the villages they would pass through on the way to Canterbury just to fill her head up with something else. Brunington, Lewisham, Wricklemouth, Bexley, Stone. No.

She had forgotten Crayford. Crayford, Stone, Greenhithe. Chris had walked away from the man he loved saying 'one day', but that day wouldn't come for him and Edmund. Nor would it come for her and Will.

The villages. She must think of the villages. After Greenhithe came sad, little Denton, then Chalk, Godshill, Frindsbury, and what was next? The thin wooden bridge, yes, Twydall. She thought of waking to find Will beside her. The villages weren't working. The carter shouted for any more passengers to climb aboard. There were some of her neighbours perched on the cloth bales looking down at them so she couldn't really hug him, but she did anyway. He was trembling so she held him tighter. Bopping, Sittingbourne, not really a village, Snipeshill, Bapchild, Radfield, Boughton-under-Blean, Rough Common, Harbledown, and then they were there, her destination. She didn't want to say it. It wasn't a village anyway. The carter was shouting at her.

'Give me a leg up then,' she said to Will. He cupped his hands for her to stand on, and she clambered up and sat on her bag.

She leant down over the side and whispered to Will, 'Listen, I'll have to come up to London to trade cloth and leather. When I do, if you want I can spend the night with you.' His eyes widened. Surely after all they'd been through together, he couldn't be shocked at this. 'I'm doing what a man would do,' she said, 'but obviously, it's only if you want to.'

'I do,' he said, and then smiled wryly at the marriage oath he had accidentally repeated.

Let's face it, adultery was the least of her worries. There was no point worrying about breaking the seventh commandment now, for she had broken the sixth when she killed Strange. She wondered if Will knew. Hadn't it been obvious, pretending to be sick on his cloak, and when he came to look, slipping the poison she'd got from the Friar into his wine? He had promised that the tiny vial of gu was enough to kill a man, and he'd been right.

The carter whipped the oxen and she looked at the crowds thronging the street ahead of them.

'This cart is going to take about five minutes getting to the first corner,' she said. 'I can't bear watching you all that time. Do you mind going now?'

'Oh, Ann,' he said, and turned and went.

POSTSCRIPT

You may want to know what is true and what is not. I have changed several facts because they got in the way of a good story. Also, I am sure there are many more details I simply got wrong through ignorance. I imagine those who know a lot about Elizabethan London will spot them.

But what is true?

Kyd was arrested in 1593, brought before the Queen's Court and tortured. He is believed to have given them the name of Marlowe as an atheist. Christopher Marlowe was summoned to appear before the Court, but a few days beforehand he was killed in Deptford by Frizer, Pooley and Skerries, men with links to the spy networks of Walsingham and Cecil, (still only a 'sir' in 1593). Skerries had been a double agent in the Babington Plot.

The inquest was conducted by Danby, the Queen's Coroner, because the killing took place just within three miles of a royal palace. The killers were found to have acted in self-defence, temporarily imprisoned but freed by a royal pardon four weeks and a day after the murder. Frizer was reportedly rewarded. Eleanor Bull did have a cousin who was a lady in waiting to the queen.

Marlowe and Watson, the poet, killed Bradley in a brawl in Hog Lane. They too were imprisoned but subsequently freed. Watson, in reality, died around six months before Marlowe.

Curiously, the 1592 play *Arden of Faversham* has been variously attributed to four writers... the four writers in this book: Shakespeare, Marlowe, Kyd and Watson.

I suppose Alleyn could have been the real pamphleteer who railed against Dutch immigrants, using the nom de plume 'Tamburlaine', but that is ridiculously unlikely. Whoever it was may have had influence, however, as no one betrayed them for the massive reward of one hundred crowns.

There are doubts about the order and date of both Shakespeare and Marlowe's plays. Shakespeare is believed to have written *Richard III* and *Romeo and Juliet* in 1593. Marlowe's last play was most probably *The Massacre at Paris* but some do think it was *Edward II*, which was placed in the Stationers' Register on July 6th 1593, five weeks after his death.

There is nothing to connect the tragedy of *Sir Thomas More* with the Babington Plot, though Shakespeare did help to rewrite it; barring signatures, it is probably the only example of his handwriting that remains. Essex, however, did pay for a revival of *Richard II*, another play about a rightful king being murdered, as propaganda for his attempted coup in 1601.

There is nothing connecting Sir John 'Rich' Spencer to any plots. (He was, in fact, not yet a 'sir' in 1593.) Intriguingly, Shakespeare gave, as Richard III's address in London, the house in which Spencer subsequently lived, so perhaps he didn't like him. He had one daughter and there is no record of an illegitimate son. It is true that during a performance of *Tamburlaine* live ammunition was accidentally fired into the audience – something that didn't happen when it was the first ever play staged at the Olivier Theatre... health and safety gone mad.

1593 was the worst plague year in London for thirty years and it killed about thirteen per cent of Londoners. They painted red crosses on the doors of plague victims and, reportedly, the penalty for emerging before the end of their quarantine was to be buried alive in a plague pit. Similar measures could have led to a more satisfying ending to the Dominic Cummings saga.

Lord Ferdinando Strange was an impresario who ran London's most prestigious company of players in 1593. He was mentioned in Henry VIII's will and descended from Henry VII , and Hesketh led a Catholic plot to install him as king in 1593. Strange reportedly went to Lord Cecil and told him about it and Hesketh was executed.

Strange was poisoned later in the year. His contemporaries blamed it on Jesuit priests but history is written by the winners.

Danby most likely also died in 1593 and Thomas Kyd died in 1594, probably from the injuries suffered during his interrogation.

Finally, we come on to Ann Marlowe. Her sister Jane was married at thirteen already pregnant, and she died in childbirth. There is no evidence whatsoever that Ann had an affair with Shakespeare, but it's true she married John eleven days after Christopher's death and that she too was already pregnant. While everyone else seemed to die young she lived to eighty and would have seen the Civil War and Cromwell's rule. She was called a scold, but perhaps that was just how men described women who stood up for themselves. She did, however, have a police record and was arrested three times in her fifties for fighting with her neighbours using a sword and a knife.

William Shakespeare, subsequently, did quite well as a writer.

Finally, what I've just said is true may not be true. That is the joy of the 16th century: nobody knows.

ACKNOWLEDGEMENTS

I have many people I'd like to thank, starting with Cari Rosen who has been a wise and whipsmart editor and who was the first to see possibilities in this book.

Big thanks to Lucy Chamberlain, Olivia Le Maistre, all the legendary team at Legend, and to Rose Cooper who designed the cover. Ross Dickinson copyedited the book, had excellent suggestions, and, rather annoyingly, was always right. I salute Katie Johnston who grappled with the scrawl of my handwriting. Thank you to the Lockdown Bakehouse who caffeinated me during the long hours my dog and I took up one of their tables while I wrote it.

I am lucky to have Marc Berlin as my agent who I have been with for 45 years – for many good reasons. Thank you also to Lara, Louis, and Jack who have helped me wrangle computers, printers, and life generally. My greatest thanks go to Bernadette Davis who proved how wise it was to marry another writer. Despite her dismay at my terrible grammar, she read many versions, saw what was wrong, and came up with ways to make it better.

And thank you to anyone who read it, and particularly to anyone who gets to this bit.

Follow Legend Press on Twitter
@legend_times_

Follow Legend Press on Instagram
@legend_times